OTHERWORLD CHRONICLES

THE INVISIBLE TOWER

OTHERWORLD CHRONICLES

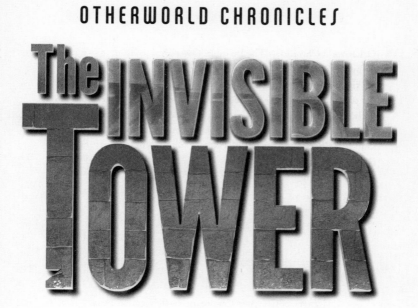

The INVISIBLE TOWER

NILS JOHNSON-SHELTON

HARPER
An Imprint of HarperCollinsPublishers

Library of Congress Cataloging-in-Publication Data
Johnson-Shelton, Nils.
   The Invisible Tower / Nils Johnson-Shelton. — 1st ed.
    ISBN 978-0-06-207086-9 (trade bdg.) — ISBN 978-0-06-213192-8
(int'l ed.)
      1. Arthur, King—Juvenile fiction. [1. Arthur, King—Fiction.
2. Adventure and adventurers—Fiction.] I. Title.
PZ7.J6398In 2012   2011022928
[Fic]—dc23   CIP
                                                            AC

Typography by Torborg Davern

12 13 14 15 16   CG/RRDH   10 9 8 7 6 5 4 3 2 1

❖

First Edition

TABLE OF CONTENTS

OTHERWORLD CHRONICLES
THE INVISIBLE TOWER

Long ago an old man—a wizard in fact—was imprisoned in an invisible tower. It was built by strong magic above a snaking brown river and rolling green hills, and it shut the world away from the wizard. From this tower he could see nothing but the interior walls of his prison.

For many years he was so angry that he could do nothing but seethe at his absent, far-off jailers. But then, after much time, his anger flagged, and he realized that while he was unable to go out into the world, he could will parts of the world to come to him. And so he summoned men, women, and children; beasts, insects, and plants; stone, soil, and sand. For nearly a thousand years all of these suffered as he attempted to extract from them a means to escape, which was pointless. Escape was impossible.

But then he began to hear of a people landing in great-sailed wooden ships on faraway shores. These newcomers were outcasts and vagabonds and ministers from lands called England and France and Nederland, among others. The world that he had once inhabited was returning, and a plan took root in the wizard's mind. It would require dedication, cunning, and a lot of luck, but if it worked it would provide him with his freedom.

Once free, his gray, ancient eyes would behold the world again. Once free, his great power would be reborn.

Once free, he would set right all that had gone wrong so long, long ago.

IN WHICH WE HEAR OF THE DRAGON SLAYER'S DUMB LUCK

1

𝕬rthur "𝕬rtie" 𝕶ingfisher—twelve, rail thin, and not nearly tan enough for a kid in late July—had just finished slaying Caladirth, a female green dragon with sharpened rubies for teeth and curved golden spikes for horns. One of the horns lay shattered on the ground like a splintered broom handle. Artie thought it was a pretty clever weak spot. Seriously, everyone in the Otherworld knew that dragon horns were always best avoided.

The beast lay at Artie's feet, orange blood draining from her broken horn. Her cave felt suddenly empty, which was remarkable considering it contained a dead ten-ton dragon, three huge black dragon eggs, and a trove of sparkling treasure that would hardly fit in Artie's empty shoulder bags. He had a lot of work to do.

Artie fell to the ground and examined his double-edged ax, which was named Qwon, for battle damage. It was a little nicked but nothing that couldn't be fixed by the town smithy. He let out a long breath. He felt satisfied. And totally pooped. There wouldn't be any new quests for a while.

He closed his eyes and took stock of himself. He was all in one piece and sweating a little, even though the air around him was very cool. The only sounds were his breath, the small *kerplunks* of dripping water, and the crackling torchlight. After the excitement of battle, he suddenly felt very alone.

But then his neck tingled familiarly, like it was being tickled with a handful of feathers.

Artie always knew when his sister got within a dozen or so feet of him, and at that moment Kay was creeping into their subterranean cave, trying to get Artie. An image of her jelled in Artie's mind: her long red hair was pulled back in a ponytail, and she was wearing cargo pants and that blue T-shirt with a garden gnome doing karate on it. He could see, without looking at all, that she thought she had a real chance at finally scaring him.

This was predictable. Artie knew that *she* knew that *he* knew that she'd be trying to frighten the cookies out of him. They'd spent the better part of their childhood playing this game, and it had yet to work.

They always knew.

"Ha! Gotcha!" Kay blurted as she pushed him hard but playfully in the back, knocking the 3-D virtual reality goggles off his face. Artie gasped, and Kay was shocked to see that Artie was sweating. She asked, "Wait—did I really just get you?"

He wiped his forehead with the back of his hand and smiled. "Of course not. I felt you about thirty seconds ago." He took the Xbox controller and paused *Otherworld*, the game he'd been obsessed with since he'd gotten it for his birthday in April.

"'*I felt you about thirty seconds ago,*'" Kay goofily mimicked. "Whatever, Chico. I got you good."

"Nope."

"Whatever."

Kay, already thirteen and a ridiculous six feet tall, with limbs like those of a praying mantis, cruised past Artie into the game room. "Whatcha up to?" she wondered.

The video game that Artie had been playing inside his goggles was duplicated on the flat screen bolted to the wall. Seeing the fallen dragon bleeding from her golden horn, Kay yelped, "Artie! You did it?" She leaned closer to the TV. "Holy cow! You did!" She wheeled around and beamed at Artie with her fantastically unusual eyes, one being sky-blue, the other being clover-green. "How'd you figure out how to kill her? How? *How?*" She grabbed Artie by the shoulders and gave him a little hug.

Artie and Kay were as close as a twelve-year-old boy and his thirteen-year-old sister could be—especially since for some reason they'd always shared identical-twin-level ESP, which was even weirder considering that Artie was adopted. Artie was happy that Kay was giving him some props. Usually it was the other way around. Kay was no slouch when it came to gaming—or anything else for that matter. She wasn't as good as Artie at *Otherworld*, but she was so good at *Call of Duty* and *Fallout* that she'd already won about five grand playing in tournaments. Artie was certain that she would notch yet another win the following week when their dad, Kynder, took them to a huge tournament Kay was set to compete in.

Artie put the controller and the goggles on the floor and kicked his feet in front of him. He took a sip of Mountain Dew from an unlabeled plastic bottle and told her how he'd done it.

Basically, after a lot of tries he got lucky. There was a nook high on the eastern wall of the cave that he'd maneuvered his mage-warrior, Nitwit the Gray, into. The dragon knew Nitwit was there but she wouldn't attack because in the nook were the three black dragon eggs. Essentially, Artie was using them as shields—she wouldn't dare sacrifice her unborn hellions just to down Nitwit. The dragon didn't like this and she made a big dance in front of the nook, wagging her head back and forth and slapping her tail on the ground, but Artie wasn't scared. He was, however, very frustrated because, no matter what, he just could not kill the thing. He decided to try another fireball. It was the strongest spell he had.

However, due to some clumsy button pushing, he cast Find Item, which revealed the nearest and most powerful magic item that was not in the caster's possession. Caladirth's horns were immediately haloed in a red glow. Artie said to Kay, "At first I thought that if I could kill her, a sword made out of her horns would be pretty sweet, but then it came to me. It was, like, an inspiration or whatever. Just to double-check, I cast Find Item again, and sure enough, her horns glowed red again. So I flipped to hand-to-hand, targeted her horns, and went to work with Qwon. As soon as I got a direct hit, she screamed and fell over. And that was it."

Kay stared and shook her head. "Wow. The horns. Who'da thunk it?" She grabbed the soda from Artie and drank three big gulps. She shrugged and said, "You'll have to let the Dr Pepper heads on the boards know about that." Artie could never figure out why, but to Kay *Dr Pepper heads* meant "geeks."

"C'mon, Sis, you know I hate the game forums."

"Yeah, yeah, 'gaming purist' and all that. Never go to walk-through sites. Whatever, Artie. You deserve the kudos.

Go show off a little!"

Easy for her to say. Artie loved his sister, but the fact remained that he wasn't her. While she was a supergamer, crazy, fast runner, ex–Little-League all-star, straight-A student, who could also dance—in other words supercool—he was a pretty good gamer, wispy, lightweight punching-bag bully target, and straight-B-minus student, who never danced and was only somewhat cool on account of his supercool sister.

But the main reason Artie didn't like getting recognition was because of Frankie Finkelstein. Years of bearing the brunt of Frankie Finkelstein's anger issues had taught Artie that a low profile was best. Even a medium-low profile provided ample opportunities for Finkelstein to punch, kick, headlock, noogie, push, and swear at Artie.

All of which sucked big-time.

However, as these things ran through Artie's mind, he realized his sister was probably right. He'd slain Caladirth, for crying out loud! Why *not* gloat a little?

Artie looked at Kay and said, "Yeah, okay. I think I will."

"Great!" she chirped. "But not yet, Chico. First you and me have to help Kynder in the yard."

"Oh yeah."

So Artie and Kay made their way up the stairs and into the kitchen. Artie recapped his Mountain Dew and stashed it in the back of the refrigerator. Kynder didn't approve of soda pop in general and especially hated Mountain Dew, swearing up and down that "it will literally turn you into a drug addict," even though it hadn't yet and Artie had been drinking it for three years (okay—and six cavities). Then they went into the backyard to the little vegetable garden that, after his kids, was Kynder's pride and joy.

Kynder was also tall and thin and redheaded. Both of his eyes were hazel. He wore a nicely groomed mustache that gave his very-straight nose the look of an upside-down T, and on his nose rested a pair of large, squarish glasses that might—*might*—have been cool in 1980. He still wore his ridiculously short running shorts from his morning jog but had replaced his sneakers with a pair of green wellies that must have been boiling, since it was nearly ninety degrees outside.

Yes, Kynder was a Dr Pepper head, too. A modest, pseudowealthy, semiretired geek, and his kids loved him.

"Hey, guys, done practicing?" Amazingly, this was what playing video games was called in the Kingfisher house.

"Yeah. Hotshot over here finally killed Caladirth."

"No kidding? That's great, Arthur! You've been working on that since the day Qwon kissed you on the cheek, huh?"

This was how the last day of sixth grade would forever be known in the Kingfisher house, and Kay and Kynder had been ribbing Artie about it ever since. Artie had no idea how Kynder knew that Qwon—not the virtual battle-ax, but the schoolmate who it was named after—had kissed him, but he did.

"Nice going on that one too, Slick," quipped Kay.

"Oh, shut up, both of you," Artie moaned. He plunked down by the tomatoes and began weeding, wondering what would come next in that crazy game he loved so much.

𝔄rtie, 𝔎ay, and 𝔎ynder liⱱed in a yellow clapboard house on Castleman Street in Shadyside, Pennsylvania, about four miles east of downtown Pittsburgh. Both Kay and Artie had been calling their dad by his first name since they were around eight years old. That's when Artie learned he was adopted, and while Kynder was the only father he'd ever known, he stopped calling him Pop and started calling him Kynder. Within a few months Kay was doing it too. Kynder thought it was a funny quirk and liked it, so he never insisted on being called Pop, or Dad, or anything else.

Kay's mom had left them when Kay was three and Artie two, and Artie had lived with them since he was exactly one year and three days old. Kynder rarely spoke about Kay's mom, and never talked about why she left. Artie didn't even know her name, and Kay never bothered to share it with him. When it came to her mom, Kay never shared anything with Artie. Hey, all kids have secrets, right? Even sisters like Kay?

That night after dinner Artie logged onto Otherworld's game forums to share a little secret of his own. He started a new thread called "killed Caladirth w/o walkthrough" and waited. Within minutes there were over a dozen posts patting Artie on the back. He read all of them proudly. Artie thought that this was what it must feel like to be Kay.

Most of the posts were from registered members, but some were anonymous, and some of these were trolling. One of the trolls called Artie a wimp on account of him choosing to play the mage-warrior class. Apparently that guy had it in for mage-warriors. Artie could not have cared less. The heck with trolls.

Artie was about to log off and go to his room when the board live-updated with a post titled "Arthur's Easter Egg." Curious, he double-clicked it. It read:

Arthur, you need to find your Easter egg tonight. Look in the most obvious place. —MrT

Everyone who's really played video games knows what an Easter egg is: it's a secret, usually a joke, that's hidden in the game, kind of like, well, an Easter egg. As hard as Easter eggs could be to find—usually you had to look them up on the internet to have any chance of uncovering them—they were there for everyone. How could it be that Arthur had his *own* Easter egg in *Otherworld*?

Also strange was that MrT's post was private—only Artie could read it.

Artie clicked the reply button on MrT's entry and simply wrote, "Huh?!" and clicked Post.

Within twenty seconds came the reply:

Arthur, it has begun. Find your egg. It is with Caladirth. You must do this. I have already said more than I should. Go to your egg, and to your destiny. —MrT

What the heck was this guy talking about? Artie had a *destiny*? In a *video game*? This was too weird to ignore.

Artie logged off and ran down to the game room. He turned on the TV and picked up the controller and unpaused the game. The soundtrack played over the stereo system as he moved Nitwit the Gray from one end of Caladirth's lair to the other, looking for something out of the ordinary. He didn't see anything. He sifted through the pile of treasure. It was a good haul, and it got him excited to continue playing, but nothing about it stood out.

"Look in the most obvious place," the post had said. The most obvious place . . . the most obvious place . . .

The eggs!

Artie guided Nitwit to the dragon's three large, stone-black eggs. Nitwit picked one up—nothing strange—and put it back. He picked another one up and turned it over. On the bottom it said, "Break me."

Artie shook his head and made Nitwit throw the egg to the floor. It exploded in a sparkling orange haze. There was no dead dragoling or gooey egg white—only dust.

But then the dust settled, and there, cradled along the inside curve of a large piece of shell, was a note.

Nitwit picked it up and went into the Inspect Item mode.

Artie was overcome with nervousness.

The note read, "Arthur. In one week's time you will come to me at the IT. You are special, Arthur, and I have need of your service and power. I have been waiting so long for you. Your humble servant, M."

Wait. He was special? And he had a servant? A *humble* one?

What?

Artie stood rooted to the rug for two minutes. He felt a little woozy. The controller slipped from his grip and when it hit the floor, Artie came to. He read the note again. What was going on? Artie was suddenly scared, like Finkelstein was bearing down on him with a baseball bat and no lunch money.

He shut down the system, ran to his room, and dived under the covers, where he concluded that, yes, he'd just had his leg pulled and it was just coincidence that his name was Arthur, and there was an Easter egg in *Otherworld* that was addressed to somebody also named Arthur. Yes, that's what it was. A coincidence.

Eventually Artie fell into an uneasy sleep.

Six days after Artie's Easter egg hunt, about which he had decided to never tell a soul, as Artie was reading the latest *X-Men* on his bed, the telephone rang. He didn't move to answer because he knew Kynder, who was in his room packing for their trip to the tournament in Cincinnati, would get it.

After a pause Artie heard a muffled but insistent "Who?" through the wall but didn't pay it much mind. Then he heard something in Kynder's voice he'd never heard before: fear. It was sudden and undeniable.

"My ex-wife? Oh my. It *is* you." Artie sat bolt upright and dropped his comic book. A call from her was about as likely as a call from a giant saber-toothed tiger.

Artie crept to the wall and pressed his ear to it. Kynder said, "Why on earth are you calling me now? And why do you sound so far away? No one sounds far away anymore."

Kynder's fear was gone. It had been replaced with anger. Artie felt proud of his dad.

"Really, I don't care. What do you want?"

Pause.

"What? How do you know about that? What do you mean?"

Pause.

Kynder sounded extra flabbergasted when he asked, "Why on earth not?"

Short pause.

"What do you mean, it's not safe? It's Ohio, not Afghanistan."

Pause.

"What? Since when do you care about the children? Since when do you care about anyone but yourself?"

Artie remembered that there was an old corded phone with a busted ringer in the hall. He left his room and tiptoed to it and carefully picked up the receiver. A weak voice finished saying, "not safe for me—or you, either."

For a moment Kynder said nothing. Then, very forcefully, he said, "Listen. You're loony. I'm hanging up now. For the last time, *good-bye*! Don't ever call here again!" And he hung up. Kynder had cut her off so abruptly that Artie was sure she'd call back. But she didn't. The phone didn't ring again at all.

𝕬𝖗𝖙𝖎𝖊 𝖉𝖎𝖉𝖓't 𝖐𝖓𝖔𝖜 𝖜𝖍𝖆𝖙 𝖙𝖔 say about the phone call. He wanted to tell Kay but he couldn't bring himself to. Kynder didn't mention it either.

So the Kingfishers left for Cincinnati early on Thursday morning, as if the phone call had never happened.

They pulled into a downtown Hilton at one o'clock and checked in. Then Kynder left Artie with the room service menu while he took Kay to register for the tournament, which was slated to get started at noon on Friday.

Artie ordered a hamburger with curly fries and a Coke and hooked up the Xbox to the room's TV. He looked in Kay's bag for her lucky controller—a shiny silver number that she'd adorned with faux jewels—but he couldn't find it. She must have had it with her. Room service came, and he reclined in the lounger while eating and channel surfing.

When Kay and Kynder got back, Kay went over to the game console and said, "Thanks, Homey, for hooking this up."

"No sweat, Kay."

She picked up the standard-issue controller and turned it in her hand. "Where's my lucky controller, though?"

Kynder pilfered a fistful of Artie's fries.

Artie said, "Dunno. I thought you had it with you."

"No. It's in my bag."

"Uh, no, it isn't."

"Uh, yes, it is—*oh no*!" Kay's eyes widened as she dug through her stuff. "Omigod, I can't believe it but, but . . . I think I left my controller at home!" She stood in front of the TV and started to pull her hair. "Seriously, Kynder, what am I going to do?"

Kynder sat on the foot of one of the beds. He put his hands on his knees and said, "Kay, let's try to stay calm. Maybe we can get someone to FedEx it, or maybe we can get you another controller and have it blessed or something before the tournament starts."

Kay plopped down next to Kynder. "No way. I can't win with some vanilla out-of-the-box thing."

Artie suddenly remembered something. "Kay, you know Erik? He used to live here. We could call him to see if there's a good place to get a custom controller."

"Erik? Ugh." Kay sighed. Erik sat behind Kay in art class, where his favorite pastime was pelting her with eraser nubs he'd yanked off number two pencils. In other words, he liked her. "Okay. I guess so."

Kynder stood up and clapped his hands. "Great. Why don't you give him a call, Arthur?" He stole another fistful of Artie's fries.

Artie got out Kynder's cell phone and dialed Erik. Kynder pointed at Artie's hamburger and said, "You know, Arthur, you really shouldn't eat that. Do you know what they feed those cows?"

Artie did and honestly didn't care. He was twelve.

Erik picked up, and Artie had a quick conversation with him near the window. He hung up and said, "Well, Erik said he'd go over to our house and get the controller if you want—"

Kay interrupted. "I don't think so. I don't want Erik Erikssen poking around my room. Like, at all."

"Right. But he also said that there's a crazy store we should check out—some place called the Invisible Tower. It's like a comics-slash-gaming-slash-D-and-D shop run by a really strange old dude. They sell custom controllers— Erik has two from the store himself. I've seen them. They're pretty sweet."

Kynder, now fixated on Artie's meal, held up the Coke. "Arthur, you know how I feel about soda pop! You know I think you drink more than you should, right?"

"*Dad!*" Kay yelled. Kay reserved the use of that word for only the direst of circumstances.

Kynder put down the soda. "Oh, right. Okay. Arthur, since you've already 'eaten,' why don't you find out where this Invincible Tower place—"

"*Invisible* Tower, Kynder," Artie corrected.

"Whatever it's called, find out where it is and take a cab to check it out. Kay—why don't you and I go get some lunch? You'll feel better."

Kay reluctantly agreed and shuffled off to the bathroom. Artie looked up the place on their laptop. "It's only six blocks away, Kynder."

"Fine. Here's some money. Only spend it on cabs and the controller, if there's a good one."

"Got it."

"Bring me the receipt. And try not to be gone for more than an hour."

"Right."

"I mean it."

"Okay, okay."

As Artie passed the bathroom, he could hear his sister sniffling. He resolved to help her however he could.

The doorman flagged a cab and Artie climbed in. The young driver was huge and wore reflective aviator sunglasses and he would have been menacing-looking if he hadn't also had a baby face that was smiling the whole time.

After a short ride they pulled up to the store. As Artie paid, the driver lowered his sunglasses and gave him a pronounced—and slightly creepy—wink in the mirror.

Artie hopped out of the cab and hurried away, but when he saw the Invisible Tower for the first time, he immediately forgot about the weird cab driver.

It was located on the ground floor of a squat, hundred-year-old red-brick building with gray granite lintels and stonework lettering in an arch below the roofline that read "Vine Street Cable Railway." There were plenty of tall plate-glass windows lining the sidewalk, and displayed in them were the contents of every twelve-year-old's dreams.

There were action figures, masks, books, posters, costumes, games, swords and axes and arrows. There were Batman, Spider-Man, Iron Man; there were Halo warriors, rogue-looking special ops members, not-to-be-messed-with lady commandos; there were Frankenstein, Dracula, and the Mummy; *Star Wars*, *Lord of the Rings*, *Avatar*; all manner of Tolkienesque wizards, elves, trolls, orcs, fairies, and sprites; robots, Transformers, droids; dragons, snakes, hydras; screaming manga heroes on motorcycles and doe-eyed anime girls in private-school miniskirts; generic monsters and godly titans of every kind and at every stage of decay or anger or sorrow. The logos in the windows included Marvel, Dark Horse, Wizards of the Coast, DC, D&D, Transformers, Sony, Xbox, and Lucasfilm.

Artie pulled open the store's heavy oak front door. A brass bell attached to it tinkled. He could swear that in the little bell's ring was a voice that said, "Welcome, good sir."

But bells couldn't talk, right?

He crossed the threshold. Artie couldn't explain it, but as he did, he felt *stronger*. It was like he'd gained twenty pounds of muscle. His fingertips tingled. His hunched back—the default posture for any tallish preteen who preferred to keep a low profile—straightened out. He turned his neck from side to side and it cracked. He took a deep breath. He felt amazing.

The inside of the store was dimly lit. The windows were totally blocked by all of the stuff on display in them, and Artie couldn't see outside at all. Not even a crack of sunlight. Artie blinked as his eyes adjusted.

The shop was narrow and high ceilinged. There were three rows of lofty shelves stretched out before him. On the end of one of the shelves was a large sign in silver letters that read:

SHOPLIFTERS WILL BE PUNISHED. MALCONTENTS WILL BE BANNED. LOYALISTS WILL BE BLESSED.

—MANAGEMENT

Something about its lettering conveyed its seriousness. Artie instinctively doubted that the Invisible Tower was robbed very often, if at all.

He walked around and touched the shelves and the spines of the books and comics with reverence. Things were crammed together and not always well organized. Low, Celtic-sounding music played over a tinny sound system from beyond the bookshelves.

Artie suddenly remembered what he was there for and wandered deeper into the place, looking for the video game stuff.

At the back of the store was a checkout counter unlike any he'd ever seen. Instead of the usual waist-high case with a cash register on top, there was a hulking ebony-black desk that looked plain ancient. Its legs were carved in the shape of a draft horse's—hooves, muscles, tendons, and all. On top of the table was a gigantic and ornate cash register. There was also a normal-looking ledger, a brass desk bell, and a liter bottle of water.

No one was behind the desk. Artie stepped forward to ring the bell, and that's when he saw them.

In a locked case to his right were the customized gaming controllers. There was one for PlayStation encased in snakeskin, another that was fire-engine red, and an Xbox one that was striped like a tiger and had little cat eyes for buttons. There was a pink one with orange flames on it, and a glittery purple one with silver buttons. There were also several boxes of standard controllers that hadn't been opened. But, above all these, on the highest shelf and with a light shining on it, was a golden Xbox controller that looked like it was made of real metal. All of its buttons were jet-black, and its connector cable was red velvet. It was, without a doubt, one of the coolest things Artie had ever seen. In front of it was a small placard with golden hand-lettering that read, "Display Only."

"Ahem."

Artie turned. Standing behind the black desk was an old man in a red long-sleeved T-shirt and billowing linen pants. He was shorter than Artie, and thin like Kynder, but he had a little gut that filled out his shirt. His skin was very wrinkled yet very healthy-looking. He had on round eyeglasses and a black porkpie hat, and had huge sideburns that curled below his jawline. He wore a long necklace with some sort of wooden pendant weighing it down.

The old man smiled like a Buddha, and Artie couldn't help but move toward him. As he got closer, Artie realized that what he'd taken for deep wrinkles on the man's face was in fact a maze of black tattoos crisscrossing in every direction.

"Like what you see, eh?" His voice was clear and sub-stantial sounding.

"Uh, yes sir. I've never been in a place like this before."

"Yes, it is pretty cool, isn't it?" He chuckled and placed his hands palm down on the desk.

"Say, uh, I was wondering—"

"The golden one? Display only, like it says."

"So does that mean you have others like it that *are* for sale?"

The man looked down at the table and chuckled again. Without looking up, he said, "No, I'm afraid not, child. Can I ask you something, though?"

"Uh, yeah, sure. And I'm almost thirteen. I'm not really a child anymore."

"Ah, pardon me. To these eyes, everyone seems a child. Here's what I want to ask: May I try to guess your name?"

That was weird, but hey—why not? "Okay. Shoot."

"Excellent." The old man laced his fingers together and closed his eyes. He rocked easily on his feet. "Hmm. Yes. You've got a royal name, I think. An old name. English. Not Charles. Not Henry or James. Edward? No, no. I think it starts with *A*." Artie felt his palms clam up. Then the man stopped rocking, opened his hands and his eyes, and leveled a gaze on Artie that made his knees buckle. "You're Arthur!"

Artie couldn't believe it. Then suddenly the message from the *Otherworld* game, the one he'd forced himself to forget, hit him like a bolt of lightning: *Arthur. In one week's time you will come to me at the IT. You are special, Arthur, and I have need of your service and power. I have been waiting so long for you. Your humble servant, M.*

The IT. Invisible Tower.

Which made this old guy M.

Artie took a small step backward as he realized that the Easter egg had not been a coincidence at all.

Then a silly notion sprang into his mind. He said, "Yeah, and I guess that makes you Merlin, huh?"

The words, while his own, sounded utterly ridiculous. Arthur and Merlin, together alone, in some geek-fest comic-book-collectors' shop called the Invisible Tower.

The old man smiled and took a deep breath before he spoke. "I've gone by many names, dear Arthur, some kind and some horrific. Lately I've been known as Lyn. Many of the children who enjoy my shop just call me "dude," which is a little absurd but fine by me. Merlin, though. My goodness."

Artie developed a lump in his throat the size of a tennis ball. He choked it back and asked, "So wait. You *are*, like, Merlin?"

"Aha! There you go again. So easily you say it! Part of the spell has already been broken. The first stones have begun to crumble. So soon I am in your debt."

Artie was thoroughly confused, and a little scared. He asked, "What are you talking about, mister?"

The man ignored Artie's trepidation and said, "Arthur, my boy, you may find this hard to believe, but there is magic at work here that has kept me from my proper name for nearly as long as I can remember. . . ." The old man looked at the ceiling then at the huge desk. He looked back at Artie. "Merlin! Not even I have been able to say it! Merlin. *Mer*lin!" Each time he said it, he got quieter and quieter, until he was whispering, "*Merlin.*"

Artie asked weakly, "So what exactly are you saying?"

"What I'm saying is that you are special, my boy. You see me as I am. Most people look at me and maybe they *begin* to think of Merlin, but then that idea is dashed from their mind. But you! You see me as I am," he repeated with wonder. "Tell me—what is the strangest thing about the way I look?"

Artie felt supremely uneasy, but this was a simple question to answer. "Your tattoos, sir," he said.

The old man beamed. "Exactly. Come here, I want to show you something."

Artie didn't want to go anywhere with this old freak, yet something about his tone enraptured him. He had to hear the old guy out. He said, "All the same, sir, I'd like to stay where I am. If you have something to show me, you'll have to show it to me from over there."

The man waved his hands through the air comfortingly and said, "Of course, of course. Here. Look." He bent down and lifted a small color TV onto the great desk. It took Artie a second to realize that he was looking at live surveillance images of the store. The bookshelves, the toy cases, the front door, the desk. There he was, and there was the old man. The man took off his hat. Something was different. Artie took a step forward and looked closely. The man in the monitor was bald but didn't appear to have a single tattoo on his head. Artie turned quickly to the man. He nodded. His head was definitely crisscrossed by a swarm of lines and runes and shapes, all in dark ink. Artie looked back at the monitor. It was as if the man on the screen had been washed clean.

"How are you doing that?"

"That is how most everyone sees me. As I said, Arthur, you are special. You are very special, my boy."

A shiver ran down Artie's spine.

"Special? You mean something's wrong with me?"

"No, no! Nothing is wrong with you. You are King Arthur, the only one who can break the spell and say my name. Which means, of course, that I *am* Merlin!"

This was too much. The heck with Kay's special controller. No way this old guy was the real Merlin and Artie was some kind of reincarnation of King Arthur. What did that even mean? That he was the king of England? Artie had never even been to England!

Surely Artie was going insane. Yeah, that was it.

Artie backpedaled. "I, uh, I've got to get out of here, mister. I'm thinking you're probably just a crazy old tattooed dude and I shouldn't be talking to you." Not looking where he was going, he bumped into a shelf and spun around a little. He had to look away to catch himself, and when he turned back, the man had moved from behind the desk and right up to Artie's side.

Artie backed quickly toward the exit, but while he did, the old man held his hands open in front of him and pleaded, "Please, child, hear me out! You are special! A king, I swear it! Ask your father, if you don't believe me! Ask how you came to him!"

"I'm adopted, I already know that!" Artie was halfway to the door. His instincts were to turn and run, but something about the power of the man's voice held his attention. It was like a spell was being cast over him.

The old man continued, "Yes, but ask about Mr. Thumb. Ask him where you're from. Ask Kynder today, and if he tells you that you are special too, then please consider coming back here tomorrow. You've nothing to fear! If you allow me to show you something, then the controller is yours—and Kay's as well!"

"Kay—how do you know my sis—" He was so close to the door now.

"I know much about you, Arthur. You've nothing to fear from me. You are my king! You are my king and I am now and forevermore at your service!"

Artie stumbled through the door into the blinding daylight as these preposterous words rang in his ears. Barely paying attention, he tripped across the pavement and back into the same cab, and without saying a word the driver sped off to the Hilton.

IN WHICH WE LEARN THAT ARTIE IS A PERFECTLY REGULAR AND LOVELY SON

4

𝕎hen 𝔄rtie got back to the hotel room he lied, saying that the store was closed but that it would be open early the next morning before the tournament started, and that he'd be happy to go back and get Kay a controller then. Kay was soothed a little, and Kynder was satisfied that it would be taken care of, and so they passed the rest of the day quietly hanging out in the room and around the pool on the roof.

Artie didn't mention the old man—wizard—Merlin— whatever—at all. But he couldn't stop thinking about him.

Trying to fall asleep that night was torture. How had that dude known Kay's and Kynder's names? Had he used magic on Artie? Was there even such a thing as magic? Was Artie going crazy?

He had to be.

But even if he was, this Merlin guy had touched on *the* question that Artie had longed to know the answer to: Where was he from? Kynder had never told him, preferring to play it off like it wasn't important because they had such a great little family. Still, like a lot of adopted kids, Artie couldn't help but wonder if he had come from somewhere—from *someone*—special. He didn't want to take anything away from Kynder, because he loved his dad a ton, but now more than ever he needed to know if he had come from someone *important*.

He resolved to do as the old man had said and ask. So, as Kay snored away in the other bed, Artie gathered his nerve and whispered into the darkness, "Kynder?"

"Mmmm?"

"You awake?"

"A little, Arthur." Kynder turned over and rubbed his face hard. "What's up?"

Artie said quietly, "I heard you talking to her yesterday."

Kynder paused. Finally he breathed, "You . . . did?"

"Yeah. Don't worry, I didn't tell Kay."

Kynder sounded sad when he said, "Me either."

"It's okay. It's better that way. But that's not what I want to talk about. It just got me thinking. You know, about how you got me. Can you tell me how you got me? Please?"

Kynder sighed and said, "I adopted you, Arthur, you

know that. Kay's mom and I adopted you, and awhile later Kay's mom left us. That's all."

Artie took a deep breath and then he said, "Yeah, but the thing is, I've been thinking about it a lot lately and I really want to know more. Look, don't ask me how, but I've heard a little about Mr. Thumb. Please, can you tell me the rest?"

Of course Artie knew nothing about Mr. Thumb, but he had to take a chance.

And it worked. After a few moments Kynder propped himself up and began talking. This was more or less how it went:

On a clear September night Kynder and his ex-wife were woken by a horrible sound coming from Kay's baby monitor: a sudden and horrendous coughing fit.

Kynder jumped out of bed and ran to Kay's room, his ex-wife not far behind. Kay's door was half open and they could see the warm glow of her night-light coming from inside. She coughed and gasped desperately.

But then she stopped, and the light from her room got much brighter. This, along with Kay's silence, made Kynder and his ex-wife freeze in astonishment.

Kynder took a deep breath and continued. He said, "Then Kay laughed, and the light went off and we went into the room. Kay was in her crib, her hair standing on end. And next to her, out of nowhere, was you. The two of you were staring at each other. It was—well, it was disorienting to say the least."

"Where did I come from?"

"Honestly, Artie, I still have no idea."

Kay turned and grunted in her bed.

Artie and Kynder quietly looked in her direction. Satisfied that she was still asleep, Kynder continued in a low whisper, "My ex-wife was totally confused and scared, but for some reason I wasn't. I checked you out and cleaned you up and gave you a bottle. You were a plump, healthy little boy. You and Kay seemed happy together, which helped calm me even more, but not Kay's mom. The things that happened that night—and the next day—changed her forever, and not in a good way."

Artie's heart sank a little at what this meant: Kay's mom left because of him.

Kynder went on, "For the rest of that night we were in shock. You guys drifted off peacefully, but my ex-wife and I couldn't possibly go back to sleep. We went to the kitchen, made coffee, and decided that in the morning we'd call the police. I still have no idea why we didn't call them right away, but we didn't.

"Which brings me to your Mr. Thumb. As the coffee brewed the phone rang, and on the other end was a man that went by that name. He had a British accent. He wanted to talk about you. What could I say but 'Go ahead.'

"Immediately he referred to you as Arthur Kingfisher, as if you were already a part of the family. He said that it was no coincidence that you had come to us—to me and Kay, actually—that the three of us were meant for one another—and that by three that afternoon we'd get a FedEx package with a bunch of paperwork that would facilitate our legally adopting you into our family. I tried to ask him questions, but he kept interrupting me, and when he was done telling me what was going to happen, he just hung up. I had no way to call him back.

"Still in shock, we waited. You guys got up and I fed you and dressed you. You and Kay spent the morning playing together so well that, in a very real and very strange sense, you *did* feel like part of the family. In fact, to me you already were. I know this sounds weird, but it was like a spell. From that moment on, I loved you like a son. The same could not be said for Kay's mom, though, and ultimately it was too much for her to handle. Within the year she'd left, and until yesterday I'd never heard from her again. She left because she couldn't adapt to you, but, Artie, her leaving wasn't your fault. It was *her* fault and *her* fault only."

Artie sank into his pillow and whispered, "Thanks," even though he felt pretty crummy. Kynder put a hand on his son's shoulder and went on.

"Anyway, at three on the dot the doorbell rang. It was the FedEx guy. Just a regular FedEx guy with a clipboard and a smile. I signed for the package, brought it in, and opened it up. It contained everything Mr. Thumb said it would. Still feeling spellbound, and with hardly a word between us, Kay's mom and I sat down and read everything, filled the papers out, stuffed them into the proper envelopes, and put them in the mail. Within a week we received confirmation from the state of Pennsylvania that you were ours. The rest, as they say, is history."

Kynder lay back down. Artie didn't know what to say. Kay sounded completely asleep.

Finally Artie asked, "So that's it?"

"Yeah, that's it."

Artie took another breath and asked, "So, does this mean I'm special or something? That I'm, like, a freak of nature? I mean, where *did* I come from?"

Kynder took what felt like forever to answer. But when he did, he sounded simultaneously sad, happy, relieved, and full of honesty. "Like I said, Artie, I really have no idea. I've tried to convince myself that you're normal, but the fact is you're not. If for no other reason than the way you appeared in our lives, you *are* special. Heck, for all I know you could be a space alien, or a fairy, or an android from the future. But, Artie: to me, it doesn't matter. None of it. I love you more than my own heart, if that's possible. To me you're special for one reason and one reason only: and that's that you are my son. My perfectly regular and lovely son."

Well, that did it. Artie knew before he fell asleep that night that, for better or worse, he was definitely heading back to the Invisible Tower. Maybe the old man knew more about where he came from. Maybe he even knew this Mr. Thumb.

The next morning Artie got up early and told Kynder and Kay that he was going to get "the best custom Xbox controller this side of the Mississippi." He said he'd be back with time to spare.

He took another cab to the store—with a different driver this time, thank goodness—but when he got there, it was closed. Artie started knocking, and very quickly the door unlatched. Artie pulled it open, but no one was there. The bell tinkled again, saying, "Welcome." Maybe bells *could* talk.

He stepped in and made his way to the back. Behind the big black desk stood the old man, wearing a Hawaiian shirt and cutoff blue jeans and the same porkpie hat and wooden pendant as the day before.

"Hello, my boy! So glad to see you. What did—"

Artie had played through his mind exactly what he was going to say, and he stood tall and spit it out: "Hold up, mister. Let me say something. I asked Kynder like you said, and he told me some stuff that I'm guessing you already know and that I'm not going to repeat. Mainly because it sounds pretty nutty."

"Okay."

"Yeah, well, the gist is that my dad says he isn't sure where I'm from, but that Mr. Thumb helped him adopt me. Kind of. Anyway, you said yesterday that you're Merlin and I'm King Arthur. That still sounds totally crazy to me—and I really don't believe you—but if it helps me learn a couple things about myself and also get that controller before my sister's tournament starts, I'm willing to play along. You just have to promise that you'll answer some of my questions, and that I'll get out of here in time."

The old man laced his fingers together and placed them on his small but bulging tummy. All he said was, "Done."

Artie took a deep breath. He'd never been more nervous

in his life, but something about the confidence that this man seemed to place in him made him feel strong and certain.

For Artie Kingfisher this was a first. The school bully, Frankie Finkelstein, wouldn't even have recognized him.

Artie said, "Okay, so you're Merlin. Really?"

"Really."

"All right. How old are you?"

"About seventeen hundred years, give or take."

"Wow. Okay, I don't really buy that, but whatever."

"Don't worry, you will."

"And you think I'm *King* Arthur."

"That's correct. But I don't just think it—I know it. And I can prove it to you, if you give me your faith and a little bit of time."

"We'll see. Who's Mr. Thumb? My father?"

Merlin laughed. "Good goodness, no, my boy! Thumb is more fairy than man."

"Okay, then who *is* my father?"

"Hmm. That's a harder question to answer. The short answer is Uther Pendragon."

"And my mom?"

"Lady Igraine."

"And where are they?"

"Dead, my boy! Been dead for ages!"

Artie furrowed his eyebrows and said, "I don't understand."

"Of course you don't! Please, Arthur—"

"Artie. Only Kynder calls me Arthur."

Merlin nodded. "Please, Artie, come with me. Let me show you what it is you're here to see." Merlin stepped away from the desk and motioned for Artie to join him. "We have to go to the basement. Don't worry. I am in your charge, Artie. Nothing bad will happen to you. Come."

"I don't know," Artie said slowly. He really didn't. And yet, there was something inside him that wanted nothing more than to go with this Merlin character.

"It will be worth your while. Then the controller will be yours."

"It won't take too long?"

"Don't worry about the time, I can take care of that."

"What, with a spell or something?"

"Something like that."

"So you are a"—Artie cut himself off, not believing what he was about to ask—"you really are a wizard, then?"

"My dear boy, what a preposterous question! I am Merlin! What kind of Merlin would I be if I weren't a wizard?"

Artie couldn't deny that he had a point. Provided this was all really happening, of course.

Artie shrugged. "Well, you don't look like one."

"What did you expect? It's the twenty-first century. Robes are too drafty. And the pointy hat went out of style hundreds of years ago, my liege."

That was weird, being called a liege.

"I really can't believe this," Artie said, as much to himself as to Merlin.

Merlin ignored him, moved to the curtain behind the desk, and parted it. "Come with me," Merlin pleaded.

And reluctantly, Artie did.

Merlin's basement was unlike anything Artie had ever seen.

The space was very long and deep. In fact, Artie couldn't see the end of it. There were brickwork arches holding up the ceiling, three abreast and about eight feet wide each, and the arches were supported by plain iron columns. Merlin paused in the first room to hang up his hat. This was an anteroom containing racks for clothing and hats, a long line of shoes on the floor, and a pedestal sink for washing up.

After stowing his hat and grabbing a light bamboo cane, Merlin moved into the next room, beckoning Artie to follow. He did.

Passing through the first archway was like being transported from a warm house into a hot, dank jungle. Every wall and surface was covered with plants of all kinds. Merlin moved quickly through this nursery without comment, and passed into the next room.

This room was also filled with plants but it was near freezing. If the first room felt like a South American jungle, then this room felt like a Himalayan mountaintop. But things lived here too. Small, desperate plants clung to stones, and little gnarled evergreens grew from the walls and floor. Artie realized that his breath was visible. Strangest of all was that this room had a very stiff breeze, even though there were no fans to be seen.

They moved through more rooms. One had a stream running through it; another was full of computers and video equipment; one was a fully functioning chemistry lab; at least three were menageries containing all different kinds of exotic animals. There was a room engulfed in different-colored fires, none of which gave off any heat, and there was a room made entirely of blue glacial ice but that was not at all cold. There were five rooms full of books and scrolls and tapestries, each with a nice place to sit. There was a room full of hand-to-hand weapons from all over the world and all through the ages. There was a room that contained two jail cells and some chains with cuffs attached to the walls; this room was musty and dead-feeling. There were familiar places too: a kitchen, a completely modern living room, a game room, and a room with an elliptical machine and free weights.

After they'd passed through the first jungle room, Merlin started talking like a tour guide.

"You know, Artie, no person, fairy, troll, or sentient what-have-you—other than myself and Mr. Thumb—has walked through these rooms in a long, long time. For all intents and purposes, you are the first person to ever see these places. Yes, I've spent many a day down here whiling away my time. And I'll tell you that I've not been lazy! In addition to all the old-style magic I know, I've learned quite a bit of the modern sciences down here—in fact, a little secret about magic is that a good portion of it is scientific trickery. Oh, there are real magic spells that alter the fabric of space and time and substance and all that, but no small part of enchantment is just applied biology, chemistry, and physics.

"In addition to learning the hard sciences, I've also become a pretty good computer programmer and a middling hacker. That's how I got that message to you, of course, in the *Otherworld* game. Bless the internet; what a marvel!

"*Any*way . . . Listen, Artie, here is the cold, hard truth: you are King Arthur, like it or not, and I am Merlin and we have been reunited on purpose. The simple fact is that you are here to help me. And I will, to the best of my ability, do everything *I* can to help *you*."

Artie wandered behind the old man. He was no longer

nervous. Now he was just flabbergasted. "Uh, okay."

"Now, you've heard of the sword in the stone, yes?"

"I guess. That's the one only King Arthur can pull out of the rock. Excalibur, right?"

Merlin looked over his shoulder and shouted, "Wrong! Excalibur is not the one from the stone—no, Excalibur is with the Lady of the Lake. The *sword in the stone* is Excalibur's cousin, Cleomede. It's like Excalibur's gatekeeper. If you can wield it in battle then you will have proved that you are worthy of Excalibur, at which point the Lady in the Lake will give it to you."

Artie stopped in a room full of spinning gears and gyroscopes and weird coils zapping mini bolts of lightning to one another. Merlin took a couple more eager steps before realizing his guest had frozen. He wheeled around with his head cocked.

Artie said, "Wait—did you say 'battle'?"

"Of course, my boy! You are King Arthur! One of the greatest warriors the world has ever seen!"

Artie knew that was *so* not true. He asked, "By 'battle,' you mean, like, real battle?"

Merlin shook his head in an offhand, vaguely reassuring kind of way, and said, "No, fake battle."

There was a brief silence, and Artie exhaled.

But then Merlin chuckled and said, "Of course real battle, Artie! Don't worry, for you it will be no more arduous than playing *Otherworld*. I've watched you. You're quite good at video games."

That may have been true, but the fact was that Artie was not a fighter. The idea of battle—which seemed about a million times worse than the idea of a simple fight—scared Artie to no end. He was a kid who had never thrown a retaliatory punch in his life. He had no intention of following this old guy into the depths of his dungeons, or whatever these crazy rooms were, only so he could be led into a full-on fight.

Check that: a full-on *sword* fight.

Artie tried to change the subject, preferring, like he usually did, to ignore his problems. "Kay's better at video games. Maybe you should be talking to her. Hey, which reminds me—I really need to get out of here."

"In due course. Remember, if you want that controller, then you need to let me show you something."

"And what exactly is that?"

"Come. We're almost there." The old man spun around and resumed marching through the mysterious rooms.

Finally they reached the end of the line. The last room's ceiling was lower by half than the others. Artie had to stoop slightly to keep his head from banging into the heavy wooden joists overhead. The walls were made of large, damp granite stones, and the floor was dirt. Merlin fit in the room without having to bend at all.

On the far side was a stone wall and a waist-high wooden door with brass bands and hinges and a large brass doorknob right in the middle of it.

"Here we are," Merlin said. "The back room. The caboose, as I like to call it. And in the caboose is this very special door. It even has a name—Mrs. Thresher. Depending on what I tell her, she can lead to many different places."

"And you want me to go through it?"

"Precisely. I want you to go through it to a place not far from here called Serpent Mound. Have you heard of it?"

"Nope."

"Well, Serpent Mound is a pre-Columbian effigy earth mound constructed by people belonging to what is known as the Fort Ancient culture around 1000 CE."

Artie pretended to know what Merlin was saying and said, "Oh yeah, that. Sure, I've heard of it."

"Good! It's in Peebles, Ohio, about seventy miles east of Cincinnati. I've never been there, but I know a fair amount about it. The main thing for us, and the reason you'll be going, is that it's a crossover point."

"A crossover point?"

"Yes. There are thousands of such points around the world, but, with a few exceptions, they have all been shuttered for a very long time."

"But crossover to what? To where?"

"In this case, to the sword in the stone."

"The sword in the stone—it's in Peebles, Ohio?"

"No, no! Don't be ridiculous. It's in the Otherworld."

"Like the video game?"

"Not entirely, but they do bear some similarities, as you'll soon find out."

"I'm sorry, Merlin, but I'm really confused."

"Naturally! That's why we're keeping your first trip to the *real* Otherworld short and sweet—and it's also why I'll be sending someone with you who possesses a bit of local knowledge."

"You aren't going to come with me?"

"Afraid I can't, Artie. I am unfortunately obligated to remain here. But Mr. Thumb has graciously offered to help."

At these words Merlin reached behind him and spun a leather fanny pack from his back to his front. Artie couldn't figure out how he'd failed to notice the bag before, because it was huge and dorky. Most strange was that the front of the bag—the side that faced outward—was perfectly clear, like a little window, and through this window emanated a steady blue light. Merlin opened the bag and stuck his hand inside, but he didn't fumble or search—he just put his hand in and waited. Then he pulled it out, peeked into it, and said something very quietly in a language Artie couldn't understand. Finally, Merlin held out his hand.

In Merlin's palm stood a miniscule man, no taller than a thumb, dressed in white and carrying a short red cane. He smiled when he said in a voice far larger than his diminished stature, "Hello, Artie! Mr. Tom Thumb at your service. Are you quite ready to make your mark on the world?" Where Merlin's accent was hard to place, Thumb's was definitely British.

"*Tom* Thumb. Like, *the* Tom Thumb."

"One and the same, my lad, one and the same."

"I thought you were from fairy tales—not King Arthur."

"Yes, well, my story has been mashed up over the ages. In point of fact, I was and am every bit a member of the Arthurian milieu. Merlin here made me, and King Arthur the First liked me so much he made me a knight of the Round Table!"

Merlin nodded as Artie mumbled, "Tom Thumb. I don't believe it."

"Do, my lad! Look me up on Wikipedia! It's all there in black and white!"

"Uh, okay . . ."

"Right! Now, then, give us your hand." In a daze, Artie did as he was told. The little man jumped from Merlin's palm to Artie's. "Let's go. No time like the present, I always say!"

Without wasting a beat, Merlin knelt by the door and began chanting lowly. Artie considered the possibility that here people just sat around and talked to doors all the time. Why not?

He also considered turning tail and running as fast as he could back outside.

But then Merlin stopped talking and the door began to creak open. Merlin jumped back. Thumb poked Artie's hand with his cane and said, "Well, let's go then! Sally forth, lad!"

And before Artie knew it, he was gingerly cradling a miniature man in one hand as he got down on the other and crawled through a short and magical door named Mrs. Thresher.

HOW ARTIE AND THUMB VISIT THE SWORD IN THE STONE

"**Put me down, you're squeezing** me."

Artie put Thumb on the ground and stood up. They were on a low rise of grass-covered earth surrounded by forest. It was the dead of night, and as this sank in, Artie had a moment of panic. How was it nighttime? Why was he doing this? Just for a stupid game controller?

No—he was doing it to find out something about himself. Something totally strange, it seemed.

As if he could read Artie's thoughts, Thumb said, "Fascinating, isn't it? Merlin can make some peculiar things happen."

"Yeah. I don't feel so good." Artie's stomach started to fill with butterflies.

"That's because we just went from day to night. Your

internal clock is spinning out of control. Try not to think about it. Now follow me."

They took off.

The air was warm and thick. A full moon hung high in the sky. A breeze whispered through the trees, and a jet droned far overhead.

As Thumb ran along the grassy hill, Artie realized that it must have been Serpent Mound. It was definitely snake-shaped, and they quickly reached the head, which looked like it was in the process of swallowing a large egg.

Thumb came to an abrupt stop and said, "Stand there."

"Where?"

"There! You need to get on the eastern foci. I will move to the western one!" Artie didn't know what a foci was, but he followed the tiny man's instructions.

Artie looked down, and a little to his left was a patch of grass illuminated by a lance of bright moonlight. He stepped onto the light and said, "Tom? I think you're a little bigger."

"Yes, I think I am too!" He was now about six inches tall. Thumb looked for the right spot, stopped resolutely, and several things happened at once.

Thumb grew a foot and a half. He was now about two feet tall, and all his clothes were still perfectly in place. An arc of moonlight shot up from the two spots they occupied, connecting above them. From this fell a delicate curtain of light, and as soon as it touched the ground, Thumb moved from his spot and parted the curtain with his cane—except that his cane was no longer a cane but rather a curved short sword in a red velvet sheath that looked kind of Asian.

Thumb said, "Come, lad, through here." Artie moved next to Thumb, and the little Englishman indicated that he wanted Artie to step through the moonlight arch.

And so he and Thumb stepped through.

Now they were somewhere else entirely.

They were still outside, and it was still night, but there was no moon and it was as black as tar. Thumb produced a mini Maglite from his pocket, turned it on, and took off at a jog. Artie followed, and Thumb started to speak in a fierce whisper.

"Listen, things are going to happen very quickly. A door between the worlds has not been opened in some time, so we should be ready for company. Hopefully we won't see anyone, but you never know. You get what you need to get, then we get out."

Artie was incredibly frightened. He felt very stupid for following these weird people to wherever he was. But at this point he had to play along. "And what is it I'm supposed to get?" he asked.

"Why, the sword from the stone, of course!"

Oh, that.

They ran over hard ground, following the beam that danced from Thumb's flashlight. Artie couldn't make out their surroundings, but they appeared to be on a country footpath. They were running hard when suddenly Thumb stopped. He pointed his sheathed sword into the darkness. Artie froze.

"Shh!" Thumb hissed.

Thumb stuck the flashlight in his mouth and silently drew the sword a couple inches from its sheath.

Artie couldn't hear a thing. Thumb whispered through clenched teeth, "There!" Thumb swung his light to the center of a grassy circle in which stood a spur of stone about four feet high. Jutting from the top of the promontory was the hilt of a sword. He commanded, "That's it lad; go and get it!"

Artie's heart raced as he felt his blood course through his body.

He walked quickly to the rock, breaking the beam of light that Thumb had trained on their prize.

The stone was easy enough to summit. Once on top, Artie straddled the weather-beaten sword and gave it a little kick. It didn't budge. He bent over and slapped it lightly— still it didn't move. He stood and looked into the light and said, "It seems pretty in there!"

"Quiet, lad! Grab the hilt and get on with it!"

Artie heard nothing but his heartbeat and breath. "Fine," he snapped. He bent and wrapped his hands around the hilt of the sword. He felt no tingle of destiny, saw no glow of enchantment. This was stupid. The sword was stuck—it might as well have been part of the rock.

But then he started to stand, and, unbelievably and quite effortlessly, the sword moved!

It slid out easily.

So now Artie had a sword. He didn't feel any different. He certainly didn't feel kingly or anything. Artie held it in front of him, the point down, and regarded it like a bad report card or glass of spoiled milk.

He turned to Thumb to ask if they could go now, but before he could say anything, he heard something. Something that made his knees buckle and the back of his neck go cold.

Thumb's light moved erratically and then hit the ground, rolling to a stop. Whatever was out there was breaking branches and moving very fast in Artie's direction. Then Artie heard the sizzle of Thumb's sword as it was freed from its sheath; Thumb's grunts off to Artie's right; the *whisk* of his sword through the air, followed very quickly by two liquid *pops* and then a gruesomely muffled *crack*. The sounds had moved around the edge of the clearing from right to left. Thumb yelled, "Ha!" And then he said, "Behind you, lad!"

And in that instant Artie heard something take to the air.

It goes without saying that Artie Kingfisher had never held a sword before, let alone wielded one in an honest-to-goodness fight. But he'd spent countless hours wielding virtual swords, daggers, axes, spears, pikes, crossbows, maces, hammers, and longbows in video games. And with all the gardening the Kingfishers did, he was pretty handy with pickaxes, posthole diggers, and shovels.

This sword, however, was nothing like a posthole digger.

As Artie spun to face whatever it was that was flying at him, time slowed and he became keenly aware of a couple things.

First: this sword was incredibly light, and perfectly balanced, and even felt a little bloodthirsty.

Second: the thing flying at him was both familiar and horrifying. It was about the size of a Labrador. It had yellow eyes, super-long ruby-red teeth, and green iridescent skin. Its taloned feet strained toward Artie, like an eagle going in for the kill, and its golden claws had to be at least five inches long.

The sword was still pointed down, slightly across his body, and by now the thing was only a few feet away. Artie reacted and swung the sword in a long arc. It felt like hitting a hanging breaking ball over the fence. The sword sliced the thing's skin and severed its neck. Through his new weapon, Artie could feel the heat of the creature's blood.

Its head sailed over his right shoulder and its serpentine body fell with a thump on his left side, well past the stone.

Artie had just killed something that was trying to kill him.

He'd never felt so alive in his life.

"Ha-ha! Yes!" exclaimed Thumb from the darkness. He jumped into the clearing, retrieved the flashlight, and ran to the stone. "Come down from there, and let's get going," he barked.

Artie was still in shock. "Did I just—?"

"You most certainly did, my boy!"

"Was that . . . was that a dragon?"

"Righto! Or not a dragon exactly, but a dragoling."

"You mean a baby dragon? A baby, uh, *green* dragon?" For now it was as plain as day that this thing was a small version of Caladirth, the pesky serpent from the *Otherworld* video game.

"Aye, lad. Hellish things, aren't they?"

"Uh, yeah."

"Got two myself over there in the bush."

Then Artie thought of something. "Did they have a mom or dad or anything?"

"Most likely, lad. That's why we need to wrap this up and get moving!"

Thumb didn't need to say that twice.

Artie hopped from the rock. Thumb produced a short

rope and motioned for the sword. Artie handed it to him, and Thumb tied a sash for Artie to carry his new weapon. As he worked he spoke quickly. "Can't fathom why these things were here. I don't see why there would be any need to post a guard on the stone. . . ." He handed the sword back to Artie, who slung it nervously over his shoulder. Thumb, still thinking out loud, said, "Bless my stars, these dragolings are very curious, very curious indeed!"

Thumb turned back around and, judging by the look on his face, seemed suddenly to have forgotten his concern. He looked Artie over and smiled broadly. "The sword—Cleomede—she becomes you, my boy."

Artie didn't really care about that at the moment. "Tom, shouldn't we get going?" he asked.

"Oh yes! Of course we should! To the moongate, lad!"

Thumb wheeled and ran back to the path they'd come up. Artie eagerly followed him.

As they ran in silence, Artie thought, I just killed something with a sword. *I just killed something with a sword. I JUST KILLED SOMETHING WITH A SWORD!*

But then his mind went blank as a sound unlike any he'd ever heard rose up behind them. It was part wail, part scream, part three-alarm fire. He looked over his shoulder and saw a huge green glow light up the trees from where the sword in the stone had been. Artie and Thumb stopped briefly in their tracks. Thumb turned to Artie with a look of terror on his face and yelled, "Quickly, lad, as fast as you can!"

They took off at a dead sprint, and in spite of being much smaller, Thumb kept up with Artie quite easily.

The sound behind them changed. It was like a huge machine beginning to turn on, or like a gust of air pushing itself through a massive bellows.

It was the sound of two wings beginning to flap.

"Don't look back, my boy!" Thumb implored.

Artie wasn't planning on it. He saw the moongate ahead and ran fast and then faster. Thumb did the same. They hit the portal at breakneck speed and tumbled through it head over heels.

Artie looked behind them. There was nothing there. Just the woods surrounding Serpent Mound in Peebles, Ohio, on a beautifully moonlit night.

"What *was* that, Tom?" Artie asked, out of breath.

"That, my boy, was a close shave, wouldn't you say?"

"Uh, yeah! But was that really a dragon?"

"Can't be sure, but it certainly sounded like one."

Artie started to walk away from Thumb, who'd shrunk back to his smallest size. Artie reached over his shoulder to touch the hilt of the sword. It was too much.

He dropped cross-legged to the ground. Thumb walked to Artie's feet and rested a hand on his leg. He sighed and said, "I know this is a lot to take in, lad."

"I'll say. These things don't happen, Tom. I'm talking to a man the size of a baseball. . . . And we just killed three baby dragons. . . . These things don't happen."

Thumb gave Artie a grave look. "Whether you like it or not, these things *do* happen, and whether you knew it or not, these things have been happening to you your whole life. You did well back there, but trust me, you will have to do more than that before your days are done. I know this isn't making sense, but it will. I swear to you, it will."

Artie took a deep breath and nodded. "All right." He stood. "Let's get back to Merlin. I want to get that controller and go back to my family."

Thumb nodded. "Of course, lad."

They silently made their way along Serpent Mound. When they reached the spot where they'd crawled through Mrs. Thresher, Thumb tapped the ground. It started to glow and very quickly the light became so intense that Artie was momentarily blinded. When the light faded, he found himself back in Merlin's basement, in the first room at the bottom of the stairs.

The little man—or fairy or whatever he was—said, "There's the sink. Why don't you wash up?" Artie went and splashed his face and forearms. As he did, he noticed something orange swirling down the drain.

Dragoling blood.

Great.

When he was done, Thumb looked him up and down and said, "Good as new. Merlin's upstairs waiting for you. He'll give you what you came here for."

Artie looked over his shoulder and saw the hilt still hanging there. It was so light. "Okay," he said.

"I'll be seeing you right soon, lad. You and me, we're going to have lots of capital-*A* adventures!"

Artie felt like they'd already had a capital-*A* adventure and wasn't so sure he wanted another.

Dazed, Artie shuffled up a few stairs before turning back. "Hey, Tom, thanks for taking care of those things back there."

"Don't mention it, lad. Someone's got to look after you. Off you go now!"

Back in the shop Merlin was talking to a couple of kids a little younger than Artie. A grown-up behind them thumbed through a graphic novel. Artie was suddenly conscious of the sword. Merlin broke away from his customers midsentence, turned to Artie, and said under his breath, "Don't worry, they can't see it. Look in the video monitors." Artie looked and, sure enough, there was no sign of Cleomede. Then Merlin piped up and said, "Children, you are very lucky. This young man has proven himself worthy of one of my rarest possessions! He has won the Golden Controller!"

"No way!" exclaimed the boy, expressing immediate admiration for Artie.

"I thought no one could get that!" said the girl, sounding more disappointed than impressed.

"Not no one, child, just not *any*one. Artie is this young man's name, and he is quite special. Go on, Artie, help yourself. Take the controller, but come back tomorrow when the tournament is over. We have some unfinished business to attend to."

Artie went to the case, which had been opened since he'd gone on his surrealistic adventure, and picked up the controller. It was a lot heavier than he expected. He put it in a bag that Merlin held open for him, and headed toward the exit.

"I called a taxi for you," Merlin shouted. "And remember tomorrow, sire!"

Sire. That would take some getting used to.

Artie climbed into the yellow Cincinnati Checker cab idling in front of the shop and found himself back at the hotel in five minutes. He was so out of it that as he was getting out, he didn't hear the young driver exclaim, "I'll be seeing you around, kid!"

Artie threw Cleomede over his shoulder as inconspicuously as he could. No one said a thing about it or paid him any special attention.

He had an invisible sword? Really?

He walked through the lobby, got into a full elevator, and no one stared. He passed a cleaning lady in the hallway outside his room, and all she said was, "Hello there."

He had an invisible sword. Really.

He let himself into the room. Kay and Kynder were resting on the beds. When he walked in, Kynder propped himself on his elbows and said, "There you are. I was just beginning to worry."

He didn't notice the sword at all. "Nothing to worry about!" Artie said uneasily. "Here. Check it out, Kay." Artie removed the controller from the bag and held it out.

She took it without taking her eyes off her brother. Kynder didn't seem to notice, though, and he said, "Well, that looks really cool, Kay. I think it'll work great for the tourney, don't you?"

"Uh, yeah, should be fine," she said.

"Great," Kynder blurted, "I'm going to grab a shower."

"Cool," Kay said.

Kynder went into the bathroom and closed the door. Artie didn't move.

Kay asked, *"What is that?"*

Artie said weakly, "That's your stupid controller."

"I can see that, Slick, but I mean *that*." She pointed directly at him and said in a desperate whisper, *"The sword!"*

"What sword?"

"Uh, the medieval-looking broadsword hanging over your shoulder!"

"You can see it?"

"Of course I can."

"No one else can. Kynder can't. The cabbie couldn't. No one else can see it!"

"Bull."

"Not bull. Look, I'll take it off and lean it against the wall over here, and wait and see if Kynder says anything."

"Wow. Okay. But you're crazy."

"Maybe." Artie put the sword down, and as he did, everything that had happened drew into focus. He had met Merlin. Tom Thumb had guided him. He had taken the sword from the stone. He had seen and slain a dragoling. He was King Arthur and, while totally unsure of what that meant, he was proud of himself.

He couldn't explain why it all made sense, but suddenly it did.

He looked at Kay. "Later on today, after you win the tournament, I think things will get a little clearer."

"How's that?"

"You—you and Kynder—we've got to go back to that store. You'll see."

"See what?"

"I can't explain."

"Artie, *what* is going on?"

"After the tournament," he said.

Kynder walked out of the bathroom in a robe to get a clean shirt before showering. Kay said, "Hey, Kynder."

"Hey, Kay."

"Notice anything weird in here?"

"Not really. You two can be a little weird, but I like you that way," he said with a smirk.

"That's not what I'm talking about, but thanks for the compliment. What I mean is, you see anything, like, strange over in that general area?" Kay pointed directly at the sword.

Kynder looked at his daughter quizzically, then to where she was pointing, then back to her. "You all right, Kay?"

"You don't see anything weird over there?"

"Unless the wall is strange, no." Kynder shook his head. "Did you have too much Coca-Cola yesterday?" He headed back to the bathroom, mumbling, "Really, I don't know why I indulge you two like I do."

Kay was dumbfounded. "Artie, *what* is going on?" She walked up to the sword and touched it. She picked it up. "Man, it's light." She turned the sword in her hands. Then she looked closely at the blade and demanded, "Artie, what is this? Is this *blood*?"

The boy who would be king just nodded sheepishly.

𝕶𝖆𝖞 𝖈𝖆𝖑𝖒𝖊𝖉 𝖉𝖔𝖜𝖓, 𝖑𝖔𝖇𝖊𝖉 𝖙𝖍𝖊 new controller, and summarily kicked everyone's butt at the tournament in record time. Her victory was so complete that Kynder deemed her controller "inspiring." He insisted that before leaving town they visit "this Indivisible Tower place" to pay a debt of gratitude.

And so at five thirty they found themselves staring at the Invisible Tower's front door.

Kynder pulled it open, and they stepped inside.

Like Artie, Kay and Kynder were also very impressed with the place. Kynder gravitated immediately to a case full of vintage action figures. Kay moved to the comic book shelves. Artie just waited for Merlin.

After a minute or two the old man drifted up the center

aisle toward Kay, who, looking at an issue of *The New Avengers*, didn't notice him at all.

When he was next to her, he said, "Hello there!" in a velvety, soothing voice.

Kay yelped, "Oh!" She took one look at the old man and said, "Wow! Nice tats, Gramps."

"Aha! I'm glad you can see them." Artie walked toward them as Merlin whispered conspiratorially, "Not everyone can, you know. Your brother can. Your father will not."

"Like that crazy sword Artie's carrying?"

"Precisely."

"So you gave that to him?"

"No. He had to go and get it. As a matter of fact, he's supposed to give it to you once he retrieves Excalibur."

The mention of Excalibur didn't faze Kay in the least. She thumbed through the comic book, saying, "Really? Cool, I guess. Not sure why Artie has a sword, but it is pretty sweet, being invisible and all."

Artie stepped to Kay's side and awkwardly said, "Sis, this is—well, his name is Merlin—and he's got something to do with—"

Kay interrupted, "Wait. *Merlin?* Are you kidding me?"

Artie shook his head. Merlin placed a hand on Kay's shoulder and said, "He is not, my dear. I am the wizard Merlin, and your brother is a king, and you are his champion."

Kay spun to her brother and demanded, "Artie, what's this geezer talking about?"

Artie held up his hands and answered, "Just listen to him. I know it sounds crazy, but just listen, okay?"

Kay scrunched her face and turned back to the old man. "All right, Pops. I'll do what Artie says, but I want you to know that you're starting to creep me out."

Merlin smiled. "Of course I am, my dear! It's not every day you meet a wizard! Come. Let's find your father."

Kay rolled her eyes and said, "Okay, whatever."

They made their way to the back of the store as Merlin called out, "Kynder Kingfisher? Come here, please."

Kynder wandered down the far aisle and when he got to them, he stuck out his hand. As promised, he didn't seem to notice the old codger's tattoos at all. Kynder said, "Hello, sir! Seems my children already told you my name, but let's make it official. Kynder Kingfisher. It's a pleasure to meet you."

The old man took his hand and said, "I can assure you that the pleasure is all mine, Mr. Kingfisher. My name is Merlin."

"Well, it's very nice to meet you, Merlin," Kynder said casually, as if the old man was instead named "Steve."

"Likewise. If I may say, you've done a marvelous job with the children."

"Thank you," Kynder replied. "And thank you also for

selling Artie that lucky controller. I've never seen someone play a video game as proficiently as Kay did today. Really, I hesitate to say it, but it was almost magical!"

Merlin beamed. "Imagine that! I'm glad to have been of service and I thank you for your gratitude. As a gesture of goodwill, I wonder if you might allow me to give you the dollar tour?"

"That would be great, wouldn't it, guys?"

Artie and Kay both said sure.

"Fantastic!" Merlin said. He tented his fingertips. "Well, you've seen the store, so let's continue with the really interesting stuff, which happens to be in the basement."

Merlin moved behind the desk and parted the curtain, holding out his hand as an invitation. Kynder accepted and walked to the back.

"Here we go, I guess," said Kay.

Artie, bringing up the rear, confirmed, "Yep, here we go."

And they went downstairs.

Kynder didn't get to see *all* the interesting stuff—only because he was so impressed by the second room. As soon as they'd stepped into the tropical greenhouse, Kynder gawked like a kid in a candy store.

"Ghost, phantom, Florida blue!" Kynder's finger pointed around the room, indicating orchids. "A nun's orchid, a pansy.

Oh, look! What's that one, Merlin?"

"A Dracula cutis-bufonis."

"My goodness, it's hideous! It's gorgeous!"

"Thank you, Mr. Kingfisher. How about you stay here with these precious plants while Kay and Artie and I carry on? I've a few things to discuss with them."

Enraptured, Kynder absently said, "Yes, yes, that's fine."

Artie and Kay shared a puzzled look. Merlin said, "Great. Follow me, then, children."

Merlin led them through the same rooms that Artie had seen the day before, and they were every bit as fantastic the second time through.

Artie watched his sister closely. He was glad to see that he was not the only one who couldn't believe what was happening. Yet Kay's open mouth and widened eyes made him a little more afraid. What he couldn't believe was happening *was happening*.

Eventually they reached a comfy sitting room, and Merlin stopped. The room had three overstuffed leather chairs arranged around a low, round coffee table.

"Please, sit down," the old man said. They did. Merlin stood behind the chair opposite them.

Kay studied the room. Its walls consisted mostly of shelves covered with musty scrolls and hefty tomes; it smelled ancient and was lit by dim electric sconces. Aside from the books, a whole shelf was devoted to an elaborate, open-air terrarium, in the middle of which stood a large mushroom-shaped thing made of Legos. As she looked closer, she saw windows in its large red cap, and a brown drawbridge door in its sturdy stem. In front of the mushroom house on a patch of moss were a little table and chair. And then, suddenly, she noticed something move behind one of the windows. She shook her head, but there it was again: the silhouette of a small man. Her heart quickened. To conceal her anxiety she pointed at the coffee table and quipped, "So, what, is this like the first meeting of the new knights of the Round Table?"

Merlin chuckled and said, "Well, I hadn't meant it that way, but yes, it is!"

Artie clapped his hands on his knees and with a lot of uncharacteristic authority he proclaimed, "All right—if this is supposed to be the Round Table, and I'm supposed to be King Arthur, and you're supposed to be my wizard—why don't you tell us whatever it is you're going to tell us?"

Kay playfully punched her brother on the shoulder and said, "You tell him, Your Highness!"

Merlin was equally impressed. He sat and stared intently at both Kingfisher children. Then he said, "Very good. Where should we begin?"

"Why don't we tell Kay about what happened yesterday?" Artie suggested.

Merlin nodded and began, "Well, as you know, Artie

came here in search of a special controller for your tourn—"

"Wait," Artie interrupted. "Why don't we get *Tom* to tell her?"

"Aha! Good idea. Tom?"

Kay asked, "Tom? Who's Tom?"

The answer came from the Lego mushroom. A voice there said, "I am Tom. Tom Thumb. And I am at your service!"

Kay shook her head. There, near the little chair on the patch of moss, stood a man no more than three inches tall. Kay stood up quickly and exclaimed, "What's that? Is this some kind of game?"

Merlin rose and held out his hand for Thumb to climb into and then sat back down. Kay remained standing, never taking her eyes off the little man.

Artie put a hand on his sister's arm and said, "Kay, I know it's crazy, but *that* is Tom Thumb."

Kay dropped back into her chair, saying, "Like from Grimms' fairy tales or whatever?"

Thumb answered, "The same, my dear, though I was never properly a member of the family Grimm. The truth is that I have always been a friend of Merlin's, and I was very dear to King Arthur himself—for your information you are looking at a bona fide knight of the Round Table!"

"Artie, please tell me what's going on," Kay pleaded weakly.

Artie smiled and asked Thumb to explain instead.

And he did. With lots of class and good-natured British authority, Tom Thumb told Kay all about the adventure to pull Cleomede from the stone, and how together they'd killed three nasty little dragons.

When he was done, Kay asked quietly, "But how can any of this be true?"

"Well—" Artie started.

But Kay had a revelation. She interrupted, asking, "Does this have anything to do with what Kynder told you last night? About how you appeared in my crib? About Mom?"

She *had* heard. Artie's heart sank.

"My dear Kay, it has everything to do with that!" Merlin said excitedly. "Please, can I tell you some of what I know? I'll first tell you why you're here, and then tell you about the Otherworld."

"The Otherworld," Kay said flatly. "Like the video game?"

Artie said, "Kinda. The *real* Otherworld. That's where I got the sword."

"Oh, okay," Kay deadpanned.

Merlin interrupted them by waving his hands through the air. The library changed. All around blossomed a world of giant trees and purplish skies. Apparently, Merlin's tale was going to be illustrated.

Merlin cleared his throat and began, "Tom and I used to live in the Otherworld. In a place called Sylvan."

"That's one of the lands in the video game!" Artie said.

"Yes, and it's what you see now in this room," Merlin said.

"Sylvan is the emerald isle of the Otherworld," Thumb said longingly. "I spent many a fine year there."

Merlin continued, "The Otherworld is this world's sibling. It's not an alternate reality, but more a hidden place that is superimposed over and around ours in subtle and invisible ways. This side shares much with its sister: trees, plants, and creatures; the atmosphere; the planet and its location in the solar system; time. In some ways the worlds feed each other. For instance, when animals go extinct here, they move there. And in other ways they are totally different: while we get our energy from oil and coal, they get theirs from an amazingly clean source only found on their side; while we have too many people, they have too few; and while we have science and progress, they have magic and stasis. The Otherworld is where I learned all of my ancient craft, and I yearn to return to it."

"Wow," Artie and Kay said together.

"Yes. It's a remarkable place. One that I've been unable to see for a long, long time. In fact, I've not seen even a crack of sky or a patch of meadow in *this* world for the same length of time. The Invisible Tower is my prison, you see. A cabal of Otherworld witches and sorcerers conspired first to murder the original King Arthur, and then to jail me. I have been here for nearly fifteen hundred years, unable to see a path to escape. Until now."

"You mean until Artie showed up?" Kay asked.

"Precisely. Which brings me to why you are here. Artie, I need your help. Simply put, I need you to break me out of this prison." Merlin paused, and the silence was deafening. He put his hands together like he was praying. He leaned toward Artie and said quietly, "Our fates are intertwined, my liege. Only with your help, and the help of your sword, Excalibur, can I get the key that will destroy the invisible tower that rises above this building in Cincinnati, Ohio."

"You mean there really is a tower up there?" Artie asked faintly.

Merlin leaned back and said, "Hard to believe, but yes."

Kay was less impressed. "Okay, so why were you imprisoned? Doesn't that mean you did something bad? And if that's the case, why should we help you?"

Merlin wrinkled his forehead and said, "Good questions, Kay. The short answer is that I am not bad, and that I need to be freed so that I can help you and your brother save the Otherworld—and this world too."

Kay gave Merlin a sidelong glance and said, "I didn't realize the world needed saving, Gramps. Sure, it's messed up and everything, but it's not like it's going to blow up anytime soon, right?"

"No, not anytime soon. But here's the thing: energy

and life and magic for eons used to flow freely between the worlds. But those who jailed me here believed that the Otherworld—*their* world—would be safer if it was isolated from this side. So they closed all the crossover points and separated earth's twin realities. This is bad because if they remain separated, there's no chance that this side will gain access to the Otherworld's clean energy source, and if this side can't get that, then it's doomed. The Otherworlders haven't cared about this side for more than a thousand years, but what they've forgotten is that they share this world's fate. Everything is connected. Eventually they too will suffer from higher seas, and heat, and drought, and flooding, and disease. Humans and fairies and everything in between will die, and knowledge and magic will pass with them. We must stop this from happening."

"But how?" Artie asked, his knee suddenly bouncing wildly.

"First by getting me out of here. Then by reconnecting the worlds and reestablishing your kingdom. And ultimately, by defeating those who killed Arthur the First, and captured me, and sealed the worlds from each other over fifteen hundred years ago."

Thumb added, "We stop it by putting an end to the reign of the foul witch Lordess Morgaine of Fenland and her illegitimate son, Mordred!"

The rural scene around them darkened and became

overgrown with vines and hanging mosses. "Fenland. That's in the video game too," Artie whispered. He knew that Fenland was where the really hard quests took place.

"That's right, but you won't find Morgaine in the game," Merlin said. "She is real, and far too troublesome to inhabit something as straightforward as a video game. Surely she knows by now that Cleomede has been drawn from the stone. She will try to prevent you from getting Excalibur, but once you do get the sword, she will likely try everything in her power to take the sword from you. She will not want you to use it to free me. She will not want you to take your kingship."

"I have to say, Merlin, this isn't much of a sales pitch," Kay said.

"No, it won't be easy, lads, but I'll be with you, and we know that you can do it," Thumb said encouragingly.

Kay asked, "All right. So what happens if we say no?"

Merlin shifted in his chair and said, "Then there is no hope. I will remain imprisoned, and you and your children will live in a dying world. Magic—real magic—will fade. Science will cease to progress. Artie's destiny will go unfulfilled. You, Kay, will learn nothing more about your mother. And all the while you both will wonder what life would have been like if you had said yes!"

Another silence overcame them. The Otherworld scenes projected around the room faded.

Merlin and Thumb waited. Kay crossed her arms. Artie continued to bounce his leg furiously. Finally he broke the silence by asking, "But why me, Merlin? I'm just a stupid kid! I mean, why would I be able to beat the people that you and the real King Arthur couldn't?"

Thumb said soothingly, "You are not that different from the first Arthur, you know. He too was terrified of his destiny when he pulled the sword from the stone. . . ."

Merlin waved at Thumb and said, "The reason why you will succeed where your genetic sibling could not is that this time we will be ready for the treachery that befell Arthur the First. This time we will not be tricked."

"Wait. Genetic sibling?" Artie asked, his head spinning even more.

"Correct. You are kindred to Arthur the First—you were made in the Otherworld by DNA from relics of the first Arthur's parents: a finger bone from King Uther Pendragon and a lock of hair from Lady Igraine. When you were a baby, I risked much and had you brought here, so that Morgaine could not find you."

"Whoa. So you're saying that Artie's, like, a clone?" Kay asked.

Merlin said, "No. A clone is a copy—technically Artie is King Arthur's brother."

"Man. Far out," Kay said.

Artie wrinkled his eyebrows and thought hard. He put

a hand on his knee and forced his leg to stop bouncing. He looked at Thumb and then at the wizard. He said, "I don't know. This doesn't sound fun, Merlin."

"Nonsense, lad, it'll be the adventure of your life!" Thumb said eagerly.

"Yeah, it'll be great," Kay said with a heavy dose of irony. She was obviously not convinced about all of this, but even so, Artie could sense that she was more excited than she'd ever been. The idea of her being a knight, and of him being a king, really got Kay pumped.

"Please, Artie," Merlin said gravely, leaning forward. "If I've learned anything during my captivity, it is that power has its limits. I can't escape without you. You can't reconnect the worlds without me. I need you, and the worlds need us. Will you help? Will you take the next step and retrieve Excalibur? Will you answer your destiny and become our once and future king?"

Artie was dumbstruck. Should he help? If what Merlin said was true, then yes, of course he should. But beyond that there was another, more personal, reason. As the moments passed, a strange voice surged inside Artie, insisting, *You are King Arthur!* All of a sudden Artie was desperate to know where that voice had come from. He knew that if he said yes, he would find out.

Finally he looked into Merlin's deep, gray eyes and said, "All right. Let's go get my *real* sword."

Thumb yelled, "Huzzah!" while Merlin slapped his knees and stood up with a look of supreme satisfaction on his face.

Kay said, "Okay. I'm in too. It *will* be pretty cool to learn how to use a sword, I guess. We are going to have to learn how to use swords, aren't we, Merlin?"

"Indeed you are, Kay," Merlin said, beaming with enthusiasm. "I have a special swordsmanship book that I want you to read. Practice with Cleomede. You're both going to need it."

"Right," Artie said, shaking his head in disbelief. "Because, you know, we're going to be getting in lots of sword fights soon. . . ."

"Darn skippy we are, Bro," Kay said, brimming with the anticipation that Artie lacked.

"Okay. So what's next, Merlin?" Artie asked, still thinking about having a sword swung in his direction.

Merlin began to pace excitedly as he said, "Well, tomorrow, after you've gone home and gotten a good night's sleep, fire up *Otherworld*. There's another Easter egg you need to find that will help with retrieving Excalibur. Aside from that there won't be much to do until next Friday, when you will need to reconvene at Serpent Mound. Oh, and don't bother talking to Kynder about any of this. He won't really hear you."

"What do you mean?" asked Artie.

"I mean I've cast a little spell over your father. Don't worry, it's quite harmless. It's just that we can't rush him into this. I fear it would hit him too hard. For now it means that the two of you will have no small amount of power over your father. He will do many of the things you ask without question. He will also ignore many of the stranger things you do, even if you do them right in front of his eyes."

"Like practice with Cleomede," Kay said.

"Precisely," Merlin confirmed.

Artie added, "Or bring us to Serpent Mound when we ask him to."

"Precisely again."

Artie and Kay smiled at each other. This might be fun.

Merlin lifted Thumb back up to his Lego mushroom house and stretched. Artie and Kay suddenly felt exhausted. It was time to go. They got Kynder, went upstairs, said good-bye to Merlin, and walked toward their car.

Before getting in, Artie turned and tried to imagine a huge stone tower standing over them. It was pretty hard to picture. A breeze far too cold for summer blew across his face.

He peered at the store's entrance to see if there was any sign of the old man, but all the lights were out. It was as if the wizard had never been there at all.

𝕶𝖞𝖓𝖉𝖊𝖗 𝖜𝖆𝖘 𝖈𝖍𝖆𝖙𝖙𝖞 𝖙𝖍𝖊 𝖜𝖍𝖔𝖑𝖊 ride home, even though Artie and Kay hardly said a word. He talked about orchids and gardening and video games, and even carried on a very Dr Pepper–head debate about whether lightsabers were better than phasers.

They finally got home at eleven that night. Artie ambled out of the car and went to bed. He didn't wake the next day until almost two in the afternoon.

He went down to the kitchen, where Kay was studying the swordsmanship manual. Kynder was relaxing in the backyard.

Artie opened the fridge and stared into it, not sure what he wanted or even if he was hungry. Kay said, "This sword book is nuts. Can I play with Cleomede later on?"

Artie shut the fridge and turned to his sister. "Sure. It's in my room. How long you been up?"

"Hours. Couldn't really sleep. Besides all the other weirdness, I couldn't get that Thumb dude out of my mind."

"He's hard to forget."

"No doubt. So are you going to check out the game, like Merlin said?"

"I guess so," Artie answered. The long night of sleep had sapped Artie's resolve a little. At the moment he didn't feel like a king of anything.

Artie sighed, stepped next to his sister, and looked at the swordsmanship book. It was full of illustrations in gold and silver that practically leaped off the page. He turned to his sister and asked, "Kay, are you ready for all this?"

Her answer was swift. "You know I am."

Artie nodded and decided he better get ready again too. He went down to the game room, and started up *Otherworld*. His character, Nitwit the Gray, was still in Caladirth's lair. Artie had no idea where to look, so he headed out the main exit of the cave, and there he found something he wasn't expecting at all.

Just past the cave opening—which had been in a snowy wood near the Vale of Goch—was an arched, blinking electric sign that read "Welcome to the OTHERWORLD." Beyond this was a pleasant country road bursting with the colors of late spring, not a snow-covered forest. In the middle of the road stood a suit of plate-mail armor.

The armor's metal was as green as Nickelodeon slime, and airbrushed across the breastplate was a bough of holly crossing a battle-ax in front of a large evergreen tree. The visor was up and inside the helmet there was—well, there was nothing.

Nitwit took a few steps forward, and the suit raised a hand in salute. It spoke in a deep, echoing baritone.

"Hello, good sir! My name is Bercilak—though most call me Greenie—and I seek no battle, I assure you truly." This was good news because Greenie wielded a battle-ax that was twice as menacing-looking as the one Artie's character had. The armor continued, "As the sign says, I am here to welcome you to the Otherworld! Now, please, to facilitate our meeting, affix your headset and speak through the microphone as if I were a comrade of yours playing this game over your 'internets.' Is that right?"

Artie was thunderstruck, but he did as he was told. When he was ready, he corrected Greenie, "Uh, no, we call it the internet."

"Excellent! My bad. That is what you say, yes?"

"Yeah. That's right."

"Excellent again!"

Artie asked, "How are you doing this? Where did all the snow go?"

"Well, I'm not quite sure what you're talking about,

but I received a message yesterday that you'd be visiting so I hurried over here. This is where I was told to meet you."

"Who told you? Merli—"

Greenie raised his hand and shook it violently. The suit of armor rattled and clanked. "Tut-tut! Please, we try not to say that over here! At least, not yet!"

"So, what, you're really over there?"

"Yes, and you are really over there! If you get my meaning. You know, since I'm here and you're—"

"Yeah. I get it. What can I call him, then?"

"How about Wilt?" asked the knight.

"Wilt," Artie deadpanned. Kynder had passed on to his children his love of basketball, and this name made Artie think of one person and one person only. "Like Wilt Chamberlain."

"A bit long, but that would be fine too."

Clearly the green knight didn't get the reference. "How did Wilt get in touch with you?"

"Oh, it's pretty technical and not all that important. What *is* important is that I give you a little orientation and tell you what to expect when you drop by on Friday. You can still make Friday, yes?"

"I guess so."

"Wonderful! Come with me, Sir Nitwit. You don't mind if I call you that, do you?"

"Actually, you can call me Artie or Sir Kingfisher. Or, you know, sire or whatever."

"Ha! Not so hasty, young man! Why, I haven't even met you yet. Not really, anyway."

Artie started to move Nitwit down the path. Greenie fell in next to him as they walked. Artie asked, "So, what, are you playing the game too, but from over there?"

"No, no, my friend! I am as you see me. Take a close look at what you're watching. Does it look different from the other images in your game of videos?"

"Video game."

"Of course. Well, does it?"

Artie hadn't noticed, but it *did* look different. What he saw was more like an imperfect television signal than the video game he knew and loved. He watched the green knight, who turned his helmet to look at him. Artie asked, "Are you smiling?"

"I am! Are you?" the knight asked conspiratorially.

"You can't see me?"

"Of course not! I only see you as a faint column of moonlight. I have a little headset in my helmet to hear you."

"So if we ran into somebody, they'd just see you talking to a beam of light?"

"Exactly! But not to worry, I've developed quite the reputation for eccentricity. It wouldn't be the first time I went around talking to strange things!"

"Can the people that live there see you—I mean—see what's inside your armor?"

"No, no! I'm the Empty Knight. What you see is what you get!"

"Okay, Bercilak, let's get on with it then. I need to be practicing my swordsmanship."

"Of course. Swordsmanship is an essential skill. Look over there." The knight raised his left arm. Artie brought Nitwit to a halt. He turned his character to see what Bercilak pointed at.

Through the trees was a lake with the bluest water Artie had ever seen.

The knight said, "That is the Lake. You will come with Thumb and Kay. I am sorry, but I will not be able to meet you. You'll need to have a compass with you so that you can find the eastern shore. Along this you will see a gigantic chestnut tree—trust me, you can't miss it—and tethered to that tree will be a canoe.

"Great."

"You will paddle to the exact middle of the Lake, which is easy to discern because at the exact middle is a large buoy."

"Got it."

"Now, Thumb may not approve of a couple things I am going to tell you to do. So, pretend he is your father in this case and—"

"Ignore him."

"Exactly. Listen carefully. You need to do these three things in this order. First, take Cleomede and dip its blade entirely in the Lake's water. Once wet, turn it around and hold it by the blade. Don't worry, it won't cut you. It can't."

"Cool."

"Very. Holding it thus, knock the very end—*the very end*—of its hilt against the base of the buoy. Do this three times, three seconds apart. Then flip Cleomede around, hold it over your head, stand up, yell, "Excalibur!" and throw Cleomede into the water."

"Okay, got it."

"Fantastic!"

"Then what happens?"

"I'm sorry, my boy, but my time is up. Till we meet again!"

And just like that, the image faltered and reverted to the video game, and Nitwit the Gray stood in a dark, snowy wood near the frozen Vale of Goch. Caladirth's cave was in front of him, and a large ice bear was rising from behind a boulder to his left. It was a middling creature—Nitwit had slain dozens. Artie reflexively fiddled with the controller, killed the bear, paused the game, sat down on the floor, and breathed deeply as his mind spun.

IN WHICH KING ARTIE AND SIR KAY ENGAGE IN SOME SWORDPLAY!

𝕺ver the next few days Kay and Artie settled into a rhythm of sword practice and messing with Kynder. Merlin was right—enchanted Kynder was more puppet than father.

Fooling with him was a blast. They made him stand on his head in the backyard for thirty minutes. They told him they wouldn't be doing their chores for a while and he'd have to pick up the slack. They made him sing songs and dance for them. They had him make chocolate-chip pancakes with spray-can whipped cream for dinner every night.

They also had him put a bunch of stuff around the backyard: an adult-sized dummy made of burlap sacks, old sheets, and wood; plastic jugs and bottles full of water; and dozens of bales of hay. All of these were to be ravaged by Cleomede.

Courtesy of the swordsmanship book, Artie and Kay learned the following about their new weapon: that it was an arming sword, which was more commonly known as a broadsword; that it was double-edged and had a double fullered blade, which meant there were two grooves, or "blood channels," that ran its length; that the leather-wrapped handle was called the hilt; that the flared bar above it was called the crossguard; and that the heavy clamshell-shaped thing at the hilt's end was called the pommel.

To Artie and Kay, it was undoubtedly the coolest thing they'd ever seen.

The book taught them how to attack and defend, how to position themselves properly, and how to move their feet so they could most effectively slice their opponent to bits while avoiding the same fate for themselves.

And then there was what Cleomede taught Artie and Kay all on its own.

For one, Cleomede had feelings and passed them on to whoever was holding it. When it sliced through the burlap, they felt each strand of the sack breaking along its edge; when it cut through the water in the plastic bottles, they knew if it was warm or cold; when it sailed through the hay, they could tell if it was grass or clover.

Another cool thing was that no matter how long they worked with it, they never got tired or achy or run-down. It was like it refreshed them—the harder they practiced, the better they felt.

Then there was the fact that it could cut through just about anything. It effortlessly sliced through *empty* bottles that a stiff breeze would have knocked over; it chopped wood like it was made of butter; it cut a glass bottle in two without shattering either half; it also severed a steel fire poker pretty dang easily.

"This thing is freaking awesome," Artie said after halving the poker.

Kay wasn't about to deny it.

As they practiced over the course of the week, Kynder drifted in and out of the yard, being careful not to get in their way. He never criticized anything they did. He cleaned up after them without complaining, and replaced their targets with new ones whenever asked. He was so at ease with all the mayhem Cleomede had brought into their yard that, by midweek, Artie and Kay started to feel guilty about making Kynder do all the silly things they'd made him do.

At one point, as he reconstructed the burlap-and-wood dummy for the twentieth time, Kynder turned to Kay with a puzzled look and asked, "Can you remind me again what it is you're doing, Kay?"

Kay smiled at her father and said, "Sword practice, Kynder. We're learning how to use our invisible sword, Cleomede."

"Oh yes. I'm sorry, I'd forgotten."

Again Kay felt a little bad, but there you have it.

On Thursday after breakfast Artie informed Kynder that he'd need to take them to Peebles, Ohio, early the next morning to visit Serpent Mound. Then Artie and Kay decided to try cutting some really crazy things.

First they tried soft things like string, cloth, paper, and plastic wrap. All of them were cut cleanly, like Cleomede was the world's sharpest razor.

Cutting a piece of Saran wrap with a slow swing of the blade gave Artie an idea. He wanted to see if he could *slowly* push the sword through hard objects. They tried a log. It worked. They tried a cinder block. Ditto. Finally Kay got an ancient desktop computer from the garage and she very effortlessly and very slowly pushed their magical sword right through it to the hilt.

Impressed, Artie said, "Nice work, Sir Kay!"

Kay yanked Cleomede cleanly from the computer and said, "Sir Kay! I like that."

"Sir Kay it is then. I shall knight you once we've procured Excalibur," Artie said in his most kingly voice.

"Excellent, my liege."

Kay handed Artie the sword, and he started to flip it in the air, catching it by the blade and then the grip. He felt great, and fearless, and powerful.

"Ahem. What is going on back here?"

Apparently they felt so good that they hadn't noticed Qwon standing at the open gate behind their house.

Kay and Artie snapped around. Cleomede was in the air, and when Artie didn't catch the sword, it righted itself and landed point down in the earth. It wagged back and forth as its energy dissipated into the ground.

"Qwon!" quacked Artie.

Qwon Onakea stepped into the yard, a hand on her hip and a confused look on her face. She wore khaki shorts and an Amar'e Stoudemire Knicks jersey.

Qwon was a huge Knicks fan.

Kay tried to play it cool. "Hey, Qwon, how's it going?"

"Uh, fine." She took a few steps into the yard.

"How long have you been standing there?" Kay wondered.

"About ten minutes," she said incredulously.

"Wow. Okay."

"Yeah, 'wow' is right. Wow is, in fact, sticking into the ground next to Artie."

Artie coughed. "What do you mean?"

Qwon pointed directly at the sword. "That! That sword!"

"Oooohhhh, that," cooed Artie.

"Don't play dumb with me, Artie Kingfisher," Qwon said. "You have a sword, and from what I can tell, you . . . you . . . you look like you know how to use it!"

Artie mumbled something, trying to play it off, but Kay figured what the hey and pulled the weapon out of the ground. She gave it a few whistling swings through the air. "Pretty neat, huh?"

"I'll say," Qwon said. "Can I try?"

Kay looked to her brother. Artie smiled at his sister and nodded.

Kay turned back to Qwon and said, "Sure, Q, here ya go."

Qwon took the sword and held it in front of her. Then she dropped into an attack position and whipped it through the air.

Artie shook his head and said, "You sorta look like you know what you're doing there, Qwon."

"Of course I do! My grandpa is a kendo expert—that's, like, Japanese sword fighting, except they use a bamboo sword instead of a metal one—and he taught me a bunch of stuff." She swung the sword again and looked at it approvingly. "This is a good blade, guys."

Kynder came from the house carrying a tray with a pitcher of lemonade. He put it on the patio table and said, "Hey, Qwon!"

Forgetting the weirdness of the situation, Qwon looked up and said, "Hey, Mr. Kingfisher!" Then she remembered that she was holding a sword. She looked at Kynder, who was pouring out drinks. Then she turned to Artie and asked under her breath, "He doesn't mind that you're playing with this thing?"

"Uh, no." Artie said lamely.

"Yeah," Kay tried to explain, "it's kinda like he doesn't even see it. I think he's in denial or something."

Artie went to get some lemonade. He wasn't sure how he felt about this development. How could Qwon see the sword? *Why* could she see it? Was Qwon supposed to be one of his new knights of the Round Table? He wasn't sure he wanted that. He really liked Qwon and didn't want to feel like he was putting her in any kind of trouble.

Then again, she did appear to know how to use a sword, which was pretty cool.

Qwon shrugged and jammed Cleomede back into the ground. She went to grab some lemonade and asked innocently, "So where'd you get it, then?"

Artie and Kay looked at each other and then back at their friend. "Online?" Kay said pathetically.

"Ha! As if."

Artie said, "No, that's where we got it. You wouldn't believe how many people are selling swords online!"

"Really?" Qwon downed her drink as she considered what he said. "I don't believe you. That thing looks special, you know?"

"Yeah, we got lucky," Artie tried to explain.

"Whatever, Artie. If you just let me take a few more

hacks with it, I wouldn't care if you told me it fell into your hands out of a rainbow."

Artie smiled. He pulled the sword from the ground, took it by the blade, and presented it pommel first to Qwon. She grabbed it, stepped back, and gave it a few rips through the air.

Artie swore that he'd never seen her smile so big.

10   ON MEETING THE VORPAL BUNNY AND VICTOR X. LANCE

𝕿𝖍𝖊𝖞 𝖘𝖕𝖊𝖓𝖙 𝖙𝖍𝖊 𝖗𝖊𝖘𝖙 𝖔𝖋 the afternoon hanging out, drinking lemonade, teasing Kynder, and acting like normal kids on summer vacation.

If kids playing with a medieval magical sword could be called normal.

Qwon left shortly before dinner. The Kingfishers ate and turned in early. They had a big day ahead of them.

The ride to Peebles the next morning was pretty boring, except for the weather. It was like the sky was schizophrenic: it alternated between bright sun and ominous storm clouds that looked as though they were about to unleash a cascade of fierce, earth-cracking lightning.

But the lightning never came.

They arrived at Serpent Mound State Memorial after

lunchtime. They parked and got out their picnic stuff. Artie slung Cleomede over his shoulder, and they searched for a place to eat. The weather had decided to stay nice, and by the time they dug into their sandwiches, it was a steamy summertime afternoon.

The plan, arranged between Artie, Merlin, and Thumb on the *Otherworld* message boards, was to rendezvous at five o'clock in the woods just north of Serpent Mound's head. Merlin had assured Artie that Kynder would be sleeping on account of being full and happy—but also on account of a little magic.

Right on cue, at precisely four forty-five, Kynder said, "Guys, I'm pooped. Do you think it'd be okay if I conked out for a few minutes?"

Kay, unable to contain her anticipation, said excitedly, "Oh sure, Kynder!"

Kynder gave her a sidelong glare and, for a brief moment, seemed to be completely aware of what was going on. Then his face softened and he smiled. Artie thought he looked like an amnesiac who'd remembered and then forgotten his own name. It made both Artie and Kay a little sad—they wanted their old Kynder back as soon as possible.

Kynder settled against a tree and said, "Great. Thanks, guys. Just fifteen minutes or so, all right?"

"You got it, Kynder," Artie answered.

"Yeah, don't worry about us. We'll stay out of trouble!"

added Kay, knowing she was definitely lying.

Kynder closed his eyes and instantly fell asleep.

Artie grabbed Cleomede, and they made their way to the serpent's head along a paved walkway.

A small brown river to the west of the mound babbled along pleasantly. Beyond that was a large cornfield. All around was postcard-perfect rural America—big old oaks and maples and ashes and beeches dotted rolling hills with small farms. It was picturesque countryside, and the last place one might expect to find a portal to earth's sister world.

They got to the snake head and milled around while they waited for a family of four to clear out. When the family finally left, it was just past five. Artie and Kay exchanged a look of mutual assurance and moved into the woods to the north.

The woods were very thick and dark. They hadn't walked ten paces before the snake-head clearing was out of sight. The little river had gone totally silent. And the light in the west was weak and orange among the trees.

"So where'd the little guy say he was supposed to meet us?" asked Kay.

Artie concentrated on his feet. He said, "Five more paces if I'm counting right."

They took five steps and stopped. They found themselves in a little depression, the ground choked with gnarled roots. The air was still and heavy.

"Thumb? You here?" Artie asked of the trees.

No response.

"Mr. Thumb?" Kay called.

Still nothing.

A branch snapped to their right. Artie jumped and swung Cleomede from his shoulder in a smooth motion. He gripped it loosely, as the book had instructed, and held it slightly to his side, point up, ready to strike.

Then a high-pitched wail echoed through the undergrowth. They looked in its direction, where they saw a large brown jackrabbit hopping from behind a birch trunk. It reared like a mighty stallion and wailed again. Neither Artie nor Kay had ever heard a rabbit before.

The small beast settled, and that was when they noticed something wrapped around his head.

Kay pointed and asked, "Are those reins?"

Before Artie could answer, two miniscule hands parted the jackrabbit's long ears and there, framed between them, was the beaming face of little Mr. Tom Thumb. "Hello, good sir and madam!" he proclaimed.

Kay chuckled nervously and said, "Tom, you scared the you-know-what out of us!"

"Aha! Not too often you get spooked by a screaming jackrabbit, is it?"

Artie said, "Nope."

"Well, this is my steed, Vorpal."

In addition to the battle-ax, Artie's video game character Nitwit had a vorpal blade in *Otherworld*, and he found the contrast pretty funny. "A vorpal bunny, huh?"

"Quite, lad. He's got vicious teeth—"

"—and he can jump!"

This voice came from behind them, giving them a start. Artie twirled around, Cleomede at the ready in front of him.

Standing in the trees was someone who looked vaguely familiar to Artie. He wrinkled his brow and asked, "Who are you?"

The young man cleared his throat and said, "Victor X. Lance, cab driver and archer, among other things." He bowed as he added, "And I am at your service."

"No offense, but you look pretty ridiculous!" Kay blurted.

And this was the honest truth. Victor Lance, who looked to be about twenty, wore high-top leather moccasins, leather and chain-mail pants, a camouflage hunting shirt under a black bulletproof vest, and a green felt Robin Hood–looking hat with a big pheasant feather sticking out of it.

The silly hat wasn't the only merry prankster-ish thing he had, either. In his right hand was a huge compound bow that was all strings and pulleys. It was decorated with a patriotic motif, like American flags and screaming eagles. Slung over his back was a quiver of very long arrows with very ornate feather fletchings, and strapped to his waist was a commando-style buck knife.

Artie still couldn't place him. "Where do I—"

"Cincinnati. I was your cab driver. I tried to be friendly, but you were pretty preoccupied."

Kay turned to her brother and asked, "Artie, you know this guy?"

"Not really. But I remember him now. He's who he says he is."

Artie lowered Cleomede, and Kay shook her head. To the list of crazies they'd met over the last week, they could now add a militiaman taxi hack from Cincinnati. Why not? Weirder things happened. For instance, they also knew a miniature man who rode a rabbit.

Thumb interjected and said, "Artie, Kay, Mr. Lance is a friend and ally to myself and Merlin, and he will be the same to you. Quite a resourceful chap. He knows a little about you and a fair bit more about the Otherworld."

"It's, like, one of my hobbies, you know? Along with archery, I just can't get enough of the Otherworld. It's a long story, but I kinda found out about it on my own. Got pretty obsessed. Did a bunch of arcane research all over the place, and that led me to the Invisible Tower and old Lyn—I mean Merlin. Still getting used to calling him that."

"You're telling me," Artie said. Kay nodded.

Lance continued, "Anyway, I'm a tough kid and good

in a fight. Was in Iraq with the Hundred and First before getting an honorable discharge two years in. Can't hear in my right ear and I only got one lung. I can't travel with you to the Otherworld. We can't figure out why, but for now only kids and people like Thumb, who's originally from the Otherworld, can go back and forth. So my job is to stay here and watch the portal to make sure no one messes with it."

Artie and Kay looked at each other and shrugged. Sure, why not?

"I won't let you guys down."

As they were hashing this out, Thumb had arranged a strand of silver thread in a wide circle on the ground. Inside the circle were him, the rabbit, Artie, and Kay. Outside the circle stood Lance.

Thumb bounded over to their new friend and handed him the free end of the thread. Lance removed an arrow from his quiver, tied the thread to it, and nocked the arrow to his bowstring. He pulled the string to his shoulder and aimed into the canopy.

He let go, and the arrow zinged through the air. It hit its mark with an impressive thwack.

Suddenly there was a sparking electrical sound, and then a pale see-through curtain encircled all but Lance. The archer said, "I'll be here when you get back! Good luck!"

And before they knew it, the dark forest was no more.

𝕬 **blinding flash of light came** and went.

They stretched their faces and rubbed their eyes and when they recovered, they found themselves on the road that Artie had strolled along with Bercilak, the green knight.

"Everyone all right?" Thumb asked.

"Yep," said Artie.

"A-OK, Shorty," affirmed Kay. "But whoa—what happened to you and your rabbit?"

As before, Thumb had grown two feet taller. His rabbit had followed suit. He was now as big as a medium-sized mutt. At that size, his teeth really did look pretty vicious.

"I'm bigger here," Thumb explained. "Vorpal, too."

"I can see that. And you have a sword, too."

Thumb patted the sheathed sword on his belt. "Ah yes,

the Welsh *wakizashi*. An old friend."

"Great, so I'm the only one without a weapon," Kay said.

"Yes, for the time being, but don't worry. Cleomede will be yours soon enough. Artie—do you know where we are?"

Artie dug his compass from his pocket and flipped it open. "Yeah. Let me just get our bearings."

He held the compass level to the ground. The needle swirled around in both directions before grooving into the magnetic field. Maybe it had had a tough time crossing over too.

Artie pointed Cleomede in the direction he thought was right and said, "It's this way."

"Very well, lad. And remember something—Cleomede is perfectly visible here. More than a few are likely to recognize her on sight. You're no longer anonymous like back home."

"Got it," Artie said.

They started off and didn't talk because there was so much to take in.

The trees were huge. Their trunks were measured in yards rather than feet. Artie figured they must be the oldest trees he'd ever seen. Many of the flowers along the edge of the road looked like flowers from back home, but then there were tons more that Artie had never seen. There was a green flower in the exact shape of a butterfly; an orange poof that looked more cloud than flower; and a flat brown one that was a perfect square.

Also, the sky was blue, but purple too. And the clouds were mostly white but ever so slightly pink. Artie wondered if it was a trick of the light, but couldn't be sure.

But the strangest things were the sounds. These hadn't come across when Artie met Bercilak in the video game, and they were fairly unsettling.

All around, the woods produced very quiet rustles, clicks, coos, snaps, and *whispers*. The sounds were almost imperceptible, but there was no doubting they were there.

Kay asked the obvious: "Tom, are we alone?"

"My darling Kay, we are never completely alone," Thumb answered cryptically. Certain parts of the Otherworld are more alive than the corresponding parts on your side. It's perfectly normal."

They walked along in silence before Thumb added, "Besides, we have the king of all lands with us, and he is armed!" Artie wasn't sure if Thumb was being sarcastic, but it didn't make him feel any better if he was. Artie was a twelve-year-old with a sword on his way to get another sword. That made him dangerous?

After a few dozen more yards Artie caught sight of a blue bluer than blue through the trees. Thumb and Kay carried on as he walked to the side of the road. He parted a thick stand of bushes and there, not far beyond them, was the Lake.

Artie said, "Hey, guys, wait up!"

Just as both of his companions stopped, they heard a horrible wail from above. They craned their necks. At first there was nothing, but then, far overheard, emerged the silhouette of a giant vulturelike bird. It made broad turns in the sky, gliding on invisible currents; Artie assumed that it was looking for something to eat.

Something like them, perhaps.

Thumb exclaimed, "Good stars! Would you look at that!" The vorpal bunny reared, and Thumb brought him under rein. He patted him on the neck and whispered something into his ear.

"What is that, Tommy?" Kay asked incredulously. "It's huge."

Thumb answered, "That is a magnificent Argentine. The largest bird ever to have plied the skies, my girl. Extinct on your side. I'd warrant it's nearly twenty-five feet from wing tip to wing tip."

"Holy cow," Kay said.

"Quite," Thumb agreed. "But don't let it concern you. It's mainly a carrion eater. We only need worry about it if we die. In which case, we'll have nothing to worry about at all!"

"Way to make a girl feel comfortable, Tommy," said Kay.

Artie forced himself to forget about the huge bird and said, "Guys, what I was trying to tell you was that we're here. The Lake's right over there." Artie pointed through the forest on their left at the patches of brilliant blue water.

Kay and Thumb joined Artie and they abandoned the path. Artie led the way, using Cleomede as a machete.

The Lake was round and a couple of miles across. The buoy was plain to see in the middle. To their right, about a quarter of the way around the lake, stood a massive tree. It was perfectly shaped—a thick, sturdy trunk jutted from the ground and about ten feet up the branches reached straight out uniformly. The canopy was shaped more like a mushroom than a tree, and it towered over everything in sight. Next to it and turned upside down was a red-hulled canoe.

"Good stars again! The great American chestnut. Those used to be everywhere on your side, you know."

"What happened?" asked Artie.

"Can't remember the exact cause—some beetle infestation or fungus wiped them out, I think. There's a few left, but none like that. I bet it's nearly as old as I am."

They walked to the tree, and Artie flipped the boat over. Underneath it were three paddles and a cloth sack. Artie opened the sack. It contained a clunky old cell phone and a note.

Artie unfolded the note. It read, "Hello, good sir knights! I hope this finds you well. Please take this phone and keep it. Service is awful around here, but better to have one than not. I wish you the best of luck and I hope to see you all soon!" Bercilak had signed it with a stamp in green ink that depicted the same seal he had on his breastplate—a holly branch crossing a battle-ax in front of a pine tree. Under that he'd scribbled down his phone number: 2-305-67.

As they got the canoe into the water, Artie told them how they were supposed to go about getting Excalibur. Thumb squirmed at the idea of flinging Cleomede into the depths, but Artie assured him it would be okay. They got into the little boat. Artie was in front, Kay was behind him, Vorpal was next, and Thumb brought up the rear.

Kay asked, "You're sure you're good back there? I have a merit badge for canoeing from summer camp."

"Kay, my dear, I am over a thousand years old. I'm well acquainted with the J-stroke."

"Just making sure," Kay said.

They shoved off and paddled easily toward the middle of the Lake, making good time.

But after a few minutes a headwind picked up that made paddling a little harder.

Then, as they made their way, a shadow moved across the water. Artie looked up. The magnificent Argentine had blotted out the sun, training its eyes on the world below. Artie put his head back down and continued pulling against the water. The sound of wind and the bow slicing through the water was all he could hear.

But then another sound came from far off on their

right. The canoeists whipped their heads in its direction. The trees on the far bank of the Lake shook and fluttered and turned from green to black in an instant. They seemed to grow upward in a surge, like a smoke plume rising from an explosion.

But the trees weren't actually blowing up. What made the sound were birds. Millions of birds.

A swarm lifted into the sky and bulged and thinned and bulged again. It wheeled through the air and rose over the Lake like a storm.

"What are those?" yelled Artie over the noise.

"Passenger pigeons!" Thumb yelled back.

The creatures rose from the trees without pause, like the forest was a spigot gushing birds. They moved quickly and covered most of the Lake in less than a minute.

Then a terrifying screech filled the air above them and the magnificent Argentine broke through the bottom of the flock with a crash of feathers, flapped three times, and surged back upward. The flock barely registered the flying monster. It didn't seem to care that this huge bird was literally plucking its members out of the sky by the mouthful.

Artie tried to ignore the carnage above and looked back in front of him just as the bow of the canoe bumped into the buoy. They scraped alongside it, and Thumb and Kay threw out ropes to secure them in the strengthening headwind.

Artie's heart quickened.

He lifted Cleomede from the bottom of the boat and leaned over the side, dipping the full length of the blade into the water. He pulled it out. The sky suddenly got much darker. He looked over the surface of the Lake, where little whitecaps had begun to form and break.

He turned Cleomede in his hands, gripping the blade. He extended the sword in front of him. The boat began to rock, and the buoy clanged against the gunwale.

Artie knocked once against the side of the buoy. It made a dull thud. He counted to three.

The sky turned black, and he didn't know why. His hands tingled.

"Hurry, lad!" screamed Thumb.

He knocked the pommel against its target again. As he counted, he looked up.

The flock of birds suddenly dispersed, breaking from the center in all directions, leaving the giant bird all alone, its head twitching nervously back and forth.

Artie knocked the sword a third time. Cleomede was getting hot to the touch.

"Artie, hurry!" screamed Kay.

A noise broke over them like a bomb going off. It was a huge, hollow, flapping sound, far worse than that of the magnificent Argentine.

Artie craned and saw a long, iridescent green dragon

twirling overhead, practically blotting out the entire sky.

Kay shouted, "What the?"

Then it dived. The magnificent Argentine had gone from hunter to prey.

It banked defensively. Its wing tip cut the surface of the water, then it straightened and drove directly for the canoe.

Artie held up Cleomede and tried to remember what Bercilak had told him to do next. But he couldn't.

The bird strafed them, its raptorlike feet bumping the buoy and shaking the canoe violently. Everyone grabbed the boat and held on for dear life.

The dragon glided over them, moving through the air like a snake. Artie thought it looked more like a Chinese dragon than your typical European-style, Middle Earth kind of dragon. That didn't make it any less terrifying, though.

The giant bird was scared, but not for long, because in an instant the serpent plucked it from the sky. The dragon made horrible gurgling noises as it choked down its prey whole, the bird's mighty feathered wings folding into the serpent's mouth.

They were stunned.

The dragon licked its chops. The bulky, and still moving, form of the bird could be seen in the beast's scaly belly. For a brief moment the monster seemed content.

But then it looked straight at them and let out a wail

that beat upon their hearts as much as it did upon their eardrums.

It prepared to dive again.

Thumb drew his sword and yelled, "Ask for the sword, boy!"

Artie was momentarily paralyzed. Should he really be throwing the only magical blade in the boat away at a time like this?

Kay screamed. The vorpal bunny, his long ears pulled over his straining black eyes, screamed too.

Artie hoisted Cleomede above his head, shrieked, "Excalibur!" turned the sword to the water, and shoved it into the Lake's depths, letting go of his only defense.

The blade sluiced the water, and for a moment everything went black.

𝕿𝖍𝖊 𝖇𝖑𝖆𝖈𝖐𝖓𝖊𝖘𝖘 𝖑𝖎𝖋𝖙𝖊𝖉 𝖑𝖎𝖐𝖊 𝖆 slow fade-up in a movie.

Artie was still on the boat, still clutching the gunwale, still on one knee. His face was still contorted in a mask of fear and urgency.

He eased his grip and relaxed his face.

He blinked.

Calmness washed over him.

He looked at the water. Its surface was weird. It was still. No—it was moving. Only very, very slowly.

The boat also moved slowly as it righted itself incrementally.

Time was almost frozen.

Artie looked into the canoe.

Kay was on her butt, her face grimacing in confrontation.

Vorpal was ready to pounce into the air and attack. Thumb stood at full height. He held his sword above him with both hands. His mouth was wide with fury and his eyes were lit like exploding stars. He looked very brave.

Artie looked up, and there it was. A great green dragon. Bright and shimmering where the light hit it on the margins, dark and foreboding on the underside that rushed toward them.

Or had been rushing toward them. Like everything else, the dragon was practically stock-still.

Artie took the creature in. It was glorious. It had red rubied teeth and its golden horns were curled like a ram's. Its wings were powerful-looking but small. They didn't seem large enough to keep the thing aloft. It was more like the dragon swam through the air. It was pretty magical.

But most impressive were the thing's eyes. Their black pupils were shaped like a cat's, and the streaked iris was an explosion of color. Traveling around the eyeball, every hue could be seen, from brightest blue to deepest green to fieriest orange.

The dragon had rainbows in its eyes.

Which made Artie think of his sister, with her blue and green eyes, which in turn brought him back to his senses a little.

He was supposed to be doing something.

He recalled yelling, "Excalibur!" He turned back to the water, where suddenly he found two swords pointing straight up at the sky. Holding them were two light blue hands.

He looked into the water. A girl no older than five or six stared back, her clear, gray eyes open beneath the surface. Her lips, her cheeks, her hair—all were tinted blue. She smiled.

"My, Arthur, how changed is your visage," she said from under the waves. Artie wasn't quite sure what this meant. "My old friend. Take what is thine. Take both. Hold them."

Artie said, "Uh, okay. But what about the dragon?"

"Worry not, friend. Take what is thine. All will be clear."

She lifted the swords higher. Artie reached out and grabbed each by its blade.

Cleomede was cold and ready.

Excalibur was a revelation.

The blade was watered steel and about six inches longer than Cleomede. It had a single blood channel and was inlaid with golden intertwined serpents on both sides. It had Latin inscriptions running along the contours of the serpents: *Tolle me* on one side and *Iacta me* on the other. Its crossguard looked like marbled gold and platinum. Its grip was big enough for two hands and wrapped with fine, bright threads of red and blue. Its pommel was a perfect glass ball. Inside the ball was an orb of deepest black that looked like an eyeball.

As Artie grasped Excalibur, waves of knowledge coursed through him. The information was at once exact and confusing. He saw a young Merlin with the old Arthur. He heard dozens of different languages but could barely understand any. He saw Tom Thumb on the day of his tenth birthday, riding a goose to market. He saw Bercilak challenge any takers to a fight. He saw a young boy he didn't recognize, in a suit of red and blue armor, his great helmet topped with terrifying horns. He saw an owl and a man with the head of a wolf. He saw an army of children and a plain copper cup. He saw a legless man sitting on the edge of a black river. He saw an illuminated blue line surrounded by darkness that went on as far as he could see. He saw Qwon, and Kay, and Kynder, and Lance, and Thumb, and kids from school—even Frankie Finkelstein. He saw Merlin trapped in his invisible tower, sometimes screaming with rage, other times broken by solitude, yet others giddy with revelation.

He suddenly knew some Welsh and a fair amount of Latin.

And he was not sure, but it felt like he knew some magic—how to make a fire without tinder, how to heal a wound. He knew the names of plants and flowers, and some of their uses as poisons or cures.

Most important to the situation at hand, he now knew a lot more about fighting with swords.

The sword's spell was broken as the girl cooed, "Excalibur has revealed much to you, young Arthur. It will reveal more to you in time."

Artie wasn't sure if he was excited about this or terrified. Still, he thought learning more stuff in this way would be pretty cool. It sure beat sitting in class.

Then the girl said, "Do not forsake thy companions."

He turned back to the drama unfolding in ultraslow motion. They had moved a little, but were basically in the same places. The only weird thing was that all four of them—Thumb, Vorpal, Kay, and even the serpent—had turned their heads toward Artie slightly.

Artie reached behind him and put Cleomede in Kay's hand. She'd be happy for that when things sped back up.

He returned to the Girl of the Lake and asked, "What do I do now?"

"Hold high the brand."

"The brand? What brand?"

Her hands slowly sank. She was going back under. Her smile was gone. Her last extended fingertip submerged. At the same moment she winked and whispered fiercely, "Now!"

The violence of the rocking boat nearly threw Artie overboard. He got a swift hit to the gut as he slammed against the gunwale.

Kay yelled, "What the?"

The dragon writhed above them. It gurgled a foul rumble deep in its throat.

Thumb screamed, very much to the point, "What did she tell you to do?"

"How did Cleomede—" Kay shrieked, more to herself than anyone in particular.

Artie yelled, answering Thumb, "She said, 'Hold high the brand'!"

"Do it then, boy!"

"What's a brand?"

"The firebrand! Excalibur! The *sword*!"

Of course! The sword!

He thrust Excalibur up high.

The dragon reared. A hot wind wafted from its underside like a punch in the face. It reminded Artie of getting hit by Finkelstein.

Curse that Frankie Finkelstein! Even now, at the height of peril, Artie couldn't shake him!

Then Excalibur shuddered. He looked up. The glass-eye pommel of his new sword glowed white.

The dragon extended its neck at Artie. Black, crinkly

smoke began to waft from its nostrils.

Then, just as the serpent gathered itself to strike, Artie understood. He thought of light. He thought of the sun, the moon, fireworks on the Fourth of July.

Light danced off the blade in a blinding blast. Artie shut his eyes, but he still saw the light through his lids.

The dragon squealed. This time it sounded afraid. It slithered in the air and retreated a hundred feet instantly. It cried again, and the noise echoed over the Lake.

Excalibur was alive. It released another pulse of blinding light before extinguishing itself.

Artie opened his eyes. The dragon was flying away. After a few moments it stopped, turned, and looked directly at Artie. It let out a small, defeated whimper that drifted down to them. Artie knew that the creature was disappointed.

Before they knew it, the beautiful monster was gone. The air calmed, and the sweet smell of the Lake and the woods returned.

They sat in the boat for several moments without speaking, just breathing, just trying to piece together what had happened.

Finally Kay asked, "How did you move that fast, Artie?"

"What do you mean?"

Thumb said, "My boy, you were like a blur."

"I don't know. Everything was super slow-mo to me. I think the Girl of the Lake did it."

"The *Girl*, you say?" inquired Thumb.

"Yeah, the Girl. She was only five or six."

"My goodness." Thumb chuckled. "She was much older than that, I assure you, lad."

Kay let out a deep breath and cracked her neck. "Well, however it happened, that was pretty awesome, Your Highness."

Artie was happy to hear Kay sound like her old self, but was also completely exhausted. He slumped in his seat. He'd just scared off a dragon so big it could have nested on a football field. His eyes burned and his head hurt. But Artie had to agree. "Yeah, it *was* pretty awesome, wasn't it, Sir Kay?"

"Let's get back to shore," Thumb said as he wrangled Vorpal, who was still raring for a fight, into the bottom of the canoe. "I think we've had enough excitement for today. Kay, help me paddle. Artie can rest."

Kay felt that her brother was totally whipped. "Good idea, Tommy. Take a load off, Art. We'll get you home."

"Okay. Thanks, guys."

They paddled, and the sun warmed their backs. After a while the trees around the Lake shook to life again, and the passenger pigeons, free of predators, took back to the sky like a living, moving confetti storm.

The flock was so huge that, once it got going, it looked as if it had no beginning, and no end.

13 HOW THE STORM WAS LIKE A GIANT BLINDLY STAMPING HIS FEET ACROSS THE COUNTRYSIDE

𝕿𝖍𝖊𝖞 𝖕𝖚𝖑𝖑𝖊𝖉 𝖇𝖆𝖈𝖐 𝖙𝖔 𝖘𝖍𝖔𝖗𝖊, stowed the canoe, and retraced the trail they'd bushwhacked around the Lake. Their minds raced, so they didn't talk much until they got back onto the road.

Breaking their silence, Kay asked, "So what's the deal, Tommy—the pigeons, the giant bird, the chestnut tree—those are all things that are more or less extinct on our side, right?"

Thumb said, "That's right, Kay. As Merlin said, over the centuries some species have sought refuge here as they went extinct over there."

"Does that mean there's dinosaurs and stuff over here?" Kay wondered.

"No, no, my dear. It was a major extinction event that

killed the dinosaurs. The same extinction event killed many here as well. The worlds share the earth, remember; it's just that the earth is more layered and subtle in its presentation of reality than most believe it to be."

"What about dragons?" Artie asked as they walked. "Did they used to live on our side?"

Thumb raised his eyebrows and said, "Dragons are a different matter. They only come from here. Here they are very real. There, they live only in the imagination."

Artie frowned and said to himself, "Man, that's kind of how I feel right now. Both real and not so real . . ."

A roll of thunder gurgled behind them. They stopped momentarily and saw a dark, low cloud gathering in the distance. They could just make out the moongate down the road.

As they walked on, an idea popped into Kay's head. She asked, "So if things leave there and come here, does that mean that sometimes people who go missing over there end up here?"

Thumb said simply, "Not often, but it has happened. Why do you ask?"

"Oh, no reason. Just trying to get a handle on things."

Thumb glanced sidelong at Kay. He could tell that was not the real reason Kay was so curious. They carried on toward the portal.

But Artie knew full well why Kay had asked. It was

because of her mom. He knew that behind all the wise-cracks and one-liners, Kay was really a big softie when it came to her mom. In fact, Artie had begun to suspect that all the wisecracks and one-liners were compensating for the fact that Kay was kind of crushed by her lack of a mother. Needless to say, this made Artie sad. What made him even sadder was the knowledge that he had something to do with her flying the coop. Artie was starting to feel like he wanted to know what had happened to Kay's mom almost as badly as Kay wanted to, which on top of everything else (knowing a wizard, being a genetically engineered king, owning the coolest sword ever) was also a new feeling.

It was all a part of being the new Artie Kingfisher, he figured.

Speaking of the new Artie Kingfisher, he had a strong, inexplicable urge to get into a sword fight. As they reached the moongate, he said pointedly, "Tom, will you fight me?"

Shocked, Thumb asked, "Excuse me, lad?"

"Will you fight me? You know how to use that thing, right?" Artie pointed at the Welsh *wakizashi*.

"Of course I do. I am a master of the bladed arts."

"Then let's do it."

Kay interrupted, "Artie, have you gone off your rocker?"

"Maybe. I don't know. Excalibur did something to me. No, Excalibur did a *lot* of things to me. I need to see if some of them work."

"What do you mean?" Kay asked.

Artie looked around. He said, "I mean, like—you see those plants over there? I know all of them. That's witch hazel, those are Dutchman's-breeches, and that's red trillium. That bright orange one only grows here. It's called adder's nest. If you boil its roots in sheep's milk, you get a really nasty poison."

"Wow," both Kay and Thumb said.

Artie held up Excalibur. "See these words?" Kay leaned in to look at the blade's inscriptions. "They're Latin, and I can *read* them. *Tolle me* means 'Take me up,' *Iacta me* means 'Cast me away.'"

Kay leaned back. "Far out, Your Kingliness."

"On top of all this, I also think I know how to fight, like, pretty well. With a sword. So, Tom? Wanna spar a little?"

The storm cloud grumbled again. Thumb looked to the sky as he said, "I'm not sure our wizard would approve, lad. Besides, I'm a little concerned by this storm."

On cue, a deafening *crack* of thunder rode its arc of lightning to the ground, splitting a nearby pine tree to its roots. Kay jumped. Vorpal reared and turned two quick circles, looking for something to strike at.

They could tell that it would be pouring in a matter of minutes.

"We have to go. I really think we have to go now, lad!"

Thumb said with sudden urgency.

Artie said, "You're right. Let's get out of here."

They quickly stepped through the pale light of the moongate, and it frittered away like a dying sparkler as they found themselves back in the woods of Peebles, Ohio.

Where the wind was going crazy! Leaves and twigs and dirt swirled in the air, and it was much colder than when they'd left.

Lance clutched his ridiculous Robin Hood hat with one hand while holding on for dear life to a sturdy tree with the other. "Glad to see you!" he screamed hoarsely. "We need to get going! This storm came from nowhere!"

Artie picked up Vorpal and Thumb, who had shrunk back down. He slid Excalibur under his belt and grabbed Kay's hand. Thumb sounded scared as he yelled, "Follow Lance!"

They did.

They emerged from the woods to a terrible sight. Artie couldn't be sure because he'd only ever seen them on the Discovery Channel and YouTube, but he had a sinking feeling that they were about to be hit by a tornado.

Kynder was on the far side of the serpent's head. His clothes were practically being torn off by the wind. He screamed for Artie and Kay.

"Dad, over here!" Artie and Kay yelled.

Kynder saw them and started to move toward them.

"Stay there, we're coming," urged Lance, holding up his hand.

Kynder grabbed a tree. Suddenly he looked more confused than afraid.

Because here, duckwalking against the tempest, came a sight his eyes couldn't understand. His children were with a ridiculously attired young man holding a compound bow who was trying to protect them from the storm, which was pretty nice of him. Artie and Kay looked normal enough except that they—were they both carrying *swords*?

Yes. They were both carrying swords.

Plus, Artie seemed to be carrying a rabbit.

Thankfully, Kynder couldn't make out Thumb. If he had, he would have passed out on the spot.

Artie and Kay smiled at Kynder in spite of the howling wind, and Kay held up Cleomede in salute. When they reached him, Kay gave her dad a short but strong hug.

Then something in the air changed. A sound like a freight train bearing down on them came from their right.

They looked. A funnel cloud had touched down in the field across the little river.

"*We have to go now!*" screamed Lance.

They took off for the parking lot, thinking they were about to pull a Dorothy-and-Toto.

As they ran, Kynder yelled, "Who is this kid? Why do you two have swords?"

"Not now, Kynder!" Artie and Kay both implored.

The noise got worse, changing from a low rumble to a medium-high pitch. They heard a series of knee-knocking cracks. Artie glanced at the funnel, an awesome black scar joining earth and sky, and saw it lifting and eating whole trees from the ground.

They managed to reach the parking lot in once piece. There was Lance's cab, and next to it was Kynder's car—an imported 2007 turbocharged Land Rover Defender—which happened to be the perfect vehicle for dodging tornados.

They threw the doors open. Artie and Kay chucked their stuff into the cargo area and climbed in with Vorpal and Thumb. As Kynder moved to the driver's side, Lance screamed, "Let me drive!"

"What? I don't even know you!"

"Name's Victor X. Lance. It's nothing personal, sir, but I was a Humvee driver in Iraq and I personally guarantee that if you let me operate your vehicle, nothing bad will happen to you or your kids!"

Kynder believed him. He traded Lance the keys for the bow and arrows and climbed into the passenger seat. While Lance ran around to hop behind the wheel, Kynder passed Lance's weapons to the kids, who fed them into the back with the swords.

It was hardly any quieter inside the car, but at least they didn't have to yell at the top of their lungs. Lance said,

"Strap in, muchachos, I'm gonna take y'all for a ride!"

He fired up the car, threw it in reverse, and took off. They peeled toward the exit, and right before reaching the gate, Lance executed a perfect J-turn. Everyone erupted in hoots and hollers. Lance laughed heartily and took off down the road.

For a few moments the storm was at their back and its awful howl got quieter. But then, like a giant blindly stamping his foot across the countryside, a funnel touched down in front of them about a quarter mile away.

Lance slammed the brakes, and everyone was thrown forward.

The car idled eagerly.

Thumb, who'd moved up to Artie's shoulder, exclaimed, "Heavens. That is not good, lad."

Kynder whipped around. "Who said that?" It was just too much. Kynder finally saw Thumb, and he finally fainted.

Kay reached for his shoulders and tried to shake him awake. Lance, checking Kynder with a hand to his neck, said, "He'll be fine, Kay. His pulse is strong." His voice was so calm that she couldn't help but sit back.

Artie asked, "What's not good, Tom?"

Thumb said, "The thing with tornadoes is that sometimes they're like a tear betwixt the worlds, which means that while they are occurring here, they might have some manifestation there as well."

The tornado in front of them milled around the road like it was looking for something.

"What are you getting at, Tommy?" breathed Kay.

"That perhaps this particular one is—"

"Being controlled by something over there," finished Artie.

"Quite right, lad," Thumb admitted.

"Or some*one*," added Kay.

"Quite right, lass."

Lance barked, "We'll have to go back the way we came, then." He threw the transmission into reverse and executed another gut-wrenching turn. But as the car spun around, another funnel smashed into the road, even closer than the other.

Now they had *two* tornadoes to deal with. They were caught.

Thumb demanded, "Kay, can you reach Kynder's phone?"

She answered by leaning forward and fishing in Kynder's pocket, coming up with his cell phone. She handed it to Artie.

Lance asked, "You calling the old man, Tiny?"

"Correct."

"I'll buy you some time then," Lance said. On their left was a large soybean field. "Hold on!" Lance put it back in gear, crashed onto the shoulder, and took off across the field.

With Artie's help, Thumb dialed Merlin. Artie held the phone on the backseat and Thumb, once connected, had to move his body across the phone in order to hear and then talk.

Thumb's side of the conversation went like this: "Yes, that's right. You see it then? Two, possibly three of them. Pretty big, yes. No, I can't see much rain. No lightning. Yes, I can keep it open. How far? Got it. Got it. Okay. Um, north I think. There should be a state road not far. Yes, yes he did. We also have an Otherworld phone. Okay, I'll tell the boy."

He scrambled up Artie and perched himself on his shoulder, leaving the phone connected.

The way across the field was incredibly bumpy.

Artie reached to turn off the phone when Thumb yelped, "Don't touch it!" He took a breath and explained, "We need to leave the phone on so he can pinpoint our position. He's going to run some interference. Whoever is doing this in the Otherworld doesn't have a very good picture of where we are exactly. If we can put enough distance between the crossover point and us, then we'll be safe. They won't be able to see us at all if we can get about five miles distant. Can you make that happen, Mr. Lance?"

"No problemo." He ripped the wheel, and they turned due west, spraying soybean debris and dirt in their wake.

The larger funnel was at their back. The other one, which was no wimp, was on their left and gaining.

Thumb said, "Artie, you need to call Bercilak."

"What?"

A flash of blue lightning broke to their left between them and the funnel. It splintered into a thousand veins then fizzled out.

"Whoa!" Kay said.

Thumb clarified: "On the Otherworld phone, Artie. You need to call him and tell him to open the gate!"

"The gate?" Artie asked.

The funnel on their left jumped a few hundred feet in their direction. The car banked violently toward it, but Lance caught it and swerved away. "We've made it two miles, Tom!"

"Excellent!" the little man yelled.

More electricity crackled around them. It was like they were traveling inside a cage of lightning.

Artie asked, "This lightning—it's from Merlin?"

"That's right, lad. It can't hurt us," Thumb said impatiently. "Call the green one! Do you still have the number?"

"Yeah." Artie fished in his pocket and felt the scrap of paper.

The funnel off to their left suddenly disappeared. The

electrical storm surged around them, lighting the inside of the car in a thousand points of light. They could see a paved road through a thin line of trees about a mile off.

Then, *boom*! A twister crashed down to their right. Lance whipped the wheel hard to the left, and for a moment they were airborne.

Artie's face was pressed against the window, and he couldn't help but look outside. Everything there was gray and green and black. It was terrifying.

But then he saw something even more terrifying, and his body went cold. Inside the twister was the image of a person shrouded in purple and black and reaching out for the car. The face was obscured by the violence of the storm, but he could see its pointed, pale chin, and its gaping mouth. He felt its desire and its power. It reached and reached and reached. . . .

The lightning surged and the form recoiled. The car's wheels hit the ground and dug hard as they vaulted forward. The Otherworld phone was tossed into the backseat, right at Artie's feet.

"Call him, lad! Open the gate!"

Artie willed himself to forget the face in the tornado and grabbed the clunky phone. He dialed the number on the note. The earpiece made an intermittent clicking sound, like a cricket warming up its legs. Artie assumed this was its ring.

Thumb asked, "Is he answering?"

"Not yet."

"How far, Mr. Lance?" Thumb barked.

"One more mile!"

A crackly voice finally came over the other end of the phone. "Hello, good sir. I'm glad you found—"

"Not now, Bercilak! Open the gate!"

"The gate?" He paused then blurted, "So soon? Are you sure?"

"Yes, I'm sure! If you don't, we're going to get eaten by a—"

And then it was there, with a sonic boom that crushed the air around them, stealing their very breath. The lightning disappeared, along with no small amount of Artie's courage.

"Holy smokes," Kay yelped.

The twister churned in front of them. The hood of the car flew open and they lifted into the air, front wheels first, and started to spin like a top. Artie kept his eyes shut as he pressed the phone to his ear and screamed, "Open the gate! Open the gate! Open the gate!"

He could only hear snippets on the other end: "I don't— sir—are you—what."

Then there was a huge crash that shook their backs and legs. It took a few moments for them to realize that it was quiet, and that they were still.

They opened their eyes. The hood of the car had closed again, and they found themselves looking out the wind-shield—miraculously not cracked—at the sky. And there, far above them, was the diminishing form of a tornado, viewed from below, ruptured by blue lightning.

The car sat in the field on its backside, teetering on the spare tire.

Thumb asked, "Is everyone okay?"

Artie, Kay, and Lance took turns saying yes.

Artie heard Bercilak faintly over the phone. He pressed it to his ear. "Sir, are you all right?"

"I think so, Bercilak. Whatever you did, it worked."

"Thank the leaves! That sounded quite harrowing, whatever it was."

"It was." Artie was still in shock. "What did you do?"

"Why, I opened the gate."

"The gate to what?"

"The gate at the back of your court-in-exile, of course. Next time you are here, you will be welcomed home prop-erly!" Bercilak sounded triumphant. Before Artie could say anything else, their connection broke off.

Exhausted, he let the phone fall from his ear.

Artie looked at his sister. She raised her eyebrows and smiled weakly. Thumb, who'd fallen into Artie's shirt, was patting him on the chest. Lance let out a primal "Whoo-hoo!" They started to chuckle, which swelled into laughter, and after twenty seconds of this they realized that Kynder was laughing too.

As they settled down, Kynder asked desperately, "Will someone please tell me what on this green earth is going on?"

They laughed some more. They just couldn't help themselves.

𝔚𝔦𝔱𝔥 𝔞 𝔟𝔬𝔫𝔢-𝔯𝔞𝔱𝔱𝔩𝔦𝔫𝔤 𝔱𝔥𝔲𝔪𝔭, 𝔱𝔥𝔢𝔶 managed to rock the car back onto its wheels. It had been through a lot but it was still in one piece. Lance put it in gear and headed toward the road, which, without an evil gang of tornadoes chasing them, they arrived at in a few minutes.

Thumb moved to a cup holder by the gearshift and introduced himself to Kynder properly.

Kynder shook his head. Not because he was talking with a man who was only a few inches tall, but because *he knew who this man was.*

"Oh my God! You're the Mr. Thumb from when Artie came to us!"

"That's correct, sir!"

Kynder let out a small laugh and then asked, "So you

and the kids—you're friends?"

"Very much so. May I bring you up to speed? I give you my word that I'll only tell the truth."

"Why not. Go ahead."

And so, with a few flourishes from Lance, Thumb told Kynder everything. By the time they pulled up to the Invisible Tower, Kynder had learned that there was a place on earth called the Otherworld; that Artie was *King Arthur the Second*; that Merlin was *the* Merlin; that Thumb and Artie had traveled via moongate to this Otherworld place; that his son had yanked an ancient sword from a stone and slain a baby dragon with it; and that Thumb, Artie, Kay, and the jackrabbit had just been on a crazy adventure—involving a million pigeons, a canoe, a girl who lived underwater, a giant bird, and an angry green dragon—to retrieve the legendary sword Excalibur.

Kynder sat in the car taking it all in as Lance and Thumb got out and went into the store. Artie and Kay saw how dazed Kynder looked. Kay reached out to her dad and put a reassuring hand on his shoulder.

"Pretty weird, right?" Artie asked.

"Yes," Kynder said wearily.

"Just wait, Kynder," Kay said. "Just wait until you see Merlin again. Then it'll be *really* weird."

Without another word they got out of the car and entered the Invisible Tower.

Kay was right. This time Kynder saw all of Merlin's mysterious tattoos. And this time Kynder got past the first room of Merlin's vast enchanted underground home.

They spent the next few days with the wizard and Thumb recharging. They ate, slept, and bathed. They read, practiced sword fighting, and did nothing. They looked at flowers in the greenhouse rooms, weapons in the armories, maps in the libraries. They played video games and watched the news, which had a really high number of stories about strange storms ravaging the Midwest.

Mostly, though, the Kingfishers talked.

Kynder repeatedly asked both of his children, "What do you think about all of this?"

Both were too mentally exhausted to lie. So they each told him, "I don't know."

On the second night the Kingfishers found themselves in a plush living room with a fire roaring in the hearth. Merlin and Thumb were off doing whatever it was they did in the evening. Kay broke the silence when she said, "You know, Kynder, I overheard what you told Artie about how we got him—and about Mom."

Kynder sighed. "I'm sorry, Kay. I should have told you

about that sooner. I should have told both of you about that sooner. But honestly, I didn't think you'd believe me."

They were quiet for a while longer. Eventually Artie said, "I think what you said that night has a lot to do with what we're both thinking about all this, Kynder."

Kynder nodded. He wanted to hear what Artie had to say, and he could tell his son was still piecing this together.

"Here's what I think," Artie said. "By themselves, these things don't make any sense. None of them. But they didn't happen by themselves. They're connected, you know? I mean, we've seen things over the past week we never thought we *could* see—not because we were blind but just because we thought they didn't exist. A wizard? Tom Thumb? King Arthur? No way! And yet . . . these things do exist. For better or worse, this is our life."

"I admit it's hard to accept, but you're right, Arthur," Kynder said.

"But here's the thing," Artie continued. "Now that I know all this stuff? I feel like I have to know more. I mean, this is who I am! I can feel it. I *have* to know more."

Kynder looked into his lap. His kids were growing up a lot faster than he wanted them to, and in ways that he never would have guessed. He swallowed his concern and said sincerely, "It's a great thing to learn about yourself. A lot of people—adults especially—are pretty mixed when it comes to that. I think if you believe it's right for you, then you owe it to yourself to follow the path unfolding before you. Both of you."

Kay worked up her nerve and asked, "What about Mom, then?" She thought it was super cool that Artie was going to be a king and all, but this was the thing she wanted to know about most.

"What about her, Kay?" Kynder asked with obvious hesitation.

"What happened to her? Can't you tell me?"

Kynder looked his daughter in the eyes and said, "I really don't know. I'm still very angry at your mother. This isn't something I'm proud of, which is a big reason why I've refused to discuss it. I vowed never to speak her name again, but in light of all that's happened, I guess I need to get over it." Kynder took a deep breath and held it for a moment. He let it out and continued, "Cassandra—or Cassie, as everyone called her—was a strange, fragile person. She didn't do well in crowds, hated flying, and refused to drink tap water. Stuff like that. But she was also fantastic and a little, well, spellbinding. She had long red hair like you, Kay, and mismatched eyes also like you. She could sing beautifully, and was good on the piano. She was very book smart. She loved you very much, Kay." He paused for a second. "I can't say the same for you, Arthur."

The kids were quiet while Kynder gathered himself. "Your mother was very freaked out by Arthur, which is understandable. But it wasn't just that. She hated that the two of you loved each other so much. And she hated that I loved you both as much as I did—and do. As the months passed, she became less and less aware of Arthur—she just couldn't accept him at all. Eventually she would feed, bathe, and care for you, Kay, but completely ignore your brother, no matter how much he cried. I pleaded with her, but it was no use. More than once she left the house with you in tow, leaving Arthur alone in his crib, or high chair, or even in the middle of the living room floor. For Cassie it became as if Arthur literally didn't exist."

"Wow," Kay said, feeling bad for her brother.

"Yeah. One day she'd had it. She got up like she was going to the bathroom and left. Just disappeared. I looked for her, filed a police report, the whole nine. But there was nothing. Your mother was gone. I hadn't heard from her at all until that phone call a week ago. Man, that call made me mad."

Kay said, "Well, she knows something, that's for sure."

"Seems to," Kynder conceded.

"I hope you don't mind, Dad, but I *have* to find out what it is," said Kay.

"Me too," Artie said, looking at his sister in solidarity.

"Thanks, Art," Kay said.

Kynder smiled weakly. He leaned forward in his chair and placed a hand on each of his children's knees. "I understand. I understand exactly where you're both coming from. No matter what, I'll support you. I promise."

The next day they felt a little better. Over breakfast Kay quipped, "Man, that was some heady stuff last night, hey, family?" which put both Artie and Kynder at ease. It was good to see that, in spite of her concerns, Kay's spirit was intact.

After eating, Artie and Kay went to practice with their swords. Kynder joined Merlin in one of his labs, where he asked if the wizard wouldn't mind teaching him about magic. Merlin considered it briefly and thought, why not? It might be nice to have a student again after so many centuries. So Kynder followed the old man around for the rest of the day as he circulated through his labs and greenhouses and potion rooms.

Lance came over that night for dinner, and Merlin told them more about Excalibur.

Aside from what Artie already knew, his sword had a lot of other sweet bells and whistles: like Cleomede, it could slice through just about anything; and in addition to glowing with a blinding light, it could make any enclosed space completely dark; and if asked, it could find the closest source of freshwater.

Artie interrupted at one point and said, "You know, the Girl of the Lake said it would teach me more stuff too, as time went on. Is that true?"

"Indeed it is, my boy, indeed it is. Excalibur is a trove of knowledge, and it will impart it to you as needed."

Artie suppressed a giddy laugh.

"But don't get too chipper, Artie, because there's also something about Excalibur that is troublesome. The sword, you see, is very powerful, and not at all inconspicuous. That sword is like a lighthouse on a speck of island in the middle of a dark sea. Excalibur was what enabled Morgaine— surely the person who controlled those twisters—to come so close to finding you. Morgaine wants to take it from you now. She wants to take it so that I cannot be freed."

Artie remembered the vision of the person in the tornado, reaching out for him. He recalled how cold he'd felt and didn't like the idea of being hunted at all. He hung his head and shuffled slightly in place.

"You're right to be concerned, Artie," Merlin said. "Morgaine's fury grows even as we sit here, in faraway Ohio. The time we are taking to gather ourselves is an indulgence. The sooner you can use Excalibur to get the key that will destroy my prison, the sooner we can begin to confront Morgaine head-on—and together."

Kay asked, "About this key—where is it exactly?"

"You're going to tell them about Numinae, aren't you, Merlin?" Lance inquired ominously.

"Yes. I must," the wizard answered.

Kay couldn't contain herself. "Who's Numinae?"

"*What* is Numinae is probably a better question, dear Kay. The short answer is that Numinae is the great-great-great-grandson of Nimue. Nimue was one of Morgaine's minions and conspirators, and she lured me to this prison."

Kynder asked, "And what is it that my children are supposed to do with this Numinae?"

"Nimue—the one who tricked me—foolishly kept the key to this tower, and she passed it down through her line. Now Numinae is in possession of it. It is your task to find him, confront him, and take it."

Artie scratched his chin. "Okay. Where does he keep it?"

"It is in his hand."

"He's holding it? Why don't we just ask him for it then?" asked Kay.

"No, you misunderstand. It is *in* his hand. His left hand." Merlin held up his left hand and pushed his right index finger into its palm.

"Oooh. Like in*side* it," Kay said.

Merlin nodded slowly and said, "Numinae is powerful, but he won't be able to resist Excalibur's edge. All you have to do, Artie, is chop off the hand and bring it to me here. I'll take it from there."

Artie rolled his eyes and said sarcastically, "Oh, if that's all, then no problem."

Merlin said, "You're right to think it won't be easy, Artie. But that's why you're the king. Kings do things that are neither easy nor often very popular. Mostly kings must make the best worst decision, if you follow."

"I'm not sure I do," Artie said. But he swallowed hard, put some faith in his new sword and the wonder of the world he was quickly discovering, and said, "But I guess I'll find out. When do we get started?"

"That's the boy!" yelped Thumb.

Merlin stood. He looked both proud and sad as he said, "Thank you, Artie Kingfisher. I know this has not been easy—not for any of you." He regarded Kay and Kynder. "We shall start very soon. But first we have to take care of a few things. For one, we must do all that we can to conceal Excalibur from Morgaine. For the moment, everything hinges on her being kept at bay."

Kay took this as a cue and said supportively, "Don't worry, Artie, we'll kick tons of butt together!"

"Quite right, lass," Thumb chimed in. "Like I said, Artie, capital-*A* adventures are the ones we'll be having!"

𝕿𝖍𝖊 𝖓𝖊𝖝𝖙 𝖒𝖔𝖗𝖓𝖎𝖓𝖌 𝖙𝖍𝖊𝖞 𝖋𝖔𝖚𝖓𝖉 themselves in a typical chemistry lab. In the middle of the lab was a stonework cauldron that appeared to contain molten lava; opposite this was a large rectangular tank that held a brilliant blue liquid.

Merlin stood between the two and announced, "Before we attempt to hide Excalibur from Morgaine, you need to understand a couple things about Excalibur's essence. Artie, may I have the sword?"

Artie handed Excalibur to Merlin. The wizard took it casually and turned it upside down, resting its tip on the ground and his hands on the pommel. "No one knows how long ago Excalibur was forged, or who forged it. What we do know, however, is that it is made of a *very* rare magical alloy—the same alloy, incidentally, as a plain, copper-hued cup that you may have heard of."

Kynder said, "Wait—the Holy Grail?"

"That's right. The Grail and Excalibur are related. The alloy that they share is steel, basically, which is mainly iron and carbon, but added to it is another element that is completely unknown on this side. It's an Otherworld element called sangrealite."

"Sangrealite," Artie repeated uncertainly.

"Yes. It's from Old French. Literally it means 'holy grail,' but it can also be interpreted as either 'blood grail' or 'royal blood.' Regardless, Sangrealite does some very interesting things."

"And those are?" Kynder asked, his curiosity piqued.

"The first thing it does is ward off any spell that is cast upon it. For this reason Excalibur cannot be hidden with a simple cloaking spell, but we can get around this. The other thing is just as important."

"What is it?" Kay demanded.

Merlin answered by raising and then lowering Excalibur into the molten lava.

"Whoa, isn't that a bad idea?" Artie exclaimed, lunging forward.

Merlin caught Artie's hand and held it still. "Not in this case. This lava would melt normal steel, but remember—"

"Sangrealite," Kay and Kynder said in unison.

"Precisely. Come, all of you, touch the sword. It's quite safe."

The Kingfishers stepped forward and put their hands to the blade. It wasn't hot at all.

Kynder let out a low whistle, and Artie asked, "So the sangrealite is, like, immune to heat?"

"Not exactly." Merlin reached behind him and pulled out a long cable with a big clip on the end of it.

"You're going to jump-start Excalibur?" Kynder asked doubtfully.

"No. This is connected to the voltmeter over there. Watch." Merlin clipped the cable to the sword, and the needle on the voltmeter jumped instantly to its uppermost limit.

"Wow!" Kynder said, truly amazed. His knees buckled and he had to prop himself on a nearby counter. "I can't believe it!"

Artie and Kay didn't get it. "Believe what, Kynder?" Artie asked.

"Well, I'm not sure, but it appears as though Excalibur is what's called a thermoelectric converter, which is a big deal. It takes heat and makes it into electricity, like magic. If we could harness this kind of thing, that would be it for fossil fuels. No more oil, no more coal—"

"No more global warming," the Kingfisher children said together.

"Exactly," Kynder confirmed. "Merlin, this is amazing. How does it work?"

"No one knows. It just does. And that's not all—it is also a superconductor. A copper wire containing even the smallest amount of sangrealite could convey power across any distance without any resistance. A boulder-size chunk of this element from the Otherworld would be enough to quench this side's thirst for power forever." Merlin unclipped the cable, pulled Excalibur from the lava, and thrust it into the blue liquid. A hiss of steam filled the room.

As it dissipated, Kynder said, "Artie, Kay—this is huge. It makes everything Merlin has said so much more important. I have to be honest with you, I know I said I'd support you no matter what, but before I saw this, I didn't really want you to get involved. No offense, Merlin," Kynder said.

"None taken, Kynder."

"But now . . . I actually *want* you to try and do the crazy things Merlin wants you to do. And, man, for the sake of everybody and everything, you should want to do it that much more too!"

Merlin smiled contentedly as he swirled the sword in the liquid.

"So what now?" Artie asked, feeling an even greater sense of purpose.

"Now we hide Excalibur," Merlin said. "Since the sword's sangrealitic essence will reflect any spell cast on it,

I had to come up with a work-around." Merlin pulled the sword from the tank and shook it off. "This liquid is made up of lots of nanoparticles—tiny objects many thousands of times smaller than the width of a human hair—which have spells cast upon them. They've been enchanted with a cloaking spell and a spell of strong magnetism. I'm confident that once this liquid dries, the cloaking spell will stick to the sword—forever."

Kay blurted, "How confident? I mean, if it doesn't work, then it's our butts getting busted out there, not yours."

"Very confident. If for some reason I'm wrong, however, Excalibur has one final secret that will save your, er, butts quite sufficiently."

"And that is?" Artie asked, totally enthralled by his sword's powers.

"Well, if the need ever arises to move quickly from one place to another, simply drive Excalibur into the ground and say, '*Lunae lumen!*' and a moongate will open on the spot. This portal will lead to one of two locations. You can determine these locations beforehand by placing these stones"—he held out in his other hand two small, dark pebbles—"wherever it is you want to go."

"All right," Artie said, taking the stones.

Merlin said, "May I suggest you leave one with me?"

"Oh, sure," Artie said, handing one back. "I guess I'll leave the other one at home."

"Good idea," the wizard said.

Merlin clapped his hands together and said, "Well, that's it! I'm afraid today must mark the end of your esteemed visit to my caverns." He placed a hand on Artie's shoulder and intoned, "Tomorrow, my young king, you must leave for your destiny, and make your way to the Otherworld!"

𝕿𝖍𝖊 𝖓𝖊𝖝𝖙 𝖒𝖔𝖗𝖓𝖎𝖓𝖌 𝖙𝖍𝖊 𝕶𝖎𝖓𝖌𝖋𝖎𝖘𝖍𝖊𝖗𝖘, Lance, Thumb, and Vorpal convoyed home to Shadyside, Pennsylvania.

Merlin, of course, stayed behind.

In addition to everything else he'd done for them, the wizard had given them a mini trove of useful items. There was a small sack of a dozen coins that could open one-way moongates on this side, a first aid kit that would heal wounds very quickly, an "infinite" backpack that made heavy and bulky items feel light and small, and two changes of underclothes for Artie and Kay that were woven with enchanted titanium and would act like suits of armor. For Kynder, Merlin provided a basic potion-making kit, some rare ingredients, and a little spellbook.

When they got home, they lounged around and got

their stuff together. Kynder even let his kids ride their bikes to the store to get two freezing cold cans of Mountain Dew each. He figured they deserved them. They drank them in the backyard. The sweet forbidden soda pop was the best thing they'd ever tasted.

They had an early dinner that night and turned in.

Artie and Kay woke up the next day at five a.m., and went downstairs. Kynder, who hadn't slept at all, was putting the finishing touches on a huge breakfast—complete with *even more* frosty-cold Mountain Dew. They dug into it like starving prisoners.

At six fifteen they were ready to go.

They went to the yard and stood in a circle. The rays of the morning sun spiked through the neighbor's maple tree. Waking birds trilled and chased bugs over the suburbs.

Kynder handed Artie his infinite backpack. While the kids were sleeping, he'd packed it with food, changes of clothing, sleeping bags, a lighter, flashlights, a pen and paper, two small umbrellas, a picture of himself in the garden wearing those ridiculous wellies, the swordsmanship manual, the satchel of moongate coins, Merlin's first aid kit, the clunky Otherworld cell phone, and a list of phone numbers. He also gave Artie and Kay six vials each of various potions he'd made: four nourishing elixirs each and four potions that would keep them from getting too cold.

"I know they're not much, but I wanted to give you something," Kynder said.

"Thanks, Dad," Kay said, putting an especially sweet and un-Kay emphasis on the word *Dad*.

Lance said, "I wish I were going with you guys. If you can find a way for me to cross over, then come get me. I'm pretty good in a fight."

"I believe it, Lance. I'll ask around," Artie assured him.

They stood in silence, staring at the ground. Then Artie placed a moongate coin in the middle of the circle. He looked everyone in the eyes, hoisted Excalibur, and said, "Well, here goes!"

He touched the coin with the sword's pommel. Immediately twin circles of pale blue light shot up and rotated slowly around each other. Thumb rode Vorpal through first, not saying anything, just tipping his chin low to Kynder as he went. Kay patted her dad on the arm and said, "I'll be fine, Pops. I'll make sure Artie doesn't get in too much trouble." Kynder smiled. Tears welled in his eyes as Kay stepped through.

Artie nodded to Lance, then turned to the only father he'd ever known. Seeing Kynder on the verge of tears, Artie couldn't help but think that his dad didn't deserve any of this.

Artie gave Kynder a strong hug, swung his backpack

over his shoulder, and said, "I'll be back soon, Dad. Got to go save the worlds!"

He stepped through the moongate and was gone. All that was left was a dull bronze coin lying in the grass.

This time they went right where they were meant to: King Artie Kingfisher's court-in-exile. Bercilak stood in front of it with open arms, his great battle-ax leaning into a rhododendron thick with pink flowers.

When he saw them, the faceless knight boomed, "Welcome, friends!"

"Hey, Bercilak," Artie said. "Glad to see you." The green knight made a flourish with his hand.

"Greenie," Thumb said unenthusiastically.

Bercilak executed a small bow and replied quietly, "Thumb."

Kay shook her head. She said, "Wow, you're really headless, huh?"

The suit of armor shifted noisily in Kay's direction and exclaimed enthusiastically, "Headless, bodyless, toeless, you name it. I am the Empty Knight! And I welcome you all to your wonderful home away from home!"

They looked past him at the court-in-exile. And . . . ? It kind of looked like a dump.

Behind Bercilak stood a very large oak tree. Small doors and windows in various stages of disrepair were built into

its ancient trunk. A pathetic hand-painted paper sign struggled in the wind above the doorway. It read, "Welcome
Back, King Artie!"

So much for a reception fit for a king. So much for a
castle, for that matter.

A gust shook the woods, bearing leaves and small
sheets of paper. One of the papers caught on the flat side of
Excalibur. Artie peeled it off. It read:

Ofhende!
One Byrnsweord!
If unearth'd pls. post at
Castel Deorc Wæters, Fenland
C.o.D.

It was partly Old English, and Artie understood it to say,
"Lost! One Firebrand! If found, please send to Castle Dark
Waters, Fenland. Cash on Delivery."

Artie asked, "What's this about?"

"Ah, a little flyer from the lordess of Fenland," Bercilak
answered. "Ever since you gathered Excalibur from the
Lake, the continent of Sylvan has been utterly bombarded
by those leaflets. They've been a plain nuisance and have
very much irked my lord of Sylvan!"

The mention of Excalibur reminded Artie of his sword's
nanoparticle cloaking spell. He turned to Thumb, pointing

to the sword. "You think Merlin's spell thing is working, Tom?"

Bercilak shuddered and clanked.

"I'm sure it is, lad," said Thumb.

"Really, master, we should endeavor not to mention that name," Bercilak protested. "Wilt Chamberlain—wasn't that what we'd landed upon?"

"Yeah, Wilt Chamberlain," Artie confirmed.

Kay let this one go.

Bercilak continued, "Quite. I'm certain Wilt Chamberlain has been successful at hiding Excalibur from its Fenlandian seeker. At any rate, your quest is still in the offing, so we'll find out soon enough!"

"You sure sound excited, Greenie," observed Kay.

"Of course! I am thrilled to see you here. My goodness, where are my manners? Please, come in!" Bercilak turned to the oak tree and pushed open the door. He ducked through, and Artie, Kay, and Thumb followed the green knight inside.

As their eyes adjusted to the light, Bercilak stretched out his arms and boomed, "Welcome home, my liege."

What they saw was more like it.

A long hall stretched before them. The floor was black stone and the walls were lacquered wood panels. Two rows of thick wooden columns supported a vaulted ceiling. Between each column on either side were empty suits of armor. Each column had a cloth banner hanging from it. The banners on the right showed three golden crowns on alternating backgrounds of dark red and royal blue; on the left were blue banners with two white keys and white banners with a red fist sticking its thumb up. In the middle of the hall was a huge, round wooden table. Just past this were several racks full of medieval weapons. And at the far end of the hall stood what appeared to be a statue of a knight in black armor sitting on a very large white horse.

It was such an impressive sight that they didn't notice the three short, ugly people standing in front of them.

"Ahem," one of them muttered.

"Oh yes!" barked Bercilak. "These are the servants of the house. Three amiable little trolls that go by Bake, Scrub, and Hammer." As he said their names he pointed to each.

All three bowed and intoned, "Sire. Sirs." Then they shuffled into the darkness as if they'd never been there.

Bercilak led them down the long room.

"This, Artie, is your great hall. Down by the table you will find doors leading to your private quarters. Another door leads to a hallway connecting to the stables, the storage rooms, and Hammer's shop and sleeping quarters. Down at the end of the hall"—and here Bercilak pointed toward the statue of the black knight—"you will find doors to the kitchen, the cellar, and Bake and Scrub's quarters. If you need their assistance, simply ring one of the bells that can be found all over, and one will come."

"Okay," Artie and Kay said.

Bercilak continued, "Now, I suppose you're wondering what those banners on the wall are about, and the weapon racks, and the guards?"

The idea of a bunch of invisible guards got Artie pretty psyched. "So, what, these aren't just suits of armor?" he asked.

"Of course they are, sire! What else do they look like? Bananas?" Bercilak crowed.

"Ha-ha. Funny," Kay said flatly. "What he means is, are they like you?"

"Oh! Well, yes, Sir Kay. These are the court guard, and they will help you if this compound is ever overrun by your enemies." At that, each suit of armor, in perfect and deafening unison, moved as if called to attention. Those wielding swords whipped them point-up to their shoulders; those gripping polearms thrust them forward; those holding menacing maces and morning stars stuck them out fist first, parallel to the ground.

Bercilak carried on as if nothing had happened. "The weapon racks are for them, except for the silver and golden racks, which are for you. These hold additional fighting implements should you care to supplement your swords. A dagger, for example, don't you think, Sir Thumb?"

"Yes, everyone needs a good dagger," Thumb said curtly.

"The banners are also for you. The ones with the crowns are King Arthur's. The ones with the keys are Sir Kay's. Sir Thumb's, if it wasn't obvious enough, are the ones with the fist and the thumb extended."

Finally they reached the table, nearer to the back. Kay asked, "What's that statue down there? He part of the court guard too?"

"Oh, that," Bercilak said, trying to sound like it was nothing. "That is—"

"ENOUGH!" a voice boomed from the far end of the hall.

Then they saw the large horse with the black rider begin to move. They looked closer, and that's when they realized it wasn't a horse at all.

It was a white saber-toothed tiger.

It stretched and yawned silently, revealing massive tusk-like teeth.

"Tell the boy, Sir Bercilak!" the mystery voice ordered.

Kay frowned and asked, "Who's that?"

"I am Sir Bedevere the Sixty-Ninth!" the voice boomed again. The cat lowered itself and the knight in all-black armor leaped off.

He took two long strides and drew his sword. Artie knew this kind of weapon was called a claymore. It was huge. "Tell him!"

"Oh, all right, Bedevere. Calm down." Bercilak turned

to Artie and put a hand on his shoulder. "Well, as he said, that is Sir Bedevere the Sixty-Ninth. His direct forebear, Sir Bedevere the First, returned Excalibur to the Lady of the Lake after the first Arthur passed. He and all of his line have been the guardians of the court of Arthur. You remember when you called me and implored me to open the gate?"

"Of course," Artie said.

"That gate is back there, behind Bedevere the Sixty-Ninth. It is a powerful gate that hadn't been touched for an age. Cracking its seal released an amount of energy sufficient to distract the lordess of Fenland, turning her attention from the fields of your Ohio back to Sylvan. And when I opened it, Bedevere and his kitty came out. They've been waiting here ever since." He motioned to the knight and the tiger.

"Waiting for what?" Artie asked.

"For you," Bercilak said matter-of-factly.

Artie swallowed hard. "Why?" he asked.

"Because I'm the guardian of this court!" Bedevere announced. "Not just anyone can march in here and claim it. You first must prove yourself worthy!"

"Prove myself?" Artie whined. Hadn't he taken care of that already?

Apparently not. Because before he could explain about the stone and the dragolings and the Lake and the dragon and everything else, the cavernous hall filled with the awful sound of clanking metal. Clanking metal moving very quickly in Artie's direction.

Artie's first sword fight was under way.

As if that wasn't bad enough, when he turned to Kay and Thumb for help, he saw the green knight restrain them with his giant battle-ax. He could barely hear Bercilak as he whispered, "I am sorry, sire."

Artie was on his own.

Tingling with fear and excitement, Artie gingerly stepped toward the challenging knight, hoisting Excalibur with a two-handed grip. And that's when the sword wordlessly urged him to charge. Excalibur was no chicken, and Artie shouldn't be either. Artie knew the sword was right, and so he began running blindly toward the black knight.

When he and Bedevere were only a dozen feet apart, Artie saw the knight's face below his raised visor. It wasn't pretty. His teeth were yellow, and a thick purple scar ran from above his forehead to below his cheek.

Artie tensed and wailed in defiance.

Their swords struck each other. Excalibur didn't slice through the huge sword or the man wielding it the way Artie half hoped it would. Sparks flew from their scraping weapons while Artie and Bedevere were driven apart by the force of their impact. Bedevere succeeded in remaining on his feet. Artie did not.

He sprawled on his back and slid along the stone floor. But miraculously the impact with Bedevere didn't hurt that badly. Excalibur, at the precise moment of impact, had made him *stronger*. He had never felt anything like it in his life.

Bedevere heaved his gigantic sword over his head and ran at Artie full tilt.

In a flash he was above Artie, bringing down his claymore to cleave him in two.

Artie moved defensively, and the weapons met again in a song of steel. The sound spoke volumes to young King Artie, as if he'd been waiting to hear these notes of metal on metal his whole life.

Artie's block deflected Bedevere's claymore to Artie's right. Bedevere straddled him, and Artie managed to push himself very quickly between the knight's legs. Once free from the prospect of getting cut in half, Artie popped to his feet with catlike speed.

The saber-tooth growled. Kay yelled her brother's name. The two sounds echoed through the great hall.

Artie lunged, but Bedevere pirouetted and parried Excalibur with his great sword pointed down, its tip tracing an arc of electricity along the floor.

Then Bedevere did something unexpected. He punched Artie in the shoulder. And man, did that hurt.

Artie backpedaled. Just as his feet were about to give out, the golden rack of armor caught him.

Artie grabbed a small metal-and-wood shield—a buckler—from the rack. It practically strapped itself to his forearm. Excalibur instantly taught Artie everything it knew about bucklers, and in a flash Artie was an expert.

Bedevere was in midlunge, and Artie raised the little shield. The blade nicked the wood as it glanced it away.

Artie took a deep breath and sidestepped. As his lungs filled, he felt the stones under the soles of his sneakers go bumpity-bump. He was full of electricity and power.

He homed in on Bedevere. The distance between them was exactly the length of Excalibur, which rendered Bedevere's obscenely long claymore less effective.

Artie stared into his adversary's narrowed eyes. The black knight backed up to get more room, but Artie slid toward him in unison.

And that's when Artie noticed that the mighty cross-guard on Bedevere's sword had a slit in it. A slit that Excalibur would fit perfectly into.

Artie feinted a thrust at Bedevere's midsection, and the black knight brought his hands to his chest, putting the cross-guard in perfect position for Artie.

Quickly Artie stepped back, and then jab-stepped forward once more. Excalibur slid perfectly into the exposed slit. Bedevere glanced down and shook his claymore, but it was no use. Excalibur's grip on his sword was firm.

Artie raised Excalibur and Bedevere let out an "Arghh!"

as his menacing claymore rattled from his hands and onto the ground at Artie's feet.

Artie deftly kicked it away. The knight fell to his knees. Artie wedged Excalibur's tip in between two metal plates on a soft part of Bedevere's rib cage. He did not push the sword through.

Artie breathed heavily.

His first sword fight was over. And he had won it.

Kay jumped up and down and screamed, "Woo-hoo! Go, Artie!"

Bedevere turned to Artie. The knight smiled. With reverence, he dipped his head and said deeply, "Nicely done, my liege. Welcome home."

Artie lowered Excalibur and Bedevere removed his helmet. It turned out he was about sixteen or seventeen. He had long black hair pulled into a ponytail and high cheekbones. He might have been scary-looking in the heat of battle, but even with his yellow teeth he was as good-looking as one of those rugged types from the *Twilight* movies Kay liked so much.

"Sorry if I hurt you," Artie said. Blood dripped from the back of Bedevere's hand. Excalibur must have nicked it during the fight.

Bedevere glanced at the wound and said, "'Tis but a scratch, sire. I've had worse." He pointed to the long scar on his face.

"I can see that. But, please, call me Artie."

"No can do, my liege," he said with a knowing grin. "You just kicked the butt of the Guardian Black Knight of King Arthur's Court-in-Exile. You'll have to cut a lot deeper than this to make me call you anything other than my king!"

Artie shook his head. Fighting Bedevere, besting him, and then talking easily with him felt like some sort of homecoming. Artie clapped his hand on Bedevere's shoulder, and Bedevere nodded knowingly. Bedevere felt it too. It was like they'd been reunited.

Bercilak clapped his empty metal hands together and said, "Well, now that that's over, we ought to partake in an impromptu knighting ceremony. Don't you think, Mr. Thumb?"

"Absolutely," Thumb agreed. "Artie, beating the Black Knight is a big deal. Now you can use Excalibur to anoint those you choose to enter your service."

"Cool!" Artie said. "Well, I choose Kay; and you, Tom; and Bedevere; and of course you, Bercilak."

Bercilak let out a hearty laugh like a long roll of thunder. When he was finished, he said, "Good trees, no! The lord of Sylvan—whom I am bound to serve and whom you seek—would not permit it!"

"Wait. What?" Kay blurted. "The guy whose hand we're supposed to cut off and take to Merlin so he can get out of his prison is, like, your boss?"

"They are the same, Kay," Thumb said seriously. It was obvious that he already knew—and that he was pretty disappointed about it.

"That's just the way things are over here," Bedevere tried to explain. "People have conflicting allegiances all over the place."

"Well," Bercilak said uneasily, "it is true that I am somewhat flummoxed. On the one hand I want to help the returned king—but on the other I must honor the pledges I've made to my lord Numinae." He paused. "The sad truth is that, well, I know where Numinae can be found, but I cannot tell you where this is."

"Why not?" Kay barked.

Artie didn't get it either. Being a king wasn't as straightforward as he thought it was going to be.

"Because he is uncertain," Bercilak said. "If he knew surely that freeing the wizard would be the right thing to do, I deem that he would *give* you the key. But—and pardon the pun, considering where the key is kept—if on the other hand he thinks it better that the wizard stay put, then he will avoid you for as long as he can. Since he is undecided, he must try to stay clear of you. I am in his employ, and though I rank high, I lack the authority to lead you directly to him. He would have my head."

"No offense, Bercy, but someone's already taken care of that," Kay joked sullenly.

"Quite right," Bercilak chirped. "Two puns back to back!"

"How can we help him decide then?" Artie asked.

"I think I know," Bedevere said. "You, me, Sirs Kay and Thumb—we go on your quest. Put our heads down and don't worry about what these ancient leaders of the Otherworld think of you. If your actions prove you to be worthy of the title *king*, then you will be elevated. This is Numinae's realm we will be trekking through. He has eyes in many places and he will see the way you conduct yourself."

"So you're saying," Artie said slowly, "that if I act like a king, then it's more likely that I'll become one?" He felt like he'd just discovered one of life's real secrets.

"That's exactly what Bedevere is saying, lad!" Thumb shouted.

"Which is why," Bercilak intoned, "we should hasten to knight everyone here—excepting myself, obviously—so you can start your quest properly!"

Artie shook his head. "Okay. Can you at least help with that?"

"Most certainly!" Bercilak said, happy once again.

Bercilak lead them to a low dais near Bedevere's giant saber-toothed cat. Artie and Kay could hardly believe their eyes as they approached the animal. Its knifelike teeth were as long as their arms. Kay quietly said, "I'm glad that's a friendly little kitty cat."

"No kidding," Artie agreed. "Hopefully we won't ever run into a mean one."

They moved up the dais and gathered around a narrow waist-high table.

Kay went first. She wasn't too into kneeling in front of her little brother, but Bercilak insisted, and Artie promised he'd never tell anyone about it back home. He also agreed not to order her around like she belonged to him. "Remember, Your Highness, I'm still your big sister," she said.

Artie touched each of her shoulders with Excalibur, repeating words that Bercilak whispered into his ear: "In the name of the Two Worlds, the One Earth, and the Sword from the Lake, I, King Arthur, name you Sir Kay, a New Knight of the Round Table." That was it.

Sir Bedevere and Thumb followed. Each time Artie finished, a crack of thunder boomed outside, as if to announce the new knight to the Otherworld in style.

After the ceremony Bedevere presented Artie with Excalibur's scabbard, which he and his ancestors had been guarding since the sword had been returned to the Lady of the Lake. It was a weather-beaten leather thing that seemed totally unremarkable. Artie strapped it on and slid Excalibur into it.

"It's glad to be home," Bedevere said with no shortage of pride. "You know, there's something very special about that sheath, sire."

"What's that?" Artie asked.

"The injuries of whoever wears it will be healed instantly."

"Wow!" Kay said.

"Cool," Artie said as he held it up a little.

Then Bedevere gave Kay Cleomede's scabbard, which was fancier. It was wrapped here and there with silken silver rope. Kay put it on and asked, "What's this one do?"

"That? All bugs will leave you alone."

"What? That's it?"

"That's it," Bedevere said apologetically.

Kay wasn't happy. "Hey, Bro, maybe from time to time we could switch?"

Artie chuckled and said, "We'll see."

The knighting over, Bercilak suggested they get more comfortable and gather around the table. As they made their way to the center of the hall, Artie asked, "Bercilak, you said you didn't have the authority to tell us where Numinae is, right?"

"That's right."

"Well, could you at least tell us where we could find someone who *does* have the authority to tell us where he is?"

Bercilak sighed. "I don't know," he said quietly. "If you were officially seated on your throne, I would not hesitate. But of course you aren't yet."

"Speaking of my throne," Artie asked as they took places around the table, "where is it exactly?"

"Ah. Your throne is in your *real* court. And your real court is in a place that no being has been in a—"

"Avalon," Artie said wondrously. It just popped into his mind. "It's in Avalon, isn't it?"

Bercilak grabbed the armrests of his chair, cracking them with his giant gauntlets. "My stars, lad, how do you know of Avalon?"

"We know it from the video game. It's, like, where you go at the end of single-player," Kay explained.

"Ah, yes. I forgot about that," the green knight said, sounding satisfied. "And your real court *is* in Avalon. But as I was saying, no one has been there in a long, long time."

"But it is most definitely still there, lad," Thumb assured him.

"Verily, it is still there," Bercilak said, using a word Artie was sure he'd never heard anyone actually say. "Though it has been hidden. Not even Morgaine can find—"

He was interrupted by a bone-rattling growl of thunder, followed by the loud snapping of a giant tree outside being shredded to toothpicks.

Artie and Kay half jumped from their seats.

"Ack! How foolish of me!" Bercilak scolded himself.

"Apologies, good sirs. Even I am too free with names from time to time. The Fenlandian lordess has keen ears—we must remember this."

Artie's knee started to bounce furiously as he asked, "Yeah, I was wondering: You think we'll have much trouble with her?"

"Some is to be expected, there's no doubt of that," Bedevere answered.

"It is true, my liege," Bercilak said. "But worry not. She won't risk raking Sylvan with tornadoes like she did the land of Ohio. That would be far too likely to upset my lord Numinae."

"Speaking of Numinae," Kay said, "since you can't tell us *where* he is, can you at least give us a hint about *how* to find him? A clue? Anything?"

Bercilak's invisible innards grumbled as he shifted in his seat and said curtly, "Find a map. At the Great Sylvan Library."

"Not to split hairs or anything, but what good is a map if we don't know where we're going?" Artie demanded.

"Artie makes a keen point, Bercilak," Thumb interjected with a tone of disapproval.

"I see your point, of course," Bercilak said, obviously uncomfortable about what he was about to say. "You must find the one called Tiberius."

"Oh no," Thumb said, letting his face fall into his hand.

"Who's Tiberius?" Artie asked.

"Tiberius is our friend from the Lake," Thumb said flatly.

Artie slumped in his chair.

"Not the dragon?" Kay asked.

"The same," Bercilak said. "Only he has the authority to decide whether or not you will see Numinae. You will find his lair at the Font of Sylvan."

"The Font of Sylvan?" Thumb complained, standing bolt upright in his chair. "But no one knows where the Font is!"

"I am truly sorry, Mr. Thumb," Bercilak begged. "Please understand that I am trying to be honorable to all sides. The Great Library is full of maps. Really, I can say no more."

Bercilak stood, made a little bow, and turned away from King Artie Kingfisher and the New Knights of the Round Table.

He walked down the great hall toward the darkness, opened the front door, ducked out, and was gone.

"Wow. He wasn't kidding, huh?" asked Kay.

"No, I guess he wasn't," Artie mumbled.

A moment of stunned silence passed between them. But

then Thumb jumped on top of his chair. He clapped his hands and exclaimed, "Buck up, lads. We rest here today. Tomorrow, we go to find a map! Tomorrow, we begin to hunt a dragon!"

𝕬𝖗𝖙𝖎𝖊 𝖆𝖓𝖉 𝕶𝖆𝖞 𝖍𝖆𝖉 𝖘𝖕𝖊𝖓𝖙 a little time camping and hiking with Kynder, and they'd both been in scout troops when they were younger, but those things were nothing like tramping through the wilds of Sylvan.

For one, instead of just being out there to enjoy themselves, Artie and Kay were on a nutty fantasy mission to free their wizard friend from an invisible prison. This camping trip was *important*. Also, they were carrying different things. Things like magical medieval weapons and armor.

In addition to the buckler, Artie now had a blue metal great helm with curly horns, and an ancient dagger named Carnwennan that had belonged to Arthur the First. He wore this blade behind him on his belt.

Kay had grabbed a dagger, too, and a simple military helmet. Both she and Artie now wore light chain-mail shirts and leather-and-iron leggings with bendy knees. When they put all this on over their other clothes, they looked like something out of a post-apocalyptic zombie flick.

The other different thing was that they were bush-whacking through a pathless wood.

Fortunately, thanks to Thumb, they weren't totally lost.

Thumb claimed to know more or less where they were and he concluded that if they moved east for three or four days, they'd eventually hit Sylvan's main road, which ran its length from north to south, and which cut right through the town that was home to the Great Sylvan Library.

The only bummer was that by the fifth day there had been no sign of the road at all. Just forest, forest, forest, and more forest.

But what a forest! As they stamped through the woods, they saw more pigeons and giant birds. Thumb pointed out the tracks of a short-faced bear, another animal that had gone extinct on their side. At one point they glimpsed through a thicket the rack of an enormous stag-moose, and every day at dusk in the middle distance they spied a large golden laughing owl. This last sighting Thumb took to be a good omen, since over the years Merlin had been very close with owls.

For some strange reason Artie felt at home in these

woods. There was something about them that felt second nature to him. On the first night he impressed them all—Kay especially—by whipping up a raging fire in a matter of minutes, in spite of the fact that it was raining. On the second day as they forded a medium-sized stream, he showed them that he could catch fish—*with his bare hands*! He simply found a low stone and wiggled his fingers under it and waited, and sure enough, after about five minutes, he was able to grab a nice brown trout by the gills. Along with Bedevere—who with a pistol-sized crossbow was able to bag rabbits, pigeons, and squirrels—he made sure they were never hungry.

On the third night, as Artie constructed a watertight shelter from pine boughs and giant fern fronds, Kay marveled, "Man, Artie, your outdoor skills are crazy!"

Artie agreed, just as amazed as his sister. "All thanks to Excalibur. It keeps showing me things I never knew or even would've noticed before. It's pretty sweet."

"I'll say."

As they drifted off that night, they felt really good.

But it wasn't to last, because late on the fourth morning, a long howl echoed through the trees.

They stopped dead. Vorpal sank low to the ground and gathered his haunches instinctively for a strike.

"What was *that*?" demanded Kay.

Artie's hand rested on Excalibur's pommel, and his

sword gave him the answer. "It's a dire wolf," Artie said.

"Blast," Thumb said. "Big things, dire wolves."

"Best we try to ignore it, guys," Bedevere said. "It's a wild animal, and there's no shortage of prey out here. We shouldn't have any trouble."

"Are you referring to the whole 'it's more scared of us than we are of it' theory of wild animals, there, Beddy?" Kay wondered.

"I am," he answered.

"All righty then," Kay said, unconvinced.

They moved on and tried to forget it, and for the rest of the day they were successful. But as night fell and as their fire crackled, they heard the howl again. And this time, from farther off, more howls answered.

They decided to post a watch. Artie insisted that he go first.

Just before they turned in, Thumb offered this piece of unencouraging advice: "I'm not saying this is at all likely to occur, but if the wolves attack, the most important thing is that we stand our ground."

"Got it," they all said.

Artie stationed himself on a log by the fire, his unsheathed sword resting across his knees. The light of the snapping fire played on the surrounding forest. After a while a wet drizzle began to fall.

Artie opened one of the umbrellas Kynder had put in

the magical backpack and huddled underneath it. He threw a dry log onto the fire, and it quickly roared to life. The needles of a pine bough near the flames caught fire and exploded like miniature firecrackers. Artie poked the coals with Excalibur and breathed in deeply, expecting the sweet smell of wet forest and a lively fire.

Instead he was nearly bowled over by an overpowering wet-dog smell.

Artie stood, but there was nothing there.

He dropped the umbrella, hoisted Excalibur, and put on his helmet. He checked that the buckler was strapped on tight and drew his dagger.

He spun a few circles looking for a wolf, but there wasn't one.

The owl swooped out of the darkness like a stealth fighter, hooting furiously. Artie looked up, and he was not ready for what he saw.

A creature was directly overhead in a tree, not ten feet away.

Wolves didn't climb trees, did they?

Artie raised Excalibur, and the thing inched closer. Artie blinked as he tried to make sense of what he was looking at. The way it moved was mind-boggling. Clearly the creature's head was a wolf's—but the creature's body . . . the creature's body was a man's!

The thing threw back its head and began to howl.

Ahoooooool! Ow-ow-ow-ahoooooooooooooool!

The terrifying call echoed between the damp forest and the thick clouds above.

Then the wolf-man turned and scampered farther up the tree. Before it disappeared from sight, Artie saw that it definitely had human skin and hands and feet, and that it wore a red cape over a shirtless torso.

Artie felt his sword hand tingle and looked back to the camp. His knights were still out cold. How had his friends slept through that wolf cry?

"Guys?" Artie called desperately in their direction.

None of them stirred.

Artie strained, looking into the blackness of the forest. He saw nothing beyond the reach of the firelight.

That is, until a dozen pairs of wolf eyes opened at once, like a platoon of yellow lightning bugs glowing on at the exact same moment.

Artie whispered, "Some light!" Excalibur brightened, and the wolves were revealed. They crept into the circle of light surrounding Artie and his sleeping companions.

"Uh, guys? Time to wake up!" Artie yelped futiley.

Seriously, how could they be sleeping through this?

And then a communal growl erupted as the wolves bared their teeth and narrowed their eyes.

"GUYS! REALLY!"

Kay tossed and Bedevere snorted. They were still out.

Artie spun one way and then the next. He was sure these creatures could smell the blood pumping through his body. Artie checked that he was wearing Excalibur's sheath. He hoped it would keep him from getting totally mauled to death.

One of the smaller wolves lunged within reach of Excalibur. Artie stabbed at its nose but didn't make contact. The animal jumped back, a long stream of drool whipping from its jowls.

Artie sheathed his dagger and picked up a burning log. He threw it into the shelter where his so-called knights were blissfully knocked out.

Kay sat bolt upright, kicking sparks off the log. "What the . . . ?"

"Nice of you to join the party!" Artie yelled.

It didn't take more than half a second for Kay to realize what was happening. She shook Thumb and Bedevere, and as they got up, the wolf pack divided. Six stayed with Artie while the rest surrounded the shelter.

They attacked. A massive canine jumped and crashed into Artie's great helm. One of its paws raked his shoulder and neck, and Artie could tell that he was bleeding.

Then another wolf vaulted. Artie blocked with the buckler, and the creature's snout smashed into it with a loud crunch. He sidestepped as it fell to the ground, then hit the crown of its head with Excalibur's pommel. The wolf yelped and quickly ran into the woods.

Next, two lunged at Artie's heels. One got its teeth into him, the other got the glowing edge of Excalibur across the top of its head. Wounded, it ran off.

The wolf that had bitten him held on, and Artie brought the dagger back out. He stabbed at it and took a deep slice out of the wolf's shoulder. This animal released him and retreated into the woods as well.

Three wolves still surrounded him and they jumped at once. Artie spun and waved his sword furiously, keeping them from getting too close. They continued to jump around him, teeth bared. The wolves scooted back as the blade scratched two of their black, wet noses.

Artie glanced to his left as Bedevere's claymore arced up and down in a blur. Thumb's Welsh *wakizashi* buzzed, slicing the very molecules of the forest air. Vorpal bounded up and down, attacking with his long teeth. Kay, even while fighting, was saying snarky things like, "Take that, Marmaduke!"

Then two of Artie's wolves pricked their ears and briefly turned from him as Kay and another wolf tumbled into Artie's circle. Kay managed to separate herself from her wolf and stand next to her brother. She winked and threw her back against Artie's so that they had eyes on all sides.

"How's it going, Bro?"

"Pretty good now that you're here."

And that was true. For all their practicing, Artie and Kay had never actually fought side by side—or back-to-back—and adding the adrenaline of actual combat to their sibling connection made it incredibly intense.

They turned a small circle while the wolves, now four, turned in the opposite direction.

"You're hit, huh?" Kay asked, noticing blood on Artie's leg.

"Yeah, but not bad. The scabbard's working. You hit?"

"Not yet. These guys you're dealing with are a lot bigger than the ones over there, though," Kay said, pointing her chin to the other side of the campsite.

Then, without saying another word, Artie and Kay sprang on their assailants. Each sibling felt exactly what the other was doing. It was like having four arms and four legs and two minds. Their awareness and ability increased by a factor of twenty.

Artie went high and Kay went low, expanding outward in a whirl of steel. Artie hit one wolf under the jaw, and then sliced another across the shoulder. Kay stuck Cleomede between the toes of one and slapped the back of the remaining one with the flat of her sword so hard that all of the animal's legs buckled. It lay flat on the ground like an embarrassed puppy for a moment before getting up and following its brothers and sisters into the woods.

Artie and Kay looked around. The camp was clear. Bedevere, Thumb, and Vorpal had also dispatched their wolves into the night. The wet drizzle suddenly turned into a hard rain. Drops exploded on the leaves like a round of applause.

They moved toward the fire. Artie asked, "Did you kill any?"

"No, sire," said Bedevere. Thumb, sweating heavily, shook his head. Artie already knew that Kay hadn't.

Artie said, "Good. I'm glad. Something's strange about this wolf pack."

"Agreed, sire," said Bedevere.

"I saw something before it all started, while you were asleep. Which, by the way—why were you all asleep?"

"I'm sorry, Artie," said Thumb.

"Me too," said Kay. "But I was having the most wonderful—"

A crash and a quick breath of air interrupted Kay. Before they knew it, Artie was gone. Kay wheeled and saw him rolling past the shelter with the largest wolf she'd ever seen. This one had not been in the fight.

It had been waiting.

Artie felt the animal's wet fur in his fists and smelled its stale breath. It snapped at his face. They rolled for what seemed like forever, rocks and branches and roots jamming into Artie's back and sides as they moved over the ground. Finally they stopped and sprang to their feet. Excalibur was gone, but Artie still had Carnwennan, the dagger.

The wolf snarled—really, truly snarled. This was no warning. This was the sound of a protector, a thing full of hate.

Artie knew immediately that this was the other wolves' mommy.

A bolt of lightning flashed, and he caught a glimpse of his adversary. It was easily six feet tall.

Artie should have been scared but more than anything he was angry. What gave this wolf the right to be so upset that King Artie and his previously sleeping knights had dispatched her pack into the night?

"Come on!" he yelled, his voice shamefully cracking, as if he were shouting across the playground.

The wolf snarled and lunged. Artie ran toward it.

They crashed into each other. The horns of Artie's great helm caught Mrs. Dire Wolf squarely in the snout, and forced her head up and away from him. The wolf's throat was right there. Artie pushed his dagger into it and the creature cried and crumpled. He pulled the dagger free.

Artie, out of breath, stood over the vanquished creature, and the anger fell from his shoulders instantly.

Cracks of lightning shook the sky. The wolf bled out over the wet ground.

He stepped back. The rain suddenly stopped, as if shut off from above.

The forest quieted. Artie dropped to a knee, tears forming in his eyes.

He couldn't believe that he'd just killed this beautiful creature.

"Over here!" Artie yelled.

His friends emerged from the thicket, with Vorpal bringing up the rear. Kay held Cleomede and Excalibur. When the group reached Artie, Kay handed Artie his sword. He asked it for more light and it obliged.

Kay looked at the gray heap at Artie's feet. "Whoa. You did that, Bro?"

"Yes," Artie said softly.

"Well done, sire!" Bedevere said.

Artie shook his head. "I don't know, Bedevere. I don't think this was supposed to happen."

Thumb stepped next to Artie and put a hand on his leg. "You did what you had to do, Artie. I'm sorry, but this is how battle works."

Artie nodded, but his shoulders drooped. He hoped that Lord Numinae hadn't been watching as he'd killed this animal. It didn't make him feel kingly at all.

Bedevere suddenly reached for Artie's leg. "Sire—you're injured!"

Artie looked down. "I was, but the scabbard healed me instantly."

Bedevere inspected Artie's ankle. There was plenty of sticky blood but no gash. Instead there was a raised line in his flesh about three inches long, like a wound that had been expertly stitched and healing for weeks. "Amazing," Bedevere whispered.

Artie stood up quickly. "That's it! Of course!"

He dropped Excalibur and fumbled with his belt, removing the sword's scabbard. "Kay, go get the backpack!"

"Artie, I told you not to order me around," Kay warned.

"Jeez. *Please* could you go and get the backpack?"

But she was already gone. "Man, what a royal pain," she whined, her words trailing into the woods.

Artie got his belt free and pushed it under the animal. He buckled it tightly over the wound, hoping it would stanch some of the bleeding. He then carefully laid the length of his sword's sheath over the beast's shoulder.

Artie knelt and put one hand on Excalibur and the other

on the scabbard. He started talking lowly in an ancient tongue he barely understood, repeating words that just sort of came to him.

The sword started glowing as rays of intense light pierced the woods.

Artie put a hand on the wolf's chest. He pet her fur as if she was his best canine friend. The wolf's body was still warm.

But still no life was in her.

Thumb and Bedevere watched in silence. Thumb said, "Artie, I don't think—"

"Shh!" Artie hissed. Thumb bowed his head.

Kay bounded back and skidded to a stop next to Artie. "What'll it be, Art?"

"The wizard's first aid kit and one of Kynder's warming potions." Kay fumbled in the bag and pulled these out. "Okay. In the kit there's some healing balm in a little tin. Get that and open it."

"Again with the ordering!"

"*Please* open it, Kay?"

Kay found it and twisted it open. Artie took a big dollop of glittering white goop and smeared the ointment over the animal's wound. Then he placed both hands on the scabbard and repeated the strange words.

He closed his eyes.

"Sire!" said Bedevere.

"Gross! She's bleeding again!" said Kay.

"I think it's working, Artie!" said Thumb.

It was. Only things with pumping hearts bled.

Artie said, "Kay, pour the warming liquid into her mouth."

She did, and when the last drop was out of the bottle, Excalibur got so bright that they all had to close their eyes.

The animal began to breathe rapidly. Then Excalibur's light faded, and they opened their eyes.

Thumb spoke for everyone when he stammered, "I-I can't believe . . ."

Artie couldn't either. He removed the scabbard, picked up his sword, and handed these to Kay. She held Excalibur up for the light as Artie undid the belt buckle and began to reach under the animal's huge neck when the wolf yelped, opened her eyes, and suddenly stood.

Everyone jumped. Bedevere brandished his claymore, but Artie put out a hand and said, "It's okay. It's okay."

The massive wolf whimpered and darted confusedly one way and then the next. Finally she fell onto her haunches, her head resting on her forepaws.

And then the thing Artie had seen earlier in camp dropped from the canopy, landing in between the knights and the great she-wolf.

"What the?" Kay barked.

Bedevere yearned to strike, and Thumb drew the *waki-zashi* in a flash, but Artie ordered, "No!"

The wolf-head man was in a semicrouch, his palms facing the knights, pressing the air between them.

"I don't think he'll hurt us," Artie said.

"Speak for yourself, Slick, but that's a grade-A monster!" Kay said.

"We've seen each other before! I'm sorry, but let me deal with him," Artie implored.

Kay rolled her eyes.

Artie stepped gingerly toward the wolf-man. "I helped her, okay? I didn't mean to . . ."

The wolf-man was silent.

"Can you talk?" Thumb asked.

The creature shook his head.

Artie pointed at the she-wolf. "She's with you, right?"

The wolf-man nodded.

"Can you check and see if she'll be all right?"

The wolf-man pushed the air with his hands again. Artie understood. "Put away your weapons, everyone." He looked into the red and yellow eyes of the creature and said, "I have to keep mine out for the light, but I'll put it down. We won't hurt you, I promise."

Artie took Excalibur by the blade and placed it pommel first on the ground. He commanded, "Stay!" and let go, and it balanced there, perfectly on end. "Please, check to make sure she's okay," Artie requested.

The wolf-man knelt and stroked the she-wolf's mane. He leaned to her ear and made a series of low yelps and growls, and she said something back. He removed his red cape and draped it over her. She nuzzled his hand and he rubbed her ears.

He stood. He nodded.

"She'll be okay?"

The wolf-man placed his hands together and nodded again. And then he made a little bow.

Artie couldn't remember ever feeling so relieved.

Then Artie got a notion and asked, "Were you sent here to find us?"

The creature didn't move. Finally he dipped his chin, just once, very quickly.

"*She* sent you, didn't she? The witch from Fenland?"

He nodded again, his shoulders slumped. He looked ashamed.

"Why didn't your pack try to kill us? Why haven't *you* killed us?" Artie asked.

"Jeez, Your Highness, give us a little credit," Kay said. "They might have if we hadn't overpowered them."

Artie started to scold his sister, but the wolf-man made an odd sound like a chainsaw starting up.

He was laughing.

"See?" Kay said. "He gets it."

"All right, Kay," Artie said over his shoulder.

The wolf-man looked at the she-wolf.

Artie frowned. "She's your—she's your wife, isn't she?"

He nodded.

"I'm so sorry—"

The wolf-man shook his head and his hands forcefully, and then motioned to the she-wolf again.

Artie thought he got it. "I mean, you're welcome?" And the great creature bowed, then rummaged in his pockets and pulled out a crumpled rectangle of yellowing paper, which he held out to Artie.

Artie cautiously walked to the creature and took it. It was printed with very orderly block letters. It said:

CABLE
WOLFHEAD
A—OOOO—H

Artie turned the paper in his fingers and said, "Nice to meet you, Cable. I'm Artie." Artie offered his hand. The wolf-man took it in his. It was gigantic.

They released hands and each took a half step back.

Artie asked, "This is if I need you, isn't it?"

Cable nodded hard and made a quiet but high-pitched howl. Then he came very close to Artie and underlined the *A-OOOO-H* on his card with his clawed index finger.

Artie said, "So if I need you, I call your name and howl like this?"

Cable nodded again, holding up a single finger very insistently.

"It's only good once?"

The wolf-man nodded one more time, and shrugged apologetically.

"Don't worry, Cable. I won't cry wolf. Thank you, truly. But I'm wondering if you could do a couple other things for me?"

Cable looked at his revived wife, then turned to Artie, listening.

"Okay. First, is the road close?"

Cable nodded.

"Good. How far?"

He held up one finger.

"One more day?"

He nodded.

"Great. Now this one may be a little harder, but it would mean a lot. Can you hold off for as long as possible before reporting what happened tonight? We need to keep a low profile, and I don't want the witch to know about my friends and me."

The wolf-man tilted his head and frowned. He stayed like this for several moments.

Thumb stepped forward. "Please, Sir Cable. This

kindness may just buy us the time we need." And then the little man bowed.

Cable stood bolt upright and clapped his hand over his heart. He bowed deeply.

"Thank you, friend," said Artie, sounding—and feeling—more kingly than he ever had before. "I can promise that we won't tell anyone about what happened here tonight, either. You have my word."

"That's right, Wolfie, and that actually means something," intoned Kay, clearly impressed with Artie. "That's my bro, and he's King freaking Arthur."

Artie bowed low to Cable. The owl, invisible in the canopy above, hooted three times. Then it fell into the woods, and flew off.

Cable was right. They hit the road in the late afternoon on the following day.

Now all they had to do was figure out which way to go to get to the Great Library.

Down the road a ways stood a massive white pine. Thumb suggested climbing it to get the lay of the land.

When they reached the tree, Bedevere grabbed the lowest branch and pulled himself up. He quickly disappeared into the high, darkening boughs. Fifteen minutes later he came back into view, flushed and covered in scrapes and long needles.

He dropped to the ground, brushed himself off, and said, "Good news. I can see the Glimmer Stream—which in spite of its name is Sylvan's biggest river—not far to the north. Just before it is a village. I'm positive I can see the library there."

"Which means we can get our map!" Kay said.

"Which means we can *try* to get a map that will help us," Thumb corrected. "Finding the Font won't be easy, but I see no reason not to follow Bercilak's advice."

They started down the road.

Artie was next to Thumb, who hopped along on Vorpal. As they walked, Thumb said, "There's something you should know about Cable, Artie."

"Yeah, what's that?"

"Well, I can't be certain, but Arthur the First's wolf-hound was named something quite similar—Cabal. He was unerringly faithful to Arthur, and was a fierce fighter."

"You think there's a connection?"

"Perhaps. Cable may be descended from Cabal, and it may be why he was used to try to find you. The witch might have guessed that he would have stood the best chance of tracking you down."

"But then why'd he give us his card? It seemed like he wanted to help us."

"Maybe after seeing what you did for him, he realized that harming you was not in order."

Artie shook his head. "So can we trust him or not?"

Thumb took a moment before answering. "I think we can. You earned that for us by resurrecting his wife. He won't forget that."

"I hope not," Artie said quietly.

Thumb continued, "But we must remain vigilant. If the witch manages to find out where he discovered us and when, we may be in more imminent danger than we think."

They continued on in silence, passing a grove of small chestnuts and elms. In due time they came to a wooden sign with gilt lettering. It read in plain, modern English:

VELTDAM, THE TOWN OF KNOWLEDGE!

Behind the sign was a small brick building. Past this stood the beginnings of the town, which looked pretty abandoned.

Just beyond the sign in a small clearing stood a tight group of golden metal rods about ten feet high. They surrounded a very brightly glowing blue pole. At the top of this cluster was a golden upside-down bowl, out of which jutted an antenna-looking thing, and from which extended a cable that stretched to a wooden pole twenty feet away on the right side of the road. The cable went on this way down the road and into the town.

Artie was reminded of Merlin's electricity demonstration

with Excalibur back at the Invisible Tower. "Are those power lines?" he asked.

"That's right, lad," answered Thumb. "The blue rod has a tiny bit of sangrealite in it. Deep belowground its other end is immersed in a vein of lava. Capacitors and transformers are distributed along the power line as it gets through the town. And that's quite simply how the whole thing works."

"Clean energy in action," Kay marveled.

"Indeed, Sir Kay," Thumb said.

Suddenly the round door of the building swung open. Two Veltdam guards emerged, scratching their bottoms and heads as if they'd just woken from a nap.

Finally the guards noticed them. Surprised, the shorter one turned and fumbled with a halberd on a weapon rack. The larger one simply shouted, "Halt!" even though no one was moving.

The shorter guard stepped forward and lowered his weapon. "Who goes there?" he demanded.

Kay took one look at them and mumbled, "Tweedledee and Tweedle*dumb*."

Thumb stepped forward and said, "Just travelers, friends. No need for alarm."

The large one started, "Traveling where—"

"—might we ask?" the shorter one finished.

"To the library, we were hoping," Thumb answered.

"You are Sylvanian," the taller one said, indicating Thumb.

"And that one is too," the shorter one said, pointing to Bedevere.

"But where do the younger ones come from?"

Turned out they really *were* like Tweedledee and Tweedledum.

Thumb said, "The children are not Sylvanian, it is true."

"Well then—"

"—where are—"

"—they from?"

"I'm sorry but I cannot tell you that," Thumb lamented, bowing slightly.

Both recoiled, looked at each other quickly, turned back to the knights, and coughed, "Pfaw!"

The shorter one pushed the point of his halberd forward so that it was mere inches from Vorpal's chest. He said, "They wouldn't be Fenlandian—"

"—would they now?"

Everyone turned as Bedevere laughed loudly. He looked so cool—his helmet was off, his hair fell around his shoulders, his hip was thrown out, and his right hand rested lazily on the handle of his claymore.

A quick flush washed over Kay.

Bedevere asked, "Fenlandian? Please, brothers. When was the last time you saw a Fenlandian in these parts?"

The guards scoffed at Bedevere but quickly added, "We have—"

"—never seen—"

"—a Fenlandian."

Bedevere beamed. "Exactly. And as Sylvanians, as guards no less, wouldn't you think that if these were Fenland child warriors you would know it? We are all marked in our subtle ways, we can all see from where we hail. Is this not true, brothers?"

Artie was struck by how glad he was that Bedevere was with them.

The guards grunted and said, "Well, yes."

"Of course you are right."

"They are not marked. But where then—"

"—are they from?"

"*Not* Fenland," said Thumb.

And then the larger one lowered himself and said directly to Artie, "Tell me, child, where I might find your forebears!"

The sudden abandonment of the guard's habit of talking with his partner had a chilling effect, and before anyone could stop him, Artie barked, "Avalon!"

Why this word came out instead of *Pennsylvania* or

America, or even *Earth*, was anyone's guess, Artie's included. But Artie knew in his heart that it was true. He knew that when he got to Avalon he would be *returning* there. Shadyside, Pennsylvania was home, but Avalon was in his blood.

The taller guard's eyelids tensed and his head turned very slightly to the side. "Perhaps," he said.

Thumb seized on this and said, "Yes, perhaps. Have you ever seen one from Avalon?"

"Of course not. There are not many alive who have ever seen one from Avalon."

"No, there are not," confirmed Thumb. "Do you think you might let us pass now, friend?"

Before he could answer, the other guard started to ask, "Do *you* think—"

But the tall guard cut him off, saying, "Shush! Enough, Larry. The little ones are not Fenlandian, and the other two are Sylvanian, so they shall be granted passage." This guard seemed to be in charge, and no longer looked even remotely Tweedledum-like. In fact, he now seemed totally terrifying. "Call Lavery and tell him to expect four visitors, plus a large bunny."

Larry followed his orders and disappeared into the guardhouse. The remaining guard, still addressing Thumb, asked, "I assume you know where to find the library?"

Thumb smiled. "Yes; as I recall, you can't miss it."

"No, you cannot," the guard huffed.

With that, he went to the side of the house and dropped heavily into a yellow plastic patio chair. He picked up a book, briefly began to read, and then looked at Artie and his knights, who were watching him curiously. He squinted at them and barked, "Well, on you go then!"

And they did.

Many of Veltdam's buildings—which ranged in shape from normal A-frames to Smurf-like mushrooms—appeared empty. Artie thought that had something to do with the fact that, as Merlin said, there just weren't that many people in the Otherworld anymore. It was sad—Veltdam was a pretty little town, but it was on its way to being run-down and forgotten.

But then they arrived at the library, which was the total opposite of run-down and forgotten.

The Great Sylvan Library was housed in a massive elm tree whose trunk was no less than fifty feet across. This had been converted into a building and had windows and doors, not unlike the front of Artie's court-in-exile. It was obviously the library on account of the huge, gilt wooden sign saying as much, but also on account of the huge cats that guarded its steps; they resembled the famous lions in front of the New York Public Library on Fifth Avenue, which the Kingfishers had once visited with Kynder.

Except these cats were totally and completely alive. And like Bedevere's kitty, they were massive saber-toothed tigers.

As soon as he saw them, Bedevere said, "Aw, would you look at them. So cute!"

"Beddy, those are not kittens at a cat shelter, you know!" Kay exclaimed.

Bedevere put a hand on Kay's shoulder. She blushed as he said, "Oh, I know they'd rip any of our heads off, but look at them!" The cats squinted and licked their massive paws. Kay had to admit that they were pretty cute.

Kay and Bedevere didn't linger too long on the cats, though, because coming down the stairs between them was a greeting party of one.

He was a very tall, very thin creature that could only be described as a wood elf. His long, ponytailed hair was every color of autumn leaves; his skin was the hue of fresh-cut pine boards; and his eyes were the vibrant color of fresh spring foliage. He had reading glasses pushed onto his broad forehead and a long nose. He wore blue jeans and brown loafers and a ragged green T-shirt that read, "Choose Your Weapon!" under which sat a line of Dungeons & Dragons dice of various shapes and denominations.

Kay could barely believe it. For one, where did he get

that shirt? These Otherworld people *lived* Dungeons & Dragons—they played it too? For a second Kay thought she might be looking at the most ironic T-shirt and T-shirt-wearer combination ever. She choked under her breath and whispered to Artie, "Now *that's* a freaking Dr Pepper head!"

Still, he looked kind of cool—he was an elf, after all. And there was no doubt about this on account of that thing that gives all elves away: his ears. They were so long and pointy that they extended above the top of his head like horns.

As the knights approached, he smiled in a way that was equal parts welcoming and sinister.

"Hello, friends! I am Lavery. On behalf of Veltdam, I welcome you!" He held his arms out. Everyone exchanged greetings. Kay went last, and when Lavery got to her, he said with a tone that chilled her spine, "Hello, Sister Kay."

For perhaps the first time in her life Kay couldn't think of a snide comeback.

"Lovely cats, Sir Lavery," said Bedevere, not noticing Kay's discomfort. "I have one myself. A white one."

"A white one, eh? Quite rare, those. But thank you, yes. These are very good felines, very good." He pointed at the one on the right-hand pedestal. "That is Schrödinger," and swinging his extended arm to the other, "and that is Mrs. Tibbins. Where the guard of the road fails, these dears cover. Nothing gets by them." Then Lavery turned to his guests, stooped slightly, and with what seemed to be a signature tone of slippery kindness he repeated, "Nothing."

Lavery straightened and clapped his hands together, visibly tightening his long fingers around his hands. "Well! Shall we go inside?"

Thumb was determined not to let this elf's oddities throw them. They needed a good night's sleep, not to mention a map, and in spite of Lavery's strangeness and possible feline threats, Thumb could see no reason to be wary of a library. Quickly he insisted, "Yes, please show us in, Lavery."

Lavery led them in, pushing the doors closed. They boomed ominously. He grabbed an electric lantern from a peg on the wall and turned it up. Its light was warm and welcoming. The air smelled of wood and leather and paper.

Lavery started to walk, saying, "This way, my friends. We don't get many visitors so we don't often bother with the lights in the hall. We get even fewer overnighters, but we'll have no problem accommodating you."

Thumb said, "Thank you, Lavery. We won't be a burden. In the morning we wish to consult some of your archives and then be on our way."

Their footsteps echoed in the dark spaces around them as Lavery growled, "Archives, you say?"

"Maps," Kay corrected nervously, which was strange. Kay had never once in her thirteen years felt nervous about saying anything.

"Maps, eh, Sister Kay?" inquired Lavery. Kay found his voice to be terrifying and yet marvelous.

"That's right," Bedevere answered for her.

The elf said proudly, "Well, we have those! Subterranean or terranean?

"Terranean," Thumb said. "Really, we'd just like to have a look at a good map of Sylvan." Thumb sounded very convincing as he lied, "We lost ours while we were bivouacking in the woods and we need one before we leave Veltdam."

"Aha, I see. Never convenient, losing one's bearings, is it?" asked the elf. Something about his tone suggested he was making a prediction rather than clarifying a point of fact.

Thumb said, "Not convenient at all, no. You see, we're taking the children here on a summer trip, before their schooling resumes." The lie grew. "As a project they proposed finding and observing the nest of a magnificent Argentine. You see where a map may serve us then."

"Indeed I do, good Sir Thumb. If I recall, they prefer to nest on higher ground. A topographical map would do quite well for that."

"Exactly," Thumb agreed.

Lavery cleared his throat. "Well, we shall see about all that in the morning, but now"—and here the elf stopped at a short round door and rested his hand on the knob—"you would like something to eat, no?" The tone of his voice took yet another turn, this time becoming so gracious and welcoming that they nearly forgot that Lavery had been acting strangely.

Thumb smiled and said, "That sounds grand, don't you think, lads?"

They agreed and followed Lavery into a warmly lit room. There were coat pegs and a long weapon rack along one wall, and nightshirts folded on a sideboard along the opposite wall. There was a table set with a delicious-looking meal. Beyond the table were four comfortable-looking cots and a padded dog bed for Vorpal. At the very back was another door that said Washroom on it.

Lavery crouched in the doorway as the party settled in. He smiled and produced a small spiral notebook from one of his jeans pockets and fumbled through the pages, finally reaching the one he wanted, and looked it over. He turned down the corners of his mouth a little, drew a nib of pencil from behind his spearlike ears, and made a note. He closed the book and stuffed it back into its pocket.

The party sat at the table as Lavery clapped his hands and said, "Well, I shall take my leave. There is a bell by the door should you need anything, otherwise I will see you in the morning for breakfast. And then I will take you to the map house. Sleep tight!"

And before any of them could return the sentiment, he was gone.

Kay felt like a charter bus full of gaming geeks had been lifted from her shoulders.

They ate to their stomachs' content, took turns showering, and turned in to bed. They were happy to be sleeping indoors instead of outside under another makeshift shelter.

As they lay in bed, Artie became aware of a low, rhythmic rumble, like someone was blasting hip-hop in a faraway room. He listened to it and fell quickly asleep. So did everyone else.

That night they all had horrible dreams of tall, slimy hippies with super-pointy ears.

They had no idea how long they slept, but when they woke they were refreshed and ignorant of their nightmares.

Not long after they got out of bed, Lavery appeared in the doorway holding a tray with breakfast.

"Good morning, guests! I trust you slept well?"

Artie said, "Yup. Better than we've slept in nearly a week. Thanks, Lavery."

"My pleasure."

Lavery drifted into the room and set out a breakfast of cheese, fruit, and cold cuts as the knights seated themselves around the table. While they ate, he watched them from the low doorway.

Everyone was in good spirits, including Kay, but

whenever she looked in Lavery's direction she felt horrible and sick and empty. She couldn't figure out why this was until it dawned on her that their hair was very similar. Mostly red and silken and long and pulled back into a smart, athletic ponytail.

When she realized this, her stomach did an immediate and violent turn. Kay pushed back and left the table quickly, heading for the washroom.

Thumb asked, "So Lavery, when can we see the map house?"

"As soon as you're finished, if you wish."

"We wish it. We should probably get a move on if we're to have any chance of finding a great Argentine's nest!"

"Yes, you're right," said Bedevere a little hollowly.

"Fine, very fine," Lavery said. "I'll return in a bit and we'll see if we can get you your map." Then he stepped backward into the hall and said good-bye, making sure to close and lock the door behind him.

None of them thought this was strange at all.

Except for Kay. As soon as the elf was gone Kay returned to the table and asked, "Is he gone?"

The others looked at her curiously and answered yes.

"Good," said Kay.

No one thought to ask what was wrong, because none of them felt like anything was wrong at all.

They continued to eat their delicious meal. When they were done, they decided to take a nap.

It was hard to say how many hours they slept. When they woke, they quietly went about cleaning their weapons and making their beds. Bedevere found a deck of playing cards and he taught Artie and Thumb how to play cribbage. Kay spent the whole time sitting on her cot or pacing the floor.

Something was not right, and only she seemed to notice it.

Finally Lavery opened the door and stepped in. Behind him in the hall sat Schrödinger the saber-toothed tiger.

"Well, my friends, are we ready to see the maps?"

"Sure, Lavery. Just give us a few minutes to get our stuff together," Artie said, moving toward the weapon rack.

"No need, my friends. It is only a house full of dusty old maps. You can leave your belongings here."

Thumb laughed as if to agree, and Artie and Bedevere moved toward Lavery unarmed, ready to go.

But Kay wasn't so game. Being careful to avoid the elf's gaze, she said, "I think we should take our stuff, guys. We were going to leave from there anyway, right? I mean, we're not spending another night here, are we?"

Thumb's body shook as Artie and Bedevere turned to him for advice. Thumb looked hard at Kay, and she could see that his wheels were turning. Kay thought this was both bad and good. Bad because it confirmed to her that they were definitely all under some kind of spell; good because if Thumb was thinking, then maybe he was breaking free of it.

Kay moved to the rack and grabbed Cleomede and belted it on. She grabbed the rest of her equipment and then took up the Welsh *wakizashi* and placed it in Thumb's rugged little hand. Fighting back a wave of nausea, Kay looked directly at Thumb and said, "Here, Tommy, take this. We have to leave after we visit this map house, okay?"

Thumb's pupils widened to the size of dimes, and the color drained from his face. Kay thought Thumb was gone. But then the little man nodded and slipped his sword under his belt. He turned to Artie and Bedevere and said, "Sir Kay is right, lads, we must get going. Take your swords."

Artie and Bedevere shrugged and absently took these and the rest of their weapons and bags. They lined up at the door, Thumb in front and Kay at the rear.

Thumb said very forcefully, "We're ready, Master Lavery."

"Yes, I can see that," he hissed, no longer smiling. But since he was still dressed in his blue jeans and the stupid D&D T-shirt and was completely unarmed, he didn't look too dangerous.

Every inch of the cat, however, looked mortally dangerous. Lavery stepped backward into the hallway and scratched it under its chin. Schrödinger made a sound half-way between a growl and a purr. Kay's nerves rattled her every bone.

Lavery said with a fake smile, "Right, then. Shall we?"

With a tone of assuredness that comforted Kay greatly, Thumb said, "We shall." And they filed out.

They walked down the hall away from the main entrance for a long time. Lavery led the way and Schrödinger came last, padding silently behind Kay. Kay continually fought the urge to look over her shoulder at the cat, afraid that if she did, it would pop her head off with its ridiculous teeth.

Finally they reached the end of the hall, which terminated with a normal-sized door. Lavery unlocked it with a large silver key. It creaked open. A dark tuft of thick grass revealed itself on the other side.

Lavery held out his hand, and they passed through the doorway.

The library's backyard was as big as a football field. The boughs of the giant elm that was the library arched over the expanse of grass, obscuring the sky above. They were so dense with leaves that it was hard to tell if it was night or day, dusk or dawn.

A knee-high wooden fence marked the perimeter of the yard. The elf moved to the front and said, "This way, please." He started walking toward a low, windowless house with a thatched roof at rear of the yard. Next to the house sat the other cat, Mrs. Tibbins. Kay was not at all psyched to see her there.

Behind the house was an oak forest so thick and so dark it put everything they'd trudged through the week before to shame. Its great trees were draped with Spanish moss and, as they drew closer, it gave Kay a sinking feeling, as if something was in there, waiting.

Finally they reached the building. Schrödinger walked past them and sat down opposite Mrs. Tibbins.

Lavery said, "Well, here we are. The map you require has been pulled and laid out for you. I will take my leave now, but the kitties will stay here. If you need anything, just tell them and one will come and find me." And before anyone could respond, Lavery was off in the direction from which they'd come.

Kay looked sidelong at the cats. Artie and Bedevere still seemed to be out of it, but Thumb looked sharp. He nodded at Kay, turned the handle on the door, and pushed it open.

The map house appeared to be just a single room. Along the walls were dark wooden shelves loaded with rolled-up charts, and in the middle of the room was a large, waist-high table. A floodlight illuminated it and threw the corners of the room into total darkness. Spread out on the table was a huge, yellowing map.

They went to the table. Thumb clambered on top of it. He clapped his hands hard at Artie and Bedevere and asked loudly and deliberately, "Do you feel any different, lads?"

As if on cue, both Artie and Bedevere put their heads in their hands and groaned. Bedevere straightened and cracked his back. Artie looked from his hands into his sister's mismatched eyes—it was as if he was seeing them for the first time in ages.

"How long were we in there?" Artie demanded, sounding every bit like his old self.

"Were we really wasting time playing cards?" added Bedevere with an uncharacteristic twang of fear.

"Yes, we were wasting time playing cards," Thumb confirmed, "and I have no idea how long we were there. Best case is we were really only there for a day. Worst case . . . I don't even want to consider the worst case."

"Did any of you notice how similar that dorky elf and I look?" Kay asked. "Also, more than once he called me 'Sister Kay.' That made my skin crawl."

"Now that you mention it," Artie said a little desperately, "I do remember that. What's going on? Why would anyone want to stall us?"

"I don't know," answered Thumb. He looked hard at the map under his feet. "If I had to guess, it would be so that the Fenland witch could have enough time to get here. She may want to see you in person, Artie, before she tries to put a stop to you. Or maybe Numinae wanted to slow us down so he could have more time to make up his mind about our quest. Without knowing who's behind Lavery, we can't be sure."

Bedevere studied the map and said, "I say we just grab it and get out of here on the double."

They were about to agree when a noise suddenly came from one of the room's dark corners.

A robed figure emerged from the darkness. "No!" it squealed. "You will take nothing from this library. Nothing! The kitties! The sweet little kitties!"

The figure was hunched, about five feet tall, and looked to be very skinny under its baggy brown cloak. Aside from its creepy voice, it didn't seem to be all that threatening.

Still, they drew their swords.

"Pfaw!" the figure intoned. "I am old! Put away your weapons, put them away, put them away. . . ."

"Show yourself!" barked Artie.

"Ah, the abomination speaks, eh?" The figure put its wrists to its hips and did a little mocking dance, laughing. Then it said in a singsong tone, "Stop, young knight in black! Put that parchment back! Nothing leaves! Nothing!"

"This map does, madman!" Bedevere said forcefully, pointing at the parchment on the table.

The cloaked person cocked its shrouded ear in his direction. "Ah! 'Man,' you say? Ha! . . . He thinks me a man!"

"Elf, sprite, troll, sorcerer—I don't care!" Bedevere proclaimed bravely. "We need this map and we're taking it!"

The figure looked like it was about to yell back at Bedevere when its voice changed drastically. It stopped dancing and started to turn in circles, saying, "No! No! No! Not safe! Not safe for me—or you either! No! A trickster! A sneaky old trickster!"

All the menace of the voice had faded. In its place was the squealing, wounded voice of a woman.

It sounded very familiar to Artie.

He stepped forward and quietly asked, "What did you just say?"

"Not safe! Not safe for me—or you either!"

Artie sheathed Excalibur. He'd heard those exact words before.

"Do you have a phone?" he asked.

"Yes, yes of course!" she said desperately, pointing a shivering finger at one of the darkened corners. "Every night she calls me, every night she calls and frightens and reveals. Every night she portends the horrors the child will bring into our realm. Every night, every night . . ."

Artie asked, "Who calls? Can you call our world with it?"

"Yes! Yes!"

"Have you?"

"YES!"

"Who calls you?"

The stranger shook her hands and suddenly threw off her hood. With the sinister voice back in her throat she screamed a single spittle-filled word into Artie's face. "Morgaine!"

Artie recoiled and placed his hand back on Excalibur's grip, but he didn't draw. Thunder clapped outside. One of the kitties roared. The ground beneath them began to thump, as if it contained a great beating heart.

"Is she here?" Artie asked.

"Here? Here? Fool! No. Oh, but she has shown me! You have no chance, tinfoil king. No chance! She knows!" As she said this, she flicked a finger at Artie's chest, as if to prove his insignificance.

Artie took a couple steps back, and the crazy woman followed him, staying in his face. It was then that she stepped into the light. It was then that he saw them. The eyes!

Like any ranting, senseless person's, they were wide and watery and bloodshot, but unlike most other people's eyes, their irises were of two entirely different colors: one sky-blue, the other clover-green.

Artie breathed in sharply.

Kay took two shuffling steps forward, letting Cleomede fall to her side. Artie felt her heart racing, her voice searching for strength. She stammered meekly, "M-m-mom?"

There was no question. The woman's silken hair was

mostly gray but was streaked here and there with bolts of red. Her cheekbones were high, her nose pointed, her eyebrows full. She was old—far, far older than Kynder—but it was obvious that she had once been as beautiful as Kay surely would be.

The old woman spat a primal hiss at Kay. And then, as if overcome by shame, she turned and hid her face.

Kay stepped next to Artie, grabbing his arm for strength. She said quietly, "Cassie."

And that's how Artie and Kay found the woman who'd abandoned the Kingfishers so long ago.

"Cassie, Cassie, Cassie," the old woman lamented, as if she'd not heard her name in an age.

Kay released Artie's arm and moved closer to her estranged mother. "It's really you?"

"Yes," whimpered Cassie, unable to look her daughter in the eyes.

"But how did you get here? Why are you so old?"

The woman shifted her shoulders and sighed. "I . . . I don't remember everything—it was something like when *he* came into your bedroom those many years ago. . . ." She trailed off. "He" clearly meant Artie. And she clearly didn't like him.

Thumb said solemnly, "A dark magic has made her old, Kay; I can see it as plain as day."

"Yes, yes," Cassie confirmed. "So dark. So many false promises faded into that darkness. A new life, a new child, a new beginning . . ."

"A new child." Kay shuddered at what she was about to ask. "Not Lavery?"

"Yes, Lavery," Cassie said quietly.

"But how?" Kay wondered. "He's at least five years older than me."

"Wood elves age very quickly in the beginning, and very slowly at the end, Kay," Thumb explained.

"Yes," Cassie hissed. "He's your half brother. And he's more your true brother than this, this . . . thing!"

Artie didn't like being called a thing, but since his parents were a finger bone and a lock of hair, he silently admitted that she had a point.

Then Cassie spun and raised her arms. Bizarro Cassie was back in full effect. She yelled, "Copy! Experiment! Puppet!"

"Now, wait one moment, Miss Cassie," interrupted Thumb.

"Shh! Silver-tongued gnome, be quiet!"

With a crooked finger she pointed at Artie and said accusingly, "You think you have a destiny? Toadswill! Swallerwash! She is coming! She is sending her servants as we speak! If you escape her now, then she will use other means to draw you to her! Where is the one whose name

224

begins with *Q*? Isn't she with you?" Spittle drained from the corner of her mouth as her radiant eyes darted around the room, desperately seeking someone who wasn't there.

Kay asked, "Who are you talking about?"

But Artie knew, and his heart fell into his shoes. "Qwon," he simply said.

"Qwon! Yes! None of you are safe! None of you are safe from the fine wrath of the high lordess Lady Morgaine!"

At the mention of her title and name, two deafening sounds came at once: the roars of the saber-toothed cats, and a fierce howl of wind tearing through the forest around the little building.

Thumb said, "Artie, sire, I have a bad feeling. I think we ought to go. Now."

Thumb was right, but Artie felt that he owed his sister a big favor where Cassie was concerned; it was crazy, but he didn't think it would be right to hightail it out of there without her. He was about to say as much when Kay yelled over the din, "I think Thumb's right, Artie! We've got to leave her for now. It'll be okay!"

But they weren't so sure of that last point because the underground booming intensified, and then the map house simply disintegrated in a poof of black dust. One minute it and all its contents—including the map and the table that stood in front of Bedevere—were there, and the next minute everything was gone.

Artie's back was turned to where the cottage's door had been. Kay unsheathed Cleomede and lunged at her beloved brother with blinding quickness as if she was going to run him through to the hilt.

And she would have if Artie hadn't pivoted at the last split second; Cleomede whisked past his neck, touching it like a feather, before continuing on into the space behind him.

Which was suddenly occupied by the silent and gaping mouth of Mrs. Tibbins. In the same instant that the walls had disappeared, this cat jumped from where the door had been, landing catlike—which is to say, freakishly quietly— just a few feet behind Artie.

Cleomede slid between the cat's knifelike teeth and into its mouth. The blade effortlessly ran through everything that made up the head and neck of the feline. Cleomede sang for blood in Kay's fingers, and it was terrifying.

The cat died instantly. It was very gruesome. Cleomede's bloody tip extended at an angle into the air above the cat's scruff. The animal collapsed and whip-lashed Kay's arm, forcing her to release her sword. She had to turn around to extract Cleomede and that was when she saw her mom.

Cassie had her back to the darkened forest. Suddenly a thick and gnarled oak, draped in Spanish moss, came to life. A pair of boughs surged forward like giant arms, wrapping up the old woman in a tangle of wavering flora.

Cassie screamed. Kay ran to her mother, intent on

hacking this plant creature to pieces, but the woods were too powerful. Kay's eyes locked on her mother's, and for a moment they could read each other's thoughts as if they were written in the air between them. Cassie's eyes said, I'm so sorry. And Kay's eyes said, I forgive you, Mama!

And then the tree creature retreated into the deep forest in a blur, and Cassie was gone.

Kay fell to one knee.

Artie, standing next to Mrs. Tibbins's corpse, wanted to run to his sister and comfort her, but other stuff was going on behind him.

"Artie!" Thumb and Bedevere yelled in unison.

Artie spun.

Schrödinger reared several feet away. He looked pretty angry that his kitty friend had been killed so easily. So did Lavery, who was on Schrödinger's back. The elf was still dressed in his jeans and D&D T-shirt, but he was no longer unarmed.

He had chosen his weapon, and it wasn't some stupid gaming die. Instead it was a really odd-looking silver rifle with a sword on the end of it, and he spun it over his head like a spear.

Turned out Lavery wasn't so geeky after all. In fact, he looked pretty darn tough.

Vorpal initiated the fight. Taking a massive leap, he walloped the tiger's cheek with his hind legs. He bounced again and landed near the cat's rear, where he took a deep bite out of one of its legs.

Following Vorpal, Thumb leaped on top of the cat so he could pester the elf at close range. In seconds Lavery was covered in cuts and lashes. Thumb took some lumps too, but the little knight was possessed. After one impressive, Yoda-like flurry of twists and turns, Artie swore that Lavery lost a finger. Then the elf screamed as Thumb did him the disservice of lopping off his long red ponytail in one blazing swipe.

Meanwhile, Bedevere was busy making huge, loping swings at the cat's face. As Vorpal tormented Schrödinger's hind legs, Bedevere brought down the claymore cleanly through the cat's right forepaw.

The cat roared just as Lavery's disembodied lock of hair fell to the ground next to Bedevere.

Bedevere smiled. It was obvious that he loved to fight.

But he smiled too soon, because at that exact moment Lavery fired his rifle at Bedevere's arm, which suddenly lay on the ground, quite separated from Bedevere.

The wounded knight howled. The sound tore Kay from the forest that her mom had disappeared into. When she saw the arm, she nearly fainted.

But not Artie. He bounded forward to join the battle. As Artie arrived, Lavery fell from the wounded feline, Thumb following. Vorpal occupied the cat while Artie stood next to

Thumb so they could take on the elf.

Lavery fought hard. He made several deep gashes in Artie that instantly healed. He also managed to thump Artie in the ribs so violently that Artie felt them snap. These too healed instantly.

Still, it all hurt wicked bad.

But Artie and Thumb were too much for Lavery, and in a desperate flurry the elf was laid on the ground and disarmed. The young king lorded over him; the little man was at his head, the Welsh *wakizashi*'s edge drawn tight over the skin of his neck.

Artie breathed hard as he demanded, "Witch-elf, bring Cassie back!"

Lavery's eyes were closed. His chest heaved.

He shook his head slightly. "I didn't take her!"

Thumb, wild with anger, said, "Let me kill this thing, sire."

Artie seriously considered it. But something about Cassie and Kay—something about being even slightly-kinda-theoretically related to this wood elf—turned him off from this idea.

He looked over his shoulder at Kay, who comforted Bedevere, and turned back to Thumb.

"No. Enough killing and hurt for one day. We need to take care of Bedevere."

Artie began to turn to his fallen knight, hoping that his

sword's sheath and his healing skill might mend him like they had the wolf. Thumb continued to hold Lavery with his sword.

It was then that they all became very aware of something that didn't sound good at all.

And it was then that Lavery, his mouth full of blood-stained teeth, began to laugh.

"What is that sound?" Artie demanded of the elf.

The elf laughed more. Thumb pressed on his neck ever so slightly with his blade. The elf said nothing.

He didn't need to. An explosion went off somewhere under their feet as a section of grass about fifty feet away lifted up like a big trapdoor. Smoke rose from the scar in the ground. Somewhere from within the smoke came a series of deep, rabid chokes and burps.

Thumb moved away from the elf as he rushed to Artie.

Artie was momentarily dumbstruck.

"I think we're in trouble," Thumb said ominously.

The smoke cleared. What remained, aside from a mound of upturned earth, was an elephant-sized wild boar.

"Yes. We're in trouble," Thumb confirmed.

The animal's hair was wiry and shiny, his feet were completely bloodstained, and his nasty tusks were way longer than they should have been. He was an honest-to-goodness hellion.

Except that, for some reason, he had a dainty silver

comb tied into the hair on the very top of his head, like a bow affixed to the head of a cute little lapdog.

"I have a bad feeling, guys," Kay said from somewhere behind them.

"What *is* that?" Artie demanded as he and Thumb began to backpedal.

Thumb cleared his throat and said quietly, "That's Twrch Trwyth."

Lavery continued to laugh quietly.

"It's Welsh for 'divine boar,'" Thumb explained.

And then, before Artie could say anything, the boar charged.

Charged isn't really the right word, though. It was more like he teleported in a blurry zipping motion.

Before any of them could react, the creature had passed Artie and Thumb and was standing over Kay and Bedevere, rearing his hideous head.

Except that Kay wasn't on the ground next to Bedevere anymore—she was up in the air, in the boar's teeth, screaming.

More quickly than he thought possible, Artie ran to Kay, dragging Thumb with him.

The boar was wildly happy with the prospect of gobbling down Kay and didn't really notice Artie as he moved in under his chin.

A drop of his sister's blood hit Artie on the head.

They really, *really* had to go.

Artie hoisted Excalibur, drove it to the hilt into the ground and screamed, *"Lunae lumen!"*

Thumb grabbed Artie's leg, Artie touched his sister's foot, and Bedevere reached out with his remaining arm and grabbed Artie's hip.

Vorpal, still guarding the cat, wasn't going to make it.

The moongate crackled open and took them away, an express train to Merlin, where Artie hoped his knights would be healed.

The last thing he saw, past the electric glow of the moongate and the dripping jowls of the evil pig, was the slender form of a great green dragon, high above them, turning wheels in a purplish Otherworld sky.

The moongate snapped shut, its light running over their bodies like a dissipating electrical current.

They'd been transported to a plain stone chamber, Excalibur driven to the hilt in the earthen floor. Next to its crossbar was the stone the wizard had kept as a marker for their safe return.

But of course, with a bloodied sister and a delirious, one-armed knight, Artie didn't feel all that safe.

He screamed, "Merlin!"

The wizard immediately whisked in. Artie noticed that he had a new tattoo, right in the middle of his forehead: a solid black circle about two inches across.

"Where have you been?" the wizard barked, but then,

when he saw Kay's blood and the maimed Bedevere, he yelped, "Oh my!"

Merlin sprang into action. He unbuckled Excalibur's sheath from Artie's belt and floated into the air, holding the scabbard in front of him. He began to spin like a top, moving so fast that he blurred into a featureless gray column. Then he began to glow—blue, green, yellow. Suddenly everything went white. Artie felt disoriented and woozy. As the light began to fall away, things were completely rearranged.

Artie and Thumb were on one side of the room, separated from Kay and Bedevere by a glass partition. The wounded knights were strapped to beds that were raised past a forty-five-degree angle. Both Kay and Bedevere were fast asleep and hooked up to IVs.

Bedevere was shirtless and had a massive bandage wrapped around his torso, but his skin had a healthy hue. For having just been relieved of an entire arm, he looked pretty good.

Kay wore a hospital gown and was covered to the waist with a white sheet. Artie couldn't be sure, but he thought her gown was printed with a pattern of little baby-blue pointed wizard's caps. She appeared totally peaceful, as if nothing had happened to her.

Apparently they'd been transported to Saint Merlin's General Hospital.

Most striking, though, was the wizard. Merlin looked nothing like a doctor—or he looked exactly like one if you counted high priest witch doctors as doctors. He stood with his back to Artie and Thumb, still clutching Excalibur's healing sheath in both hands. His exposed skin was sheened with sweat, and some of his tattoos appeared to be rising and falling, as if parts of his skin were like a movie screen projected with a nest of writhing snakes.

Artie took a deep breath. Adrenaline still coursed through his system. He had a hard time not banging on the glass and demanding to know how Kay and his friend were doing.

As if he could read his mind, Thumb, back to his old miniature size, scrambled onto Artie's shoulder and said, "They're going to be fine, lad. Kay especially. She looks radiant, doesn't she?"

"Yeah, she does," Artie said with a shiver. Then he turned to Thumb and said, "I'm so sorry about Vorpal."

The little man smiled sadly. "I am too. No doubt that blackguard of an elf will be dining on him tonight."

"Jeez, I hope not," Artie said, a little shocked. Thumb didn't reply.

Eventually Artie stepped from the glass and looked around. Excalibur was at his feet, still pushed into the ground. Artie reached down and pulled it up. He bent again to pick up the stone, rose, and dropped it into a pocket.

The next room had some comfy chairs in it and a table set with water and snacks. A fire crackled in a big stonework hearth. Artie went into the room, Thumb still on his shoulder, and collapsed into one of the chairs.

After a while Artie took a deep breath and asked, "What just happened, Tom?"

Thumb jumped from Artie's shoulder and settled on the flat side of Excalibur, which lay in Artie's lap. "You saved our backsides, that's what just happened, lad. And now Merlin is fixing our comrades."

"I know, but I'm talking about that pig thing, Lavery, the tigers. . . . I just saw a dragon in the sky—maybe it was Tiberius? I mean, what the holy hand grenades is going on?"

Thumb sighed. "What's going on is you're the king of the two lands, and you are destined to see some strange things. I'm sorry if it's too much."

"Yeah, I am too," Artie said wistfully.

They sat in silence for a while. As Artie started to ask more about the boar, Merlin glided into the room wearing a long linen cloak.

Artie stood, and Thumb slid to the floor. The wizard returned Excalibur's magical scabbard and the boy-king strapped it on.

"Well, how are they?"

The wizard made a so-so kind of face, and Artie's heart

skipped a beat. "Kay will be fine," he said "Her wounds were superficial, and you got her here so quickly that by tomorrow she'll barely show any physical signs of damage. The Black Knight, however . . ."

"I couldn't grab the arm. I'm sorry, Merlin."

"Even if you had, I'm not sure we could have reattached it. The projectile that severed it had some poisonous magic on it. Thanks to Excalibur's sheath, I was able to chase this magic wholly from his body, but I'm uncertain that it would have worked as well on his severed arm. I don't think it would have mattered if you had brought it."

"But is he going to be all right?" Artie wondered.

"I think so, yes. He's very strong. We will know by morning if he'll survive. As for his future . . ."

"I'm sure being down an arm won't slow him at all, Merlin. He's a real warrior. Way more of a real warrior than me," Artie said.

"Fiddlesticks, lad," interjected Thumb. "You should see how quickly our boy has progressed, Merlin. He is the one, there is no doubt."

Merlin nodded deeply, moved to one of the chairs, sat, and poured a glass of water. Artie sat too, and Thumb clambered up to perch on Artie's knee.

Merlin sighed and said, "When I first heard you calling me, I was furious to know where you had been and what exactly had taken you so long. I tried ringing you on the Otherworld phone, but no one ever answered. You have been gone a long, long time, young king."

"How long?" Artie and Thumb asked together.

"Nearly three weeks."

Artie stood, Thumb hanging on tightly to his pants leg, and said, "What? Three weeks! That means we were in that stupid library for over two weeks!"

"It was as I feared," Thumb said.

"But why would we be kept? Why not just kill us and take Excalibur?"

"I'm not sure," Merlin said seriously.

"Tom thought maybe it was so that Morgaine—I can say her name here, right?" Artie asked, interrupting himself, remembering all the thunderclaps and saber-tooth roars that happened whenever her name was mentioned in the Otherworld.

"Aye, lad," Thumb said comfortingly.

"Good," Artie said. "Well, Tom thought maybe we were held so Morgaine could have enough time to travel to us, so she could take Excalibur for herself. Maybe she doesn't trust anyone else to take it for her?"

"Perhaps," Merlin said slowly. "Or maybe there's some reason she wants both the sword *and* you. We are drifting into uncharted waters, I'm afraid. There are things that even I do not know. Please, tell me everything that has happened."

Merlin held his chin in his hand and listened carefully

as Artie and Thumb recounted their adventures. At one point he conjured up a cup of coffee for himself, some tea for Thumb, and an ice-cold Coke for Artie. The wizard didn't like the sound of Lavery at all and was disturbed to hear that Cassie had emerged as a player in their drama, but he was most put off by the mention of the giant boar. When Thumb mentioned his name, whose pronunciation still eluded Artie's ears, Merlin stood up in a huff.

"Twrch Trwyth? Good great heavens! Are you certain, Mr. Thumb?"

"Absolutely, Merlin. We saw his comb."

"What's the big deal?" Artie asked. "I mean, he was super frightening and all, but he's only a boar, right?"

Merlin sighed. "Wrong, child. He is *the* boar. The divine porcine, if you will. And the big deal is that if Morgaine was able to summon him from his hell pit, it means that she has become even more powerful than I imagined." Merlin paused for a moment before adding, "My, she has been busy all these long years."

"She certainly has, Merlin," Thumb seconded darkly.

"So if she's that powerful," Artie continued, "do you think she's the one that took Cassie?"

Merlin furrowed his brow and said, "No, I don't think so. She would only have been able to do that if she were there, and if she had been there, well, I'm afraid *you* would not be here now."

"Okay, so the forest creature was Numinae?" Artie guessed, starting to piece things together.

"Probably, yes."

"Well, why would *he* take Cassie then?"

"I don't know that either, Artie."

Artie was getting frustrated with Merlin's lack of knowledge. "Take a guess," Artie said flatly.

Merlin wiped his hand across his bald head and said, "Well, maybe he just wanted to keep her away from Morgaine. Had Lavery and the boar beaten you, then Morgaine could easily have taken Cassie. I am sorry, my lord, but I just don't know. What I do know is that Morgaine wants Excalibur, and also seems to want you. And Numinae, as Bercilak revealed, doesn't know what he wants."

"This is all very confusing," Artie said, slumping in his chair.

"Agreed, but things will clear as you proceed with the quest for the key. Think now, Artie, was there anything else that you missed? Anything that seemed important when it happened?"

Artie put his head in his hands and thought. He took his time. Eventually he exclaimed, "Oh, right! At one point Cassie asked where the one whose name starts with *Q* was! She was talking about Qwon!"

"Qwon? Your classmate?" Merlin asked.

"Yeah," Artie said, disturbed. "Is Qwon, like, important?"

Merlin looked down and said, more to himself than to Artie, "Maybe, especially if Morgaine has divined that she's important to you. I think we need to see Qwon, and soon!"

Artie's knee began to bounce. "You don't think she could be in trouble, do you?"

"Unfortunately, Artie, I think she could be in *grave* trouble!"

Artie stood. "Merlin, can I *Lunae lumen* myself from here to the other stone, the one in my bedroom back home?"

"Why, yes, of course, but—"

Artie removed the stone he'd pocketed earlier and chucked it at Merlin, who adeptly snatched it from the air.

Artie said, "Hold on to that, I'll be back soon."

And before Merlin or Thumb could stop him, Artie plunged Excalibur through the floor and ordered his sword to take him back to Shadyside, Pennsylvania.

Artie, bathed in moonlight, appeared in his upstairs bedroom, kneeling on his bed. He fell to his side in a fit of dizziness. Moongating all over the place was beginning to take a toll.

Slowly his eyes adjusted and his head steadied. Downy white feathers fell around him like he'd just been in a massive pillow fight.

Excalibur, next to the stone, impaled his pillow, the mattress, and the bed frame.

Artie stood and withdrew his sword, showering even more feathers into the room. He looked around. Everything was as he'd left it. No one had disturbed his old, private kingdom.

His mind cleared and zoomed to its destination.

Qwon.

Artie jetted out of the room and down the stairs and skidded into the living room. Lance sat bolt upright in Kynder's favorite chair, exclaiming, "Whoa, Artie—whassup?"

Kynder came scurrying in from the kitchen. He wore his wellies and a red-and-white striped kitchen apron. "Arthur!" Kynder yelled, a broad smile on his face. "You're back!"

"Hey, Kynder! Hey, Lance! Uh, yeah, kinda. But I've got to go. Sorry."

"But you just got here," Kynder said, sounding confused.

"I mean I've got to go find Qwon. Have you seen her?"

"No, Arthur, I haven't. Can't you stay for a bit? I mean, how's it going?"

"Not now, Kynder. Really, I need to see Qwon. Lance—I might need your help. Want to come? You might need your bow."

"You got it!" Lance quickly moved to the foyer, where his bow and quiver were propped against the wall. He grabbed his preposterous Robin Hood hat from a peg on the wall and slid on his aviator sunglasses. He looked every bit as silly as the day they'd seen him in the woods behind Serpent Mound.

Kynder followed them with a look of helpless concern on his face. "Where's Kay? Is she all right?"

"She's fine, Dad," Artie lied, his heart sinking. "She's with Merlin and Tom."

"Oh," Kynder said, obviously disappointed that Kay wasn't there. "Can't you stay for dinner, at least? I just made—"

"I'm sorry, Dad. Believe me, there's nothing I'd rather do than stay here with you," which was true. Artie really missed Kynder, and he felt awful that he didn't have time to tell him about everything, especially about Kay. He forced himself to look at Lance and said, "C'mon, let's go."

Lance said, "Lead the way."

Artie threw open the front door and bolted, Lance jogging like the professional soldier he was right behind him. They jumped into Lance's cab and took off.

Qwon's house was about three minutes away.

"Right on Morewood to Ellsworth," Artie said.

"Got it. So what's up with Qwon?"

"We think she might be in trouble."

"What kind of trouble?"

"Otherworld trouble." They came to a stop. "Here's Ellsworth. Right again."

"Roger that. What kind of stuff you seeing over there?"

"Dragons, huge pigs, an elf, saber-toothed tigers, knights, a dude with the body of a man and the head of a wolf, that kind of thing."

"Far out."

"Yeah, totally. Go left here, on Colonial. That's hers—the white one on the right."

They screeched to a stop in front of Qwon's house, jumped out, and ran across the driveway.

A couple of teenage skaters in tight jeans and knit hats ground to a halt. One punched the other on the arm and said, "Get a load of these two losers."

And to a couple of pseudohipster skaters, that was exactly what Artie and Lance must have looked like. Their weapons were so out of place, and their clothing was such an odd mix of old and new, that they must have looked like a couple of nerdy Renaissance-fair castaways.

Artie and Lance ran to the front door and rang the bell. *Ding-dong.* Artie was in a desperate rush but he refused to barge in.

Lance drew an arrow and nocked it to the bowstring.

Artie rang again.

Ding-dong.

And again.

Ding-dong.

"I'm coming!" a voice shouted from inside. The door opened as Qwon's mother said, "Oh, hello, Artie. Qwon's up in her— My, my. What's all this?"

Mrs. Onakea was about five feet tall, had a neat head of black bobbed hair, and wore sea-green cat's-eye glasses.

Artie shifted nervously from foot to foot and tried to answer. "This? Oh, uh, well, um . . ."

"Ma'am, Victor Lance. Pleasure to meet you. Artie and I

are members of a kind of medieval fan club. We were going to a meet-up and thought we'd see if Qwon wanted to join us."

"Uh, y-yeah," Artie stammered. "It's pretty cool. None of this stuff is real, Mrs. Onakea. Totally plastic."

"I see." Mrs. Onakea said slowly.

"Please, Mrs. Onakea, can we come in?" Artie pleaded. "We won't stay long, I promise."

"Of course, Artie. Come in." Mrs. Onakea stepped aside and said, "Qwonnie's upstairs. Knock first. Can I interest you in some iced tea, Mr. Lance?"

"I'd love some, thanks," Lance said, nodding curtly at Artie.

Artie nodded back. He bounded up the stairs and hustled down the hall. There were several doors but it was obvious which room was Qwon's—her door was plastered with posters of pop icons.

Artie took a breath. He raised his arm and knocked.

Nothing.

He knocked again.

Still nothing.

He jiggled the doorknob and, finding it locked, knocked one more time.

"Who is it?" Qwon asked in a small, shaky voice.

"It's Artie. Can you open the door?"

"Artie! No! Get out—" Her voice was muffled as if by a pillow.

Artie yanked out Excalibur and shredded the door to pieces. What he saw on the other side didn't make him feel very good.

Qwon stood at the far end of her room, restrained and gagged from behind by a humanoid figure covered in soft, bright-green moss. Rising from the tuft on the top of its head were two short and crooked stag's horns—one red, one blue.

Artie looked into Qwon's eyes, and they showed just how scared she was. But they also showed something else. It was almost like she was trying to tell him something.

Artie moved into the room and raised Excalibur. Its blade was blackish, and little dark sparks started falling from it.

Artie glanced quickly at the glass pommel of his sword. It swirled with the darkest black he'd ever seen. Of course! Excalibur could make a room totally dark if he asked it to!

Artie demanded, "Who sent you?"

The Mossman said nothing.

"Let her go!" the young king demanded.

The Mossman shook its head.

Artie punched with Excalibur and ordered, "Darkness!"

Blackness came in waves from Excalibur's blood channel and covered everything. It was like a giant octopus had joined the fun and completely inked out Qwon's room.

At this moment Lance and Mrs. Onakea, wondering what on earth was happening upstairs, arrived at the top of the landing. When Mrs. Onakea saw the void pulsating from Qwon's destroyed bedroom door, she instantly fainted. Lance caught her and laid her down gently. Then he unshouldered his bow, strung an arrow, and without hesitating stepped into the inky air.

Lance felt liked he'd walked into an abyss. With no frame of reference, he didn't know up from down or left from right. Seeking some stability, he dropped to a knee. He pulled the bowstring hard, making it ready to fire.

Artie had also been overwhelmed by the dark, but, lucky for him, Excalibur hooked him up with some sweet night vision.

Artie easily saw Qwon and her captor. Confused, the Mossman had moved toward the bathroom door. He'd dropped Qwon to the ground and was kneeling on the small of her back. The Mossman fumbled with a bag at his waist. Artie considered throwing Excalibur at him, but then he noticed Lance.

Artie glanced over his shoulder. Lance was pointed in the wrong direction. "Three o'clock!" Artie ordered.

Without speaking, the cab driver swiveled exactly ninety degrees.

"Light the way!" Artie commanded Excalibur.

No sooner had Lance turned than a narrow tunnel opened in his field of vision. Lance didn't pretend to understand it, but at the end of the tunnel was the least menacing thing he could imagine: a green clump of thick moss.

"Fire!" Artie shouted.

Lance did. The arrow sprang from the string with a vibrant twang.

Lance strung another arrow but the wake of his first shot drew the blackness in front of him once more.

Artie had marked the Mossman's head to receive Lance's volley, but the Mossman was quick. It may have been a sixth sense or just luck, but for whatever reason, as Lance let the string slip from his fingertips, the Mossman stood, and instead of impaling his head, the arrow struck him with a sickening thump just above his hip. It passed through him and clanged off something hard in Qwon's bathroom before clattering to the floor.

The Mossman screamed in pain. Its scream sounded familiar to Artie, but in the heat of everything he couldn't place it.

The Mossman had thrown something small on the floor and a gate began to open. It wasn't like Artie's moongate—this gate arced open like one of those purple-and-pink electrical plasma lamps at a science fair. The Mossman dragged Qwon through it, and in an instant they were gone.

The charged air smelled like a lightning strike. Artie fell to his knees.

Excalibur drew the darkness from the room. Light from the late-summer Pennsylvania evening poured through

Qwon's windows. The birds outside her house were whipped into a frenzy and wouldn't shut up.

Lance exhaled. "I didn't miss, did I?"

"No," Artie sighed. "It moved at the last minute, though."

Lance stood, walked to Artie, and put a hand on his shoulder. "I'm sorry, Artie."

Artie turned to his friend with steely eyes. "I will save her, Lance. I don't care how long it takes, I most definitely will save her."

IN WHICH ARTIE WONDERS, WHAT THE HECK IS A FONT, ANYWAY?

𝕬𝖗𝖙𝖎𝖊 𝖆𝖓𝖉 𝕷𝖆𝖓𝖈𝖊 𝖜𝖊𝖓𝖙 𝖙𝖔 Mrs. Onakea, who was still out cold on the landing.

"What're we going to do with her?" Lance asked.

"I don't know. I guess we should take her to Merlin," Artie said icily.

"Right," Lance said, cluing in on Artie's mood. They stood over Mrs. Onakea while Artie thought.

Then the doorbell rang. Lance trotted downstairs and looked through the peephole. "It's Kynder," he yelled. He opened the door.

Kynder and Lance came back upstairs and Artie explained what had happened as Kynder knelt next to Mrs. Onakea and stroked her forehead.

When Artie was finished, Kynder asked, "Can you

transport all of us back home, Artie, to the stone in your room?"

"Sure. Why?"

"Pammy—Mrs. Onakea—needs to come with us. I'll take care of her. I don't think it would be a very good idea to carry her to Lance's car like this."

"Agreed," Lance said.

Kynder looked at his boy and said, "While I'm tending to Pammy, you and Kay have got to get back there and find Qwon. I don't think I'll be able to calm Pammy down until you do."

Artie nodded resolutely, drove Excalibur into the floor, and said, "*Lunae lumen.*" The moongate opened. In a matter of seconds they were in Artie's room, most of them falling off his bed.

"Ow!" Lance said, knocking his shoulder hard on the bedside table. Kynder and Artie fell without hurting themselves. Mrs. Onakea was sprawled comfortably on the mattress, Excalibur driven through the bed by her hip.

Artie sheathed the sword while Kynder picked up Mrs. Onakea and took her downstairs. Artie and Lance remained in his room.

"What now?" Lance asked.

Artie shook his head. "I gotta get back to the Otherworld and go right to Numinae. The sooner I find him, the sooner I find Qwon."

"And the sooner you spring Merlin," Lance said.

"Yes, and the sooner I spring Merlin," Artie repeated, suddenly not so concerned with the wizard. Artie began to pace. "I just don't know where to start, Lance. We tried to get a map, but that didn't work. I don't even know if it would've helped, anyway. What was it Bercilak said? Something about the Fountain of Sylvan? Man, I wish Tom were here."

"Bercilak—he's the green one, right?"

"Yeah. He's a good guy but he's super weird."

"You first saw this dude in the video game?"

"Yeah. He showed me where to find the lake that had the lady in it," Artie said, flicking the grip of Excalibur. "What would you do, Lance?"

"I guess I'd start at the beginning and retrace my steps."

"Man, that would take a week at least. I don't see how that'll help Qwon."

"Couldn't hurt to try. Think . . . where did this all start?"

"Cincinnati?"

"Naw, Artie. Right here, in your own house, right down—"

"The video game!" Artie exclaimed. "That's it. You're a genius, Lance, an absolute genius!"

Artie burst from the room and flew down both sets of stairs. He tumbled into the game room and fell to his knees before the controller. He picked up the remote and turned on the TV. It warmed up and its image glowed to life.

The game was still paused where Artie had left it. Thank goodness Kynder had the good sense to leave it alone. There was Nitwit the Gray, standing over the felled corpse of an ice bear outside the cave of the vanquished dragon Caladirth. What memories. Artie could hardly believe how happy he'd been to have finally beaten that huge, vile, virtual dragon. Now it seemed like the emptiest accomplishment he'd ever managed to, well, accomplish.

Artie pressed a few buttons and brought up a screen that displayed Nitwit's items. Between *Malodorous Mace* and *Mithril Mail* was the simple, single word he was looking for: *Map*. He pushed X and it popped open.

The screen filled with computerized brown parchment. A red blip indicating Nitwit's current position was dead center. Artie zoomed out, selected the continent of Sylvan, and zoomed back in. It was hard to fathom, but after staring at it for a few moments, Artie began to recognize some things. There was Veltdam and the Great Library! There was the Lake! There was the forest they'd traveled through for nearly a week! It wasn't quite right, though— the library, for example, was on a bluff overlooking the sea, and towering mountains surrounded the Lake—so it wouldn't have been any good for getting around or locating the Font. Still, it shared features with things that were real, so it couldn't be totally useless, right?

Artie studied the map, looking for a fountain or anything that had to do with water. Coursing from place to place on their way to the sea were various streams and rivers. By the time the freshwater of Sylvan met the saltwater of the sea it had collected into three main arteries: in the north the River Gully, in the south the River Smake, and running across the middle the Glimmer Stream. Artie recalled Bedevere mentioning the Glimmer Stream just before they'd gotten to Veltdam, so he knew that it was real. He figured the other rivers were probably real, too.

But where was this fountain? In the woods? In front of a castle? In some town? What exactly was it that Bercilak had said?

He decided that he'd just have to ask him.

Artie slipped the VR goggles over his head. He adjusted the microphone and spoke into it.

"Bercilak! Bercilak the Green! King Artie Kingfisher here; I need your help!"

Nothing happened.

He said, "*Please*, Bercy! I don't know what else to do. Kay is injured, we couldn't get a map, Qwon's been taken, Bedevere got an arm blown off by this wicked, geeky elf—I need your help!"

Still nothing.

Artie whimpered, "Please. It's nothing you haven't

already told me. I just need to remember what you said and I can't. I need to find your lord Numinae. I think—well, I'm beginning to think he might be working with Morgaine—"

A burst of light blotted out the map. When it fizzled, the green knight stood before Nitwit the Gray on the road where Artie had first met Bercilak. Even the welcome sign was still there.

But Greenie didn't look at all welcoming. He stood across from Nitwit brandishing his gigantic battle-ax with both hands, and he scolded Artie with his hollow voice booming throughout his empty suit of armor: "Do not say such things about my lord! You may be the young king of the land, but never would such an alliance come to pass!"

At this stage in his adventure Artie was getting used to being threatened, so he reflexively dropped the Xbox controller and drew Excalibur in the real world, down in his basement game room.

And something remarkable happened.

Nitwit the Gray drew Excalibur too.

Bercilak recoiled. "Where did that come from? Is Wilt Chamberlain with you?"

Artie simply answered, "No." He looked at the sword in his character's hands. There was no denying that the sword was the same in both places. When Artie moved it in his basement, it made the same movement in the game. It was like he'd been given the world's coolest and baddest Wii controller, and it happened to work on Xbox.

Awesome.

"You can see Excalibur, Bercy?"

Bercilak innocently said, "Yes. I can see the feeble projection of your character, as before, but what I see in your projection's hands is a real sword, young regent."

Artie thought this was very cool, and wished he could just do the rest of his quest from the comfort—not to mention safety—of his own home.

But these thoughts left his mind in a flash, because Artie didn't like Bercilak's use of the word *regent*. Artie had spent too much time in the fantasy worlds of video games, the internet, comics, books, and movies not to know what that meant: a placeholder for a king.

Artie shouted, "Regent! *Regent?* Bercilak the Green, I've been through too much to be called a regent. I may not be official yet, but I *will be* king! Please, help me find your lord! I command you now to repeat the last thing you told me in my court-in-exile!"

Bercilak reacted the way Artie had hoped. He bent his empty head toward the ground. "Please forgive me, Arthur, I am out of practice. We have not had a king for so long. I am most aggrieved at my choice of words."

Artie relaxed. "Yeah, yeah. Okay. I forgive you."

"Really, sire, I am most—"

"It's okay, Bercilak, really. I'm sorry if I overdid it. Please get up." The green knight stood cautiously. "Now can you remind me what you said? My mind is scrambled. I can barely remember where I was twenty-four hours ago."

"Of course. I believe I said, 'I can say no more.'"

"Not that, airhead! The important thing. Something about Tiberius's cave being near some fountain."

"Ah, that! Not a fountain, sire, the Font! The Font of Sylvan."

"What does that mean? Isn't a font, like, a computer typeface or something?"

"I am certain, sire, that I've no idea what a 'computer typeface' is, but I can say surely that the Font I speak of is not one of these."

"Well, what is it then?"

"I am sorry, sire, but I can say no more."

Great.

Artie sighed. "Okay. Thank you, Bercilak. I guess I'll just have to look it up on the web."

"The web? What web? Surely, sire, you have some strange things over there."

"The internet? That's the web."

"Ah yes, of course, the internet. I remember you corrected me on that point before." Bercilak had turned totally casual, and seemed prepared to hang out and shoot the breeze.

Artie rolled his eyes. "Okay, Bercy, I have to go now."

"Of course, farewell! I really am sorry, sire!"

The green knight disappeared, and so did the road. The map filled the screen once more.

Artie had to get online.

He sheathed Excalibur, tossed off the VR goggles, and ran upstairs to the family computer. He woke it up and Googled "font." Of course everything that came up had to do with typefaces and web design. He changed the search to "font definition," and found this:

font

n.

1. *A basin for holding baptismal water in a church.*

2. *A receptacle for holy water; a stoup.*

3. *The oil reservoir in an oil-burning lamp.*

4. *An abundant source; a fount.*

Farther down another definition read:

3. *Archaic or poetic: a fountain or well.*

Since Bercilak was definitely archaic, and Artie thought he probably also liked poetry, this was the one that stuck, along with the "abundant source" one from the first definition.

So Artie figured that the Font had to be the main source of water on the continent of Sylvan. Since according to

Bedevere the Glimmer Stream was the biggest river, Artie guessed that the Font would be its original source.

How the heck was he going to find that?

He sat in front of the computer for a few minutes, lightly tapping but not pressing the buttons of the keyboard. So many things to be confused about, so little time. Was this what it meant to be a king?

Artie leaned back in the chair and absently laid his hand on Excalibur's grip.

He hadn't realized it, but his sword had been screaming at him.

And what it was screaming was, *A divining rod am I! I will find the source of water! A divining rod am I! I will find the source of water!*

Of course! How stupid of him!

Artie flew back to the game room. He hastily put on the goggles and looked at the map. He drew Excalibur and held it in front of him, pointing directly at the heart of Sylvan, and commanded, "Excalibur, show me the Glimmer's source!"

Without hesitation the sword plunged forward into the virtual map, dragging Artie through the room. Unfortunately the sword went right into the TV too, and did a major number on it. Sparks flew, and Artie felt the electricity surging through him, doing him no harm on account of his sword's miraculous scabbard. The TV was ruined, but it didn't matter. Inside the goggles Excalibur pulsated with its white glow. Its tip pushed into the virtual parchment, pinpointing a spot in Sylvan's darkest forest. It marked a speck of blue, and from this wandered a hairline rill of water bearing the name Glimmer Stream that eventually emerged from the vast woodland.

Artie threw the goggles from his face. He yelled upstairs, "Kynder, Lance! I've got to go!" He didn't wait for an answer. He shoved Excalibur into the floor and moongated back to Merlin's invisible prison.

𝕸𝖊𝖗𝖑𝖎𝖓 𝖍𝖆𝖉 𝖆𝖇𝖘𝖊𝖓𝖙𝖑𝖞 𝖕𝖚𝖙 𝖙𝖍𝖊 stone on a narrow oak sideboard in his main kitchen, and when Artie materialized on top of it, he fell to the hard tile floor. Excalibur impaled the thick wood of the little table to its crossbar.

Artie staggered to his feet, rubbed his face vigorously, and shook out his hands.

Merlin stood behind the counter chopping garlic or onions or something. The kitchen was warm and comforting and smelled fantastic.

Artie pointed at the sideboard. "Really, Merlin? Couldn't you have put the stone near one of those nice chairs you have?"

"Ah, silly me. Sorry, child. I am preoccupied."

"Yeah, aren't we all," quipped Artie, sounding more like

Kay. He grabbed Excalibur's hilt and slid it out of the table sideways, cutting the thing in half. It collapsed to the floor in two pieces, forming a dilapidated *M*.

Thumb, sitting at a very small table in a very small chair on the countertop next to the cutting board, chortled quietly at Artie's act of petty defiance. Artie checked out his little knight. He appeared to be drinking beer from a thimble. On a plate in front of him was a dark, crisp-looking bing cherry, stem and all.

Thumb asked, "How'd it go, lad?"

Artie was put off by everything he saw. Merlin was cooking dinner and Thumb was kicking back like nothing was wrong? What was *with* that?

"As you can see, not so good, guys!" Artie waved the air around him. "You don't see Qwon here, do you?"

"No, but that doesn't mean you were too late," offered Merlin. "You weren't too late, were you?"

Artie couldn't believe this. "Yes, Merlin, I was! Some dude covered in moss—maybe it was Numinae—took her right out of her room. Lance and I tried to stop him, but he gated back to the Otherworld through an arc of lightning!"

Merlin slammed the flat side of the knife on the cutting board. Everything on the counter jumped, including Thumb and his little dining set. The little man's cherry fell to the floor. Thumb managed to steady the beer thimble.

"Blast it!" Merlin yelled.

That was more like it.

Thumb downed his beer and stepped to the edge of the counter. "Sorry for looking like we're taking it easy, lad. You must remember that we're both quite old. When we get a chance to relax, we take it."

Artie changed the subject. "How're Kay and Bedevere?"

Merlin stepped from behind the counter and said, "They're fine, child. We're watching them." He pointed at a monitor on the wall. There Artie saw his knights, recovering in bed. Kay was propped up and reading a paperback. Bedevere still slept. "I'm cooking dinner for you. Are you hungry?"

Artie was beyond hungry. He could've eaten a tin can and a pile of wet yarn right about then. "Yeah. Starving, actually," Artie said.

"Good. Now tell us what happened, and quickly. Once you've eaten, you need to get back."

Artie sat on a stool and told them everything. Merlin and Thumb were disappointed about Qwon but relieved that Artie had found the Font of Sylvan. Merlin put a plate in front of Artie, and as he devoured his dinner, Merlin and Thumb outlined the plan.

Artie half listened as he ate. He didn't mind the fact that he and Thumb were about to go after Tiberius and Numinae. He probably should have minded, but he just didn't. It wasn't because he was particularly brave (which he was turning out to be), or very stupid (which he clearly wasn't), but it was simply because he was fixed like a laser on getting Qwon back. The other things seemed like low hurdles he had to clear in order to save his friend. She was all that mattered.

As Artie speared his last bite of food, he asked, "Why do you think she was taken?"

"I can only guess, Artie," Merlin said seriously. "Numinae may have taken her for some unknown reason, of course, but it's just as likely that he didn't take her at all, and that the Mossman was an agent of Morgaine's. She may believe that kidnapping Qwon will buy her some insurance against your return to power. There's only one way to find out for certain."

Artie slapped his fork on the table. "Get back there, ASAP. Find Numinae and ask him what he knows. If he doesn't know enough, chop off his hand and get you out of this place so you can help me find out," Artie summarized with a heavy dose of kingly purpose.

"Sounds like the plan to me, lad!" Thumb exclaimed, standing up. "Shall we then? To the Font of Sylvan?"

Artie stood too and said, "Yes. But let's see Kay and Bedevere first."

"Agreed," Merlin said as he left the room. Artie grabbed Thumb and they followed.

They walked through at least a dozen rooms, passing under a fragrant peach tree laden with bursting fruit, through a cave of ice, and through a cloud. They passed under a geologic formation twinkling with earthen jewels of every color: purples like those of a sunset peeking underneath a thunderstorm, reds like those of a quickening volcanic crater, greens like the skins of a million chameleons in a limitless field of young wheat. They passed through run-of-the-mill closets and storerooms, pantries and wine cellars.

As they walked, Artie couldn't fight the feeling that he was going to a place that would change him forever. When they came to a stop in the hospital room, Artie smiled, tingling with anticipation. His immediate future was alive and waiting. *This was who he was.* He was a kid who grew up in the suburbs of America, but who had come from a place that most people thought only existed in their imaginations. And it turned out he was so special that he could even become king of this place, and help save it and the world in which he'd grown up. It was pretty amazing.

He snapped out of it as he became aware of Kay. He looked up and was surprised to see that she was dressed, Cleomede strapped to her side. She flashed her brother a sad, knowing smile. She was half turned to Bedevere, and had a hand on his side where his right arm should have been. The knight was still asleep.

Kay pointed at Artie and said, "Merlin and Tommy told me where you went. No Qwon, huh?"

"No," Artie said, looking at the floor. "Someone took her to the Otherworld. I couldn't save her."

Kay stepped over to her brother and said, "Well, let's go and save her then. That cool with you, Bro?"

Artie looked up at his big sister. "I think it'd be better for you to stay here and get some rest, but I also think there's no point in arguing with you."

She put a hand on his shoulder. "You got that right, Art."

Merlin asked, "Are you sure you're ready for this, Kay? You *were* recently bloodied by a divine boar, after all."

"And I hope I see that pig again," Kay said, shooting daggers at Merlin. "Lavery too. I can't believe he stole two weeks of our summer vacation in that stupid library of his."

The old wizard smiled and shook his head. Artie retrieved the infinite backpack from a peg on the wall and removed a moongate coin. Then he slung the bag over his shoulders and tightened its straps. He drew Excalibur, and its blade rang through the wizard's endless, living chambers.

"Well then, children, Mr. Thumb, off with you. I have nothing left to give. When you return, I expect you to bring me my freedom. If you do not also have Qwon, rest assured that I will do all that I can to help you retrieve her."

Artie placed the coin at his feet and gently put his

sword's pommel on it. He pictured the dark forest that contained the source of the Glimmer Stream and whispered, "Take us to the Font of Sylvan!"

The gate twirled open, and in a flash the Kingfishers and old Sir Thumb vanished, returning to the Otherworld once again.

𝕬fter 𝔰𝔥𝔞𝔨𝔦𝔫𝔤 𝔬𝔣𝔣 𝔱𝔥𝔢 𝔢𝔣𝔣𝔢𝔠𝔱𝔰 of the latest Moongate Express, Artie and his knights found themselves standing on a low mossy rise next to a picturesque brook. The surrounding woods were every bit as dark as those beyond Serpent Mound back in Peebles, Ohio—and way creepier.

The tightly packed, towering softwoods choked the sky from view. Their massive trunks gave the woods a cathedral-like feeling. The air was dank and there was no breeze. The stream babbled pleasantly to their left. The occasional buzzing mosquito flew around them, except for Kay, of course, thanks to Cleomede's scabbard's bug-off magic.

"Man, Artie, these are, like, *Avatar*-level creepy

woods, right?" Kay marveled.

"Yeah," Artie confirmed.

"What's *Avatar*?" asked Thumb, back to his two-foot height.

"Oh, nothing. A movie," Artie answered.

"Ah," Thumb answered offhandedly as he drew his sword and checked its blade.

"There should be a gorge around here. We should walk upstream a little," Artie said.

They went to the stream and immediately found what they were looking for.

The trees had obstructed a massive black basalt boulder in the middle of the brook. It was about fifteen feet high and half as wide and it cleaved the running water in two. It was perfectly egg-shaped and propped up by smaller rocks forming a stony nest. On its top grew a gnarled tree with golden leaves. The tree's roots encased the rock's crown with a tangle of long, crooked talons.

"Wow, that's beautiful," Kay breathed.

"No kidding," Artie said.

"Almost looks like it was placed there by a giant hand," Thumb commented.

"Or a giant green dragon claw," Artie added.

"Yeah, or that," Kay said unenthusiastically. They

looked to each other for courage and moved around the rock.

Behind it rose a high, imposing gorge about a hundred yards away.

"Bingo," Artie said, and they moved toward the stone crevasse.

The rocks that formed the gorge's walls were angular and jumbled. Their edges looked like knives.

As they got to the proper opening of the gorge, they found a worn single-track path on the right side of the stream. Artie took the lead, followed by Kay and Thumb.

The stream, which had been quaint and babbling near the egg-shaped boulder, was now hard and jabbering. The air in the gorge was cooler than that in the forest, and countless drops of spray exploded from the water's dismal roar.

Eventually they reached a curtain of high ferns. Artie passed through it while Kay and Thumb took a break to drink from the stream. When he got to the other side, Artie called, "Guys, come check this out." Kay and Thumb shook the icy water from their hands and pushed through the plants.

Even Thumb, who knew a lot about the mysteries of the Otherworld, couldn't believe what he was looking at.

Not twenty feet away, the jagged gorge made a

ninety-degree turn to the right, swallowing the stream, the path, and their sight line. No sensible course of water would have made such a hard-angled turn. But the thing they couldn't believe was that in this turn there was a raging, misting waterfall . . . that fell in *reverse*!

A turbulent pool turned in front of them. A white churn of water followed this as it hit the surface. But instead of coming from above, the cascade came from below, and this fell quickly through and around the sharp bend in the gorge.

"By the trees!" Thumb gasped.

Artie and Kay were speechless.

They moved to where the water dropped off. The path ended and was replaced by a series of rusted iron rungs and chain links driven into the rock face. These went down the gorge and disappeared around the bend.

"Guess we're going down," Artie yelled.

They sheathed their weapons, and Artie climbed onto the first rung.

The wet metal was slick and, judging by the thin coating of slime and algae, not used very often. They made their way gingerly.

They went straight down about twenty feet and stopped on a very narrow ledge just before the turn in the rock. Artie pushed his back to the cliff and scooted to the right to make room for his knights. Kay and Thumb clambered down and they stood shoulder to shoulder (though of course Thumb's shoulder only came to Kay's knee), panting and sweating. The ledge was so thin that both Kay's and Artie's toes tickled the edge of the precipice.

Thumb yelled above the hiss of the water, "Why in the blazes didn't we bring some rope? We should be tied together!"

He was right. If they had been smart, responsible knights, they would definitely have had a long length of strong rope. But they didn't. Artie promised himself it was a mistake he'd never make again.

Artie slid to the bend and peeked around.

The scene below was even more mind-boggling. The stream fell fifty more dizzying feet, the water still rushing in the wrong and impossible direction. At the bottom the water bent in a smooth right angle and continued on for a distance of a hundred feet or so before disappearing into a huge cave at the end of the gorge. Artie couldn't really see inside the cave, but he could tell that somewhere in there was a dim, orange light.

He turned to Kay and Thumb and yelled, "Well, it looks like we're on the right track."

"Good, I guess?" hollered Kay.

Artie peeked back around the corner and looked for the next set of rungs and chains. He saw them continuing down and across all the way to the floor of the gorge.

The only problem was that the nearest rung was about ten feet away.

He turned to his knights and told them the bad news. They discussed jumping for it, fashioning a makeshift rope out of their wet clothes, or attempting to traverse it rock-climbing style. Ultimately they ruled out all three.

They stood there for a few minutes without speaking. Between the wet and the cold they all felt pretty crummy.

Then Kay yelled, "How stupid! The swords!"

"What about them, Sir Kay?" demanded Thumb.

"Excalibur and Cleomede! They'll cut through anything if we want them too! We'll just stick them into the rock and monkey-bar our way down. The last one will pull them out, and we'll keep going!"

They agreed that it was a great idea. They rearranged themselves on the ledge, Thumb and Kay switching places by climbing back up a little, squeezing around each other, and coming back down. Artie drew Excalibur and flipped it around, holding its point down. He went to the end of the narrow ledge, took a deep breath, and leaned out as far as he could. Thumb held on to his leg to steady him.

Artie stuck out his arm and twisted his body around, straining at Thumb's strong grasp. It took a little bit of effort, and a lot of sparks flying from the point of entry, but considering it was solid rock, Excalibur easily slid into the cliff wall. Before Artie let go, he asked it to stay put. He pushed it with his fingertips, and it held fast.

He barked, "Okay. Next!"

Kay handed over Cleomede.

The next move was going to be hard, and they all knew it. Artie emptied his mind and Kay willed her body to help her brother.

Artie took three quick, deep breaths.

"Here goes! One! Two! Three!"

With one hand holding Excalibur, he turned and fell, and it was one of the scariest things Kay had ever seen.

Artie whip-lashed around the corner, stopping himself with his left forearm and the length of Cleomede, along with a little bit of his face, against the rock. His grip held. For her part, Kay was clenching her fists, and Artie could feel this. Excalibur helped him hold on too, and it urged him to keep moving.

Artie spread his dangling legs on the rock to steady himself. Then he took Cleomede, reached as far as he could, and pushed it into the rock. A tingling, magical current coursed from Excalibur through Artie's arms and chest to Cleomede.

Once Cleomede was in place, Artie let go of Excalibur and moved his right hand to join his left on Cleomede's hilt. He let go with his left hand and stretched out for the rung. It was just out of reach.

He gripped the sword with both hands again and began to swing, running a little along the rock face with the sides of his feet. Then he lunged with his left hand, and this time he caught the wet iron bar.

Dropping down, he quickly brought his hands together and his feet found their way to the rung below.

He was across. Artie had never felt so alive. He moved down to make room.

Thumb came next. He executed a series of acrobatic moves that would definitely have gotten him a medal finish at the knighthood Olympics. Swinging easily and strongly, Thumb came down to land above Artie's head. Seeing his little, ancient knight do this eased Artie's nerves.

But then, of course, came Kay. She not only had to get down but also had to pull out the swords.

Kay peeked around the corner and when she saw what she had to work with, her eyes opened wide.

Artie wasn't too psyched by the look on her face.

"It's okay, Sis, just go for it!" He concentrated the muscles and tendons of his body on hers, just as she had done for him.

Kay blew out her cheeks in disbelief. Then her face disappeared back around the corner.

Suddenly her arm whipped around and grabbed Excalibur. She gripped it hard, and Artie clenched his fists, and he felt her body count off—*One! Two! Three!*

Kay swung around, slammed into the rock, and yelped. Her eyes were closed tight. Her left hand quickly joined her right on Excalibur.

She opened her eyes and looked straight at her brother. "I don't like this, Artie!"

"Don't worry!" Artie counseled. "I did it, you can definitely do it!" Which had to be true, right? Since Kay had always been so headstrong and so good at everything she did?

Thumb said, "Don't look down!"

Which, of course, caused Kay to look down.

Artie felt her body tense. She was on the verge of freezing up.

"Kay! Look at me!" Artie ordered. She did. "You're Kay freaking Kingfisher! You don't think—you do! Now move!"

Her brother was absolutely right. She was Kay freaking Kingfisher.

She retightened her grip. Then she let go with her left hand. She was Kay freaking Kingfisher. She reached out and grabbed Cleomede. She swung between the two swords and when she drew closest to Excalibur, just as her momentum was about to shift back to Cleomede, she switched her grip on her brother's sword from underhand to overhand. It was a good move. She shifted her weight and hung as straight as she could under Cleomede. Then she pulled hard at Excalibur. The sword came out. She was Kay freaking Kingfisher and now she was swinging like a monkey. Fear shot back into her. With Artie's help she willed it out. She threw Excalibur to Thumb, who caught it easily and passed it down to Artie. She switched hands on Cleomede, then reached out for the rung. Being slightly longer than Artie, she reached it just by the tips of her fingers. She worked at the wet iron and finally got a good grip. She moved over to the topmost rung, then reached for Cleomede and asked it to come out of the rock. The sword slid eagerly away. Kay sheathed her weapon, her heart going *rat-a-tat, rat-a-tat-tat*, and let out a deep, long breath.

She was Kay *freaking* Kingfisher.

Wordlessly, with the water rushing away behind them in the wrong direction, they made their way to the floor of the gorge. When they all reached the bottom, Artie and

Kay knelt so that the three of them could share a group hug at Thumb's height.

They pulled away after a few moments, their arms locked over one another's shoulders. Thumb took turns looking each Kingfisher in the eyes. "That was fantastic, lads, just smashing. No matter what happens, I want you to know that I'm proud of you both."

Artie and Kay smiled, feeling for a second more like kids with their uncle at an important game than a pair of knights on a foolish, Otherworldly errand.

They caught their breaths. Then they broke their embrace and rose. Kay removed the helmets from Artie's backpack and they slipped them on. They drew their weapons and resumed walking.

They moved wordlessly on a well-worn footpath next to the stream, which at the bottom of the gorge flowed easily and pleasantly.

The mouth of the cave was a perfect and dark semicircle carved out of the same black basalt as the egg-shaped boulder. Framing the immediate opening of the cave were two red cedar trees that had been forced to grow in great curves. They met and joined into one giant tree at the top of the cave's opening. High above the cedars' deep-green needles hung a low, gray sky. It was breathtaking.

"Tiberius must have a serious green thumb to make

a couple trees do that," Kay joked. Artie and Thumb chuckled a little but not much.

The water flowed out of the cave from the dim light deep within.

Thumb ripped his sword through the air twice. Artie nodded. Kay slapped her helmet. Walking side by side, they entered the cave of Tiberius.

𝔄fter a dozen yards the cave opened from a wide, rugged hallway into a soaring natural cathedral of stone and earth. Tiberius appeared to be out.

As they gathered in a circle, Thumb said, "There's something you should be aware of regarding green dragons."

"Yeah, what's that, Tommy?" Kay asked, gaping at the tip of a stalactite high overhead.

"They don't breathe fire—or acid, as I believe they do in your video game, Artie—but they do expel something that can freeze things into rock."

"Great," Artie said, sounding totally unpsyched.

"I hear that you're quite safe—but a little uncomfortable—if a green dragon freezes you. I hope it won't happen, but if it does, the important thing is to remain calm. You have my word that I'll get you out."

"Check, check, and ditto, Tommy," Kay said. Artie nodded.

Then they took a closer look at the dragon's home. It was very tidy. There were neat piles of bones and tree branches and a massive heap of something that looked like cotton. It also smelled incredibly fresh—which was exactly the opposite of what Artie expected of a dragon's cave.

As for the stream, it was, without doubt, the Font of Sylvan. The flow of water originated from a gentle whirlpool about ten feet across. Erected over it was a gazebo of twisted branches, many of which still had leaves on them. These were of every color in the rainbow, even blue and purple, and they were beautiful.

Finally Kay said, "Well, looks like nobody's home, huh?"

She'd spoken too soon.

Artie saw it first. The dirt and rock of the near side of the cave appeared to rearrange itself like an earthen Transformer. He gasped. Kay and Thumb wheeled. The "wall" began to shimmer like a pattern of water reflections on a ceiling, and within seconds the whole form turned green and was revealed in all its scaly magnificence.

The tail was what came to the ground first, with barely a whisper. Then the hind legs, and the forelegs, and the neck and head. All completely without noise.

Once its heft was settled on the cave floor, it turned, and at last the three startled knights came face-to-face with the great green dragon.

Its mouth was closed. Its nostrils flared. Its ruffled, Chinese-dragon mane moved as though a soft breeze blew over it. Its eyes blinked.

It remained eerily silent.

There was no question in Artie's mind that this was the same dragon that had attacked them over the Lake. It had the same golden, ramlike horns, the same rubied canine teeth, and the same brilliant and beautiful rainbow eyes.

Thumb bowed low and said, "Keeper Tiberius, Guardian of Lord Numinae, I, Sir Tom Thumb, greet you humbly on behalf of His Eminence, King Arthur Kingfisher, and his Knight of the First Order, Sir Kay."

Kay said quietly, "Nicely done, Tommy!" but the little man, still low to the ground and standing on ceremony, shot her a stern glance.

Artie bowed but was otherwise clueless. The dragon turned his head slightly and grunted "Hmmmph" through his nose. Something black rose from his nostrils, but it wasn't smoke. It seemed impossible . . . but it looked like glass.

Thumb continued, "We request an audience—"

But before he could finish, the dragon reared and spit something black and shiny on Thumb. At first he looked like Han Solo encased in carbonite—his arms up, his sword out, and his face grimacing—but then the black substance unfolded around him, making sounds of breaking glass and sliding stone. In moments, Thumb was hidden from them in an egg-shaped hunk of black basalt about three feet tall.

The Thumb-egg teetered and fell to the side, rocking back and forth.

Kay screamed and began to move on the dragon, but Artie stuck out Excalibur and stopped her. The dragon ignored Kay and homed in on Artie.

"Needn't worry," the dragon sang. Its voice was so low and heavy that they felt it more than they heard it. "The small man is safer there. Quite alive."

"Why'd you do that?" Kay demanded.

Tiberius continued to stare at Artie. He said, "Hmmmph. I feltn't like talking to him. Not yet. And aside, he'sn't to see Lord Numinae. You are."

Tiberius settled nonchalantly on the ground and placed his chin on his forelegs like a fat housecat.

Thinking of Qwon, Artie said, "Fine. Let's see Lord Numinae, then."

The dragon looked away. "Hmmmph. You mightn't be a new pretender?"

Kay blurted, "Look, I don't know who you think you are, but—"

"Who'm I? And who're you thinking you are, infant child?"

"Infant!" Kay started, but the dragon loudly snapped one of his long, pointy ears, and Kay shut up.

"I'm older'n Merlin, Numinae, and Jester Thumb added into one. To me, an infant you are."

Artie asked, "What do you mean, 'pretender'?"

The dragon slowly blinked. He looked sleepy. "Hmmph. I know who you are, *byrnsweord* bearer. I was just wonder'n who *you* think you are."

Artie was amazed. This fantastic creature had cut to the heart of the matter. Wasn't this the question Artie wanted answered more than any other? Wasn't this question the reason why Artie had agreed to go along with all of this craziness in the first place? A dragon he'd known for less than five minutes had pegged him. A dragon.

"Well," Artie answered, "I'm King Artie Kingfisher, and as Tom said, I wish to see Lord Numinae. He has something I need, and someone I want back."

The dragon looked away casually and batted Thumb's egg like it was toy. He said, "The something perhaps he'll give. The someone I doubt he'll return. But this is for Numinae to say. He wants to see'n you too, little king, though I don't know why. If't were my choice, I'd freeze you both and return Excalibur to its sleep'n place. Too much trouble otherwise."

"But it's not your choice," Kay said, seeking assurance. Talking with this creature gave her the creeps, and she was eager to get on with things.

"No. 'Tisn't. Hmmph." Tiberius was clearly disappointed about this.

Artie was relieved. He said, "Okay, then take us to Numinae."

The dragon smiled. "Hasten not, little 'uns. Three conditions must be met. The first'n has." He stuck his chin at Thumb.

"You mean freezing Thumb?" Artie asked. The dragon nodded. "When we come back, will you release him?"

Tiberius said, "*If'n* you make it back, he'll be a-resting here." For emphasis the dragon stuck a claw into the ground—really, *into* the ground. He drew it out and it made an awful, claw-on-chalkboard kind of noise. "Quite alive he'll be."

"Okay," Artie said uneasily. "What're the other conditions?"

"No moongates. If you flee and ever come back, I'll freeze'n you like your companion. Forever."

"Okay, we have to get it done now," Kay said. "What else?"

The dragon reached across to Artie. Its front paw was the size of a love seat. Artie recoiled instinctively but he knew, somehow, that for the moment Tiberius was harmless.

The dragon flicked Excalibur's scabbard. "This'n stays here."

"Great," Kay said sarcastically.

Artie asked, "Can Kay come with me?"

"Hmmmph."

"That's a yes."

"Yes."

Artie unstrapped the scabbard and laid it at his feet. "Fine, then. We'll go together to Numinae, both vulnerable."

Kay tried to protest, but Artie held up his hand. "It's only fair."

All the dragon said was, "Hmmmmmmph," but it was so weighty and guttural that it was clear that he didn't hold the concept of fairness in high esteem. Since dragons probably were always at an advantage, this made perfect sense to Artie.

At last the dragon stood. Artie and Kay held their breaths as it backed up. It raised its relatively small wings as it lumbered back and forth on its muscular haunches. It came to a stop and looked down. In the wall was a low, black hole.

"A test lies through there. Get the comb. Only then will Lord Numinae be awaiting."

"*Another* test? Man, these guys love tests. You all should have been teachers instead of crazy dragons and wizards and spirits or whatever," Kay said. Then she grabbed Artie's hand and squeezed it tight.

Artie asked, "Ready, Sis?"

Kay nodded. "Let's do this."

Hand in hand, they walked into the small cave and disappeared.

Kay hollered, "See ya later, Tiberius!"

But the dragon, standing over their departure, said nothing.

𝕬𝖗𝖙𝖎𝖊 𝖆𝖘𝖐𝖊𝖉 𝕰𝖝𝖈𝖆𝖑𝖎𝖇𝖚𝖗 𝖋𝖔𝖗 𝖘𝖔𝖒𝖊 light. They were in a narrow capillary of rock, and after about a hundred feet they emerged in a wide field of ankle-high grass. The sun was screened behind a sheet of clouds, its bright disk clear and sharp.

They looked back. A large boulder was buried in the ground, and in the middle of this was the cave's mouth. Surrounding the field in a neat circle were thick woods of oak and ash.

Kay grasped Cleomede with both hands. She asked, "What do you think he meant by 'the comb'?"

Artie held Excalibur in his right hand and drew his dagger, Carnwennan, with his left. He hit his buckler, fastened on his left arm, with the sword's pommel, making sure it was tight. "I think I know but I don't want to say it."

Suddenly the treetops in front of them shook to life. Unseen branches snapped. The woods seized, and whatever was making the commotion moved from left to right over a distance of about thirty feet.

And then two massive oaks bent and parted as the thing pushed by them.

It was Twrch Trwyth.

"Oh fudge." Kay sighed.

"Yeah," Artie said halfheartedly.

The boar jumped and pawed the ground ferociously. It was about a hundred feet away. Steam rose from its snotty nostrils, and its eyes glowed like embers. Its wiry hair bristled. The bright silver comb atop its head was plain to see.

A wind kicked up as the animal lowered its head and began to pace tightly, never dropping the Kingfishers from its sight. The treetops hissed and danced, and the wind carried a whisper that was more rustling leaves than insistent voice: "Bring me the comb."

The whisper was clearly Numinae.

Then the boar charged.

Shoulder to shoulder, Artie and Kay backpedaled furiously. At the last minute they bumped into the boulder with the cave entrance—which was now gone—and upon hitting this, each jumped sideways, away from each other.

The animal came hard and headfirst into the rock. It

made an awful noise, like a massive tree trunk snapping under the weight of a tornado.

The boar grunted and backed up, the Kingfishers flanking it. It should have been bleeding but it wasn't. Then it reared, shuddered its head, and turned on Kay.

Artie quickly attacked its hindquarters. Excalibur easily sliced through skin and tendons, but again, there was no blood.

The animal growled like a dog and spun to Artie. Kay saw where her brother had cut the creature and, unbelievably, its bloodless wounds closed and healed themselves.

Suddenly Artie's sword hand tingled. Excalibur was trying to tell him something.

But he didn't have time to contemplate this because the boar charged again. Defensively Artie drew the flat side of Excalibur between his body and the boar's pointed, filthy tusks. As they hit him, flecks of putrid spittle lashed Artie's face.

The force of contact was awful. Artie's guts sloshed as the pig lifted him high into the air. Twrch Trwyth tossed its head and caught Excalibur crossways through its tusks. Artie held on for dear life as he stabbed furiously at the hard ridge of the animal's nose with his dagger. But the dagger was to the boar like a mosquito to an elephant.

Twrch Trwyth jostled its head again, and suddenly Artie found himself in arm's reach of the comb. This was his chance. Time slowed slightly. He reached out with the dagger and cut the hair that held the comb.

It was free!

But then, right before Artie's eyes, the hair of the boar reformed, and creepily tied the comb back into place.

Artie couldn't believe it.

The animal reared, and Artie was nearly turned upside down as Kay swung and chopped off the boar's right hind leg just below the knee.

There was a great hissing sound from the stump, and the creature toppled. As it fell, Artie's dagger drove into one of the boar's reddened eyeballs. It exploded like a rotten tomato. As the boar hit the ground, Artie came free and rolled to safety.

Artie and Kay were still many paces apart when his hand tingled so much it almost hurt. And suddenly Artie understood: Excalibur wanted to be paired with Cleomede.

Artie started to move toward Kay as Twrch Trwyth twisted its powerful body like an acrobat. It didn't seem to be bothered in the least that it had three legs instead of four.

"What now, Bro?"

"I think we need to get our swords together!"

"Sounds good!"

But then, as it hopped and retreated a little, the boar found its severed leg. It lowered its mouth and in a single motion picked up the thing and gobbled it down. Not more than a second later, its rear right leg grew back. It lowered its head and took a few careful steps toward them. Its empty eye socket began to smoke, and then flame, and then it went out.

Its eye was back too.

It raised its head and appeared to smile.

Kay rolled her eyes. "Oh *super fudge*!"

"No kidding. We need some help," Artie said.

And that's when Artie remember Cable and his calling card!

Immediately Artie screamed the wolf-man's name, and then he howled at the top of his lungs.

Twrch Trwyth paused for a moment, a look of uncertainty crossing its face. It twitched one way and the next.

But nothing happened.

Artie and Kay moved next to each other. Each felt the other's heart quicken, and each felt the other's despair deepen.

The boar lowered its cinder-block head and charged again.

And then something did happen.

Cable joined the battle so quickly they didn't even see him arrive. He was faster than Twrch Trwyth. Much, much faster. When he skidded to a stop, tearing massive clumps of grass around his legs, they'd never been so happy to see someone in their lives.

Cable had grown in size and was as big as Twrch Trwyth, and more frightening by half.

Artie and Kay gazed in amazement at their canine friend. For some reason he had a bone in his mouth.

No—not a bone. A tusk!

Artie looked at the boar. It was minus a tooth.

Artie and Kay cheered as Twrch Trwyth turned from them and confronted Cable.

The wolf juggled the long tusk in his own powerful mouth and then bit down hard and snapped it in two. The pieces fell to the ground and disintegrated to dust.

The boar squealed.

Kay yelled, "Yeah!"

Artie held out his sword and said, "Kay, cross Cleomede with Excalibur!"

She did. Excalibur and Cleomede sparked at their point of contact. They spoke a language to each other that Artie and Kay could not understand, but they felt it. Boy, did they feel it. Like the Kingfishers, Excalibur and Cleomede had a special relationship. And Excalibur seemed to know that put together—the Kingfishers *plus* their swords—they would form a powerful quartet.

They moved to within a few feet of the buried stone. Artie said, "I think together our swords can cut that thing's hair and then we can get the comb!"

"Got it," Kay exclaimed.

Cable continued to turn as the boar mirrored him. The wolf's eyes made quick stabs at Artie and Kay, assessing their readiness. The Kingfishers braced themselves against the rock. Cable was going to drive the boar right to them.

The wolf-man lunged, lightning fast. The boar managed to catch Cable under the chin with its remaining tusk. It made a deep gouge and cast a spray of red blood over the field.

On all fours, Cable swung his rear end behind him and lunged again, leading with his enormous pawlike hands, catching the boar on the top of its nose. Then the wolf-man brought his weight down on the pig's face, and its forelegs buckled. Cable was on top. He cocked his head to one side, opened wide his jaws, and came down violently on the back of the boar's neck.

Again, there was no blood, and again there was the hissing sound, like air being let out through a small hole.

The boar squealed.

Still locked on the pig's nape, Cable stood. With great effort he dragged the boar toward the Kingfishers.

Cable struggled as the animal screeched and twisted. Making one great turn down the length of its body, it finally managed to get free. Cable was thrown a few yards, and the boar stood.

It had paid a big price for working itself free, though.

A massive chunk was missing from the back of its neck, exposing its black, bloodless spine.

Kay watched the neck, expecting it to close and heal. But it didn't. Cable could injure Twrch Trwyth where they couldn't.

The wolf-man dropped to all fours and spat out the part of the boar he'd torn free. Blood gushed from Cable's wound, and for a moment he faltered.

"Cable!" screamed Artie.

The boar pranced to the wolf-man and leaped on top of him. With its filthy, mud-caked feet, it pounded Cable's body. He was driven to the ground as his ribs broke audibly. His backbone buckled. More than once the boar's hideous feet punctured Cable's frame, and more than once their friend's blood gushed forth.

A serving of bile rose into Artie's mouth. He spit it on the ground.

Suddenly Excalibur tingled fiercely in Artie's hand. He concentrated and tightened his grip, and a spear of intense light shot from Excalibur toward the boar like a sunray parting heavy clouds. The creature's skin curdled with the impact.

The boar cried out and Cable took advantage, gnashing hard on the thing's throat. Its eyeballs bugged out of their sockets, and its nostrils streamed snot. Cable got his feet under him, and with two quick bounds the wolf-man presented the head of Twrch Trwyth to the scissoring X of Excalibur and Cleomede.

The Kingfishers moved their swords over the hair, and the comb came free. Kay grabbed it and pushed it into one of her pockets.

Then Cable swung around so that the Kingfishers were out of harm's reach. His strength was flagging. He scuttled away, dragging the animal. Finally and with all his remaining energy, he flung it toward the edge of the field. And there, as if on cue, a horrid gash opened in the ground, and with a rake of stone and black earth it quickly swallowed the thing called Twrch Trwyth.

Artie and Kay ran to Cable. His breath was quick and shallow, and blood flowed from his nose and panting mouth. His tongue was peaked and limp, his eyes sad.

Artie pushed his hand into the wolf-man's thick mane. Cable looked at him. The heroic creature was dying.

Cable nudged his nose at Kay, who moved closer, putting a hand on the ridge of his snout. She drew the comb from her pocket, showing it to him, and he closed his eyes and smiled.

Kay asked, "Can that thing live without this?"

Cable shook his head slightly.

"So that's the last we'll ever see of it?" Artie clarified.

The wolf-man nodded. He coughed and spit more blood.

The Kingfisher children felt so ecstatic, and yet so sad. They hugged Cable like he'd been their dearest, truest friend. They felt his fur and smelled his blood and cried. They stayed like this for some time, until he finally succumbed, and lay motionless in the bright green grass.

The Kingfishers eventually pulled themselves from the wolf, wiping their eyes. They didn't know what to do.

But then the wind picked up, and a whisper drifted into their ears: "Bring me the comb."

They turned, and saw the thing that was Numinae, his left hand outstretched.

𝕺𝖗 𝖜𝖆𝖘 𝖙𝖍𝖆𝖙 𝖍𝖎𝖘 𝖍𝖆𝖓𝖉? It was hard to tell.

A major reason it was hard to tell was because Artie and Kay were suddenly in a completely different place. As they turned from their fallen friend, the scene around them morphed from the field of battle into a high, rocky hill. Cable was gone. Now they were just above the tree line. A few thousand feet below the mountaintop, the sprawling forest of Sylvan carpeted the countryside.

Another big reason it was hard to tell was that they were distracted by the sudden presence of not only Numinae, but also the snaking body of Tiberius, who was coiled behind his master.

But the biggest reason it was hard to make out Numinae's hand was because of Numinae himself. He was a preposterous creature. It was kind of like he couldn't make up his mind as to what kind of tree he wanted to be.

Numinae shifted from a stout oak to a wide chestnut to a thin alder; he became hemlock, and cedar, and fir; then he was beech, then birch, then black ash.

And yet he was certainly also a man. The trunk was cloven for his legs, and the long branches at his sides were clearly his arms. His head changed shape but it was always in the same place, and through the leaves and twigs and needles Artie and Kay made out his features: drooping eyes, a long nose, high cheeks, but no sign of a mouth.

He stood before them, his left hand still outstretched. Kay implored Artie, "What are you waiting for?"

This was the key they had been searching for. It was right there, palm up, waiting for the comb—or for Artie's sword.

But Artie refused to cut it so quickly.

First he needed to know what this creature had done with Qwon.

Artie took the comb from Kay and passed it into the hand of Numinae. Kay huffed. She couldn't believe it.

Numinae curled his hard, knobby fingers around the comb. They made snapping noises like breaking twigs. He pulled back his fist and stashed the comb somewhere in his body. Then he took a short step backward, and finally stopped changing.

Numinae now stood before them in his true form.

He was as tall and powerful as a pro-basketball center, with huge hands and broad shoulders. His skin was a seamless patch of vibrant, living moss. Designs were plowed through some sections of his moss-skin, reminding Artie of Merlin's tattoos, and small trees like bonsai were arranged all over him in patterns. From the crown of his head grew a stunted miniature birch, and over one ear rose a gnarled cedar like a radio antenna. His eyes were stunning. The part that should have been white was black, and his irises were shocks of green, and his pupils were as white as new snow.

Then he spoke, his mouth breaking through the moss on the lower part of his face. It was creepy as all get-out. "Thank you for the comb," he said, bowing slightly and presenting both of his hands in gratitude. His layered voice was like wind through the needles of a pine forest. When he finished talking, his mouth resealed and disappeared beneath the seamless moss.

Artie knew for certain that this was not the Mossman that had taken Qwon. That creature was like a peasant, and Numinae was his undisputed prince. Still, Numinae probably had some idea what had happened to Qwon, and Artie desperately wanted to ask him about it. The only problem was that Artie, finally faced with the magnificent forest

301

lord, was completely dumbstruck and frozen stiff.

Kay, however, was not. She wanted to know where Qwon had gone too, but more than anything she wanted to get the key and have Artie moongate them out of there. As Artie stood gaping at the forest spirit, Kay took action and quickly flicked Cleomede in the direction of Numinae's fuzzy green wrist.

But the dragon, which Kay had somehow managed to forget, whipped his head and snorted. Before she could strike, she was hit with a blast of Tiberius's rock breath. Her arm stopped and she nearly fell over. She looked at her body in disbelief. Her entire right side, Cleomede included, was encased in grating, writhing black basalt.

Kay blurted, "Tiberius, why would you—"

The dragon cut her off. "Hmmph. I am his keeper. The lord and the infant king must parley."

"But my—"

"Quiet!" the dragon boomed frighteningly. "Or I will do you whole, as Jester Thumb!"

Kay bit her lip and marveled at the statue that was her arm, which felt all pins-and-needly, like it had fallen completely asleep.

Numinae, ignoring this exchange, said to Artie, "Ask your question. We haven't much time."

And as if on cue, the sky darkened. A heaving storm was moving in quickly from the east.

"Where's Qwon?" Artie demanded.

"I did not take one named Qwon. I took one named Cassie."

Artie asked desperately, "What do you mean, you didn't take Qwon? There was a Mossman there, kind of like you but smaller. You *had* to have taken Qwon."

"I did not take one named Qwon," Numinae repeated.

"Who did then?"

Numinae answered by looking to the east. The storm was going to be a whopper.

"Morgaine?" Artie guessed feebly.

"Yes," Numinae said. He continued, "You have proven yourself, young king-in-the-making. The comb of Twrch Trwyth is a fine prize." He took a knee and placed his right hand on Artie's shoulder. Artie felt uneasy letting Numinae touch him. The tree-man continued, speaking softly and only to Artie, "I am still unsure what Merlin wants to do, but I know that what *she* wants will not suffice. I am not sure that I believe in a savior, which is to say you, but I do feel that she will seal our destruction if she prevents the worlds from rejoining."

Artie was struck by how casual Numinae was, as if everything had already happened. Considering how desperate Artie was to find Qwon, this nonchalance upset him a lot, but he tried to keep his feelings in check.

"You and Morgaine, then, you're not working together?"

Numinae answered slowly, "In the past, yes, but not for a long time—and not now. It may have appeared that I was aiding her, but rest assured that it was merely indecision that made this seem so. Bercilak did not lie to you on this point or any other."

"Okay. So you're kind of on my side then?"

"Yes. But it would be better if *she* did not know. So we should fight, to make it look like we are at odds."

Artie understood perfectly. If Morgaine was coming, that meant she'd be watching. And she needed to see that Artie was having trouble with Numinae. Artie stepped back and brandished Excalibur in the space between them.

Numinae rose. Even though Artie knew it was an act, it was really frightening. The tree-man's eyes narrowed. He may have been smiling or frowning, but it was impossible to tell. Artie kind of hated that unless Numinae was speaking he didn't appear to have a mouth.

Kay asked, "What's going on? Are we all like bosom buddies now?"

Numinae looked at Kay and threw his head back a little. "Not quite, Kay Kingfisher." He turned slightly to his dragon. "I like this one, Tiberius."

"Hmmmph," came the dragon's ambiguous reply.

The storm was closer. Lightning illuminated the billowing clouds. Wind gathered and blew across them in quickening gusts.

Numinae said, "The girl you seek is in Fenland, I am certain of it."

"So we have to go to Fenland to get Qwon?" Artie asked dispiritedly.

"Yes."

"How will we get there?"

"The wizard will know!"

The wind was terrible now. Artie made some token swipes at the air between them and asked, "So if you're not in cahoots with Morgaine, then how does she know where I am?"

Numinae pointed at Excalibur. "The sword is no longer hidden. Something has been scraped from it."

Artie glanced at Excalibur. Sure enough, its blade looked different in one very small section. It was where it had cut the hair of Twrch Trwyth. There he saw a small, dark, trembling splotch. The nanospell Merlin had cast on the sword had been compromised!

Numinae suddenly made an awful slithering sound that was like a nest of snakes careening through coarse grass. Then he said, in a low, shaking voice, "She is coming! We must be convincing!"

A fierce downdraft tore from the black clouds, hitting the forest around the mountaintop like a freight train. The trees below exploded like they were made of toothpicks, and a great circle of destruction was laid down in the woods.

Even at their distance, the devastation was immediate and impressive.

Numinae recoiled as the swath of forest was laid waste. Artie's voice cracked as he yelled, "Are you ready, Lord Numinae?"

"I am, young Arthur Pendragon!" came his high, loud reply.

Arthur Pendragon.

Artie didn't have to hear those words a second time to know that, in spite of his life with Kay and Kynder, *that* was his *real name.*

And in that instant the storm was on them. Tiberius hunkered around Kay to protect her, and even though she was still angry at the dragon for turning half of her into a tingling chunk of rock, she leaned into the dragon's side.

A crack swelled in their ears. Two, then three, giant twisters pulled down from the clouds and began to climb up the incline of the mountain.

Artie and Numinae locked eyes. They were ten feet apart and pretending to hold each other at bay with their weapons.

And then Numinae charged, raising his gigantic hammer-hand and tearing it through the air, aiming for Artie's head.

Artie had been in enough fights by now to know how to sidestep an attack like this. The hammer came down with a resounding boom on the rock next to him.

It was a close call and, he had to admit, pretty convincing.

Artie swiped at Numinae's exposed side and scratched his thigh. The tree-man pretended it was worse and yelled. He then jumped back twenty feet, looking like he really wanted to kill Artie.

He hoped this was part of the act too, because it was *really* convincing.

Numinae pushed his left hand into the air, palm forward. A stream of green and brown leaves shot from it on a beam of light. Artie pointed Excalibur at it. His sword took a direct hit, and gobbled up everything the spell delivered.

Numinae pulled his arm back and clenched his hand into a fist. "Ack!" he yelled. He was a good actor—either that or Excalibur's deflection really did hurt.

Kay heard some of this over the scream of the storm but saw none of it. "What's going on, Tiberius?" she wailed.

The dragon said nothing. Rain and hail like buckshot began to hurl from the clouds. Tiberius held a wing over her like an awning.

Artie ignored the hail and held up Excalibur, dashing sidelong to the wind at Numinae.

Numinae cried out as Excalibur hit the maul-arm with a cracking, hollow knock that echoed over the rocks.

By some miracle—or more assuredly by some powerful magic—the sword failed to slice through the club. Instead it was embedded in Numinae's arm about two inches deep.

Numinae stood quickly and swung his arm through the air, throwing Artie up and into the wind. And as he flipped around, getting caught momentarily by the vicious storm, Artie realized to his horror that he was no longer holding his precious sword.

He landed hard and slid to a stop. He looked to Numinae, who still had Excalibur stuck in his club. Artie stood and held up his arm against the searing hail and wind, and without thinking ran back to Numinae as quickly as he could.

Just before reaching the tree-man, though, he felt something vaguely familiar. His skin began to tingle and the hair on his head began to stand. A funny smell, like the one he'd noticed in Qwon's room right after she'd been taken, filled the air. And then everything went momentarily white and blue.

When the light cleared, he saw Numinae before him, his right arm ravaged by fire and split down the middle. He was on his knees, screaming, holding his maul with his left hand.

And Excalibur was gone.

Artie scanned the ground and then the air, and he saw it. Excalibur was being lifted into the blackness above, borne on strong invisible wings. It was being taken by the dark lordess of Fenland!

Artie fell to his knees. The unexpected loss of Excalibur knocked the wind from him.

Numinae writhed in pain at his stricken arm. The twisters were gaining, and the damage they wrought on the forest greatly weakened the Sylvan lord.

But then, from somewhere above, came Kay. Her arm was free, and Cleomede was bright and fierce. Tiberius was in the air above her. Kay skidded in front of Artie, holding out the hilt of her sword for him to take.

Artie grabbed Cleomede and pushed through the wind to Numinae. The dragon pummeled the air above, and he boomed through the gale, "Arthur Pendragon! Now you must get what you need'n we'll go!"

As Artie reached Numinae, he looked him in the eyes and said, "I'm sorry." Then he swung for the fences at Numinae's shaking wrist, and the tree-man's hand fell free at Artie's feet, clenched in a tight fist.

Artie took it. He felt so badly for Numinae. The green lord looked the young king in the eyes once more, and a mysterious wave of connection passed between them.

And then Numinae became a swirl of leaves and twigs and grasses, and his parts were scattered on the wind. Artie knew that he had not been destroyed but that he had done the only logical thing to do: run.

Which he and Kay really had to get around to doing as well.

The tornadoes were upon them. The dragon landed on the stone in front of Artie, and Kay rushed to his side. Tiberius lowered his massive head and instructed, "Grab my ears. Hold'n tight!"

The Kingfishers swung onto the monster's neck, and before they could count to three, they were up and in the storm, dodging through and around the twister funnels as though they were gates on a ski-slalom course.

Horizontal fissures of lightning crisscrossed the ether. The ironlike smell of ozone was everywhere. Tiberius banked and rolled frantically, avoiding the lightning at all costs.

But then he was hit with a crackling broadside, and Kay was struck momentarily deaf.

She turned to her left, to see if Artie was okay.

But he wasn't okay. He was gone.

Kay screamed. They were falling. Tiberius was knocked out. She yanked hard on the dragon's ear and leaned over to look at his eye. It was open and rolling around in its socket.

Then something caught her attention. Farther down, she saw the free-falling body of her brother, and just next to him the speck of greenery that was Numinae's hand.

"Tiberius," she wailed, kicking the dragon's head with

one of her legs. "Tiberius, wake up now!"

Miraculously, the dragon heard her. His pupil narrowed and his wings suddenly came to life, righting them instantly. Lightning veiled the air. Kay risked letting go with one hand and pointed to the forest floor. "He's there! The hand too!"

The dragon folded his wings and bent to the ground like a dart. Within seconds they were above Artie, and then well past him. Tiberius hissed, "Hold on!" Kay clenched his ear with both hands and shut her eyes as the giant serpent twisted upside down, catching Artie gingerly in one of his massive hind paws.

The dragon twisted again, completing the barrel roll, and yelled, "I have him!" Kay could feel that it was true. Artie was hurt and limp but he was alive. In that instant she both loved and hated the dragon—loved him for saving her brother, and hated him for making him leave behind Excalibur's healing scabbard.

She opened her eyes. They were above the forest and in danger of dragging Artie through the up-reaching branches. The dragon snaked his magical body through the air and rose fifty, then a hundred feet.

She looked up. The skies were still black. The witch of Fenland was still on the hunt. She had gotten the sword but she wanted more. She wanted Artie too.

The dragon dived into the forest through a large gap

in the canopy. They cruised through the dense woods, Tiberius avoiding ancient trees and boulders and hillocks. Very soon they reached the gorge they'd hiked through earlier, and dived over the backward-running waterfall. The dragon folded his wings behind him as he snaked through the gorge and into his lair.

They pulled to a stop in the great cathedral cave, and Tiberius gently placed Artie on the ground next to Thumb and the scabbard. Kay vaulted off Tiberius and clambered for the sheath. She grabbed it, ran to her brother, and laid it on top of him.

His left leg was seared and caked in caramelized blood. His hair was on end, full of charged particles. His skin was white and his breathing quick and shallow.

Kay pressed hard on the scabbard and begged it to work.

"It's not healing him!" she said desperately, looking over her shoulder to Tiberius.

He dropped something from his mouth. "Open this and try what's inside."

It was Numinae's hand, clenched in a fist. Kay snatched it up and worked at the fingers. They were difficult to peel back, but soon enough she had it open. Inside was a dark, cloudy orb of glass. Excalibur's pommel! Somehow Numinae had kept it!

"What should I do?"

Tiberius made a series of licking sounds behind her. In between licks, the dragon said, "Place it atop the scabbard."

She did, and very quickly it began to work. Within moments Artie's color returned, and his breathing grew less labored. But his leg still looked and smelled like a hunk of neglected barbecue.

Kay stood. Tiberius finished licking the rock away from Thumb's prison. The little man stood before her, wet with dragon saliva, dazed and speechless.

The dragon fetched a large goatskin and handed it to Kay. "Give him water." The dragon propped Artie up, and Kay put the spout to his lips. Artie began to stir and took a few much-needed sips.

Kay helped herself and offered more to Artie. He moaned and refused.

Kay looked at Tiberius. Thumb was still confused and speechless. Kay said, "Why isn't the scabbard fixing his leg?"

"Hmmph. It is not as powerful. It misses its companion," the dragon mused.

"Well, how can I get him better? I need to get him better, Tiberius!"

"Take him to the wizard. He'll save him."

"But without the sword, how do we get back?"

Finally Thumb said, "What's happened?"

Tiberius ignored him. "The pommel will open the gate.

The boy must ask though."

Kay ignored Thumb too. She knelt before Artie and shook him by the shoulders. Thumb began to understand what was going on. He took the goatskin from Kay and offered Artie more water. The boy lapped at the refreshing draft and coughed. His eyes opened.

"Hey, Bro," Kay cooed, forcing herself to stay calm. "We need you to say that thing that opens the gate."

Artie was delirious. His head lolled, and he moaned, "But Excalibur . . ."

"Don't worry about that, Artie," Kay said, caressing his filthy cheek with the back of her hand. She suddenly realized that she must look awful. Tears welled in her magnificent eyes. She took her brother's face in her hands and concentrated her breathing. "Just put your hand on the scabbard and say the words. That's all you have to do. You remember them, right?"

Artie frowned. He so badly wanted to go to sleep. He whispered, "*Lunae . . .*"

"That's it, c'mon!"

"*Lunae lum . . .*"

"That's the boy!" urged Thumb, gazing at Artie's charred leg and finally comprehending the seriousness of the situation.

"*Lunae lumen,*" Artie said weakly.

Kay pleaded, "Now think of Merlin's cave! C'mon now! We gotta go to Merlin's cave!"

Artie moaned, "Okay," and finally the young king fell into unconsciousness.

But it worked. The moongate flew open from the pommel. Kay smiled and grabbed Numinae's hand. As they were carried away, they heard Tiberius imploring, "Hmmph! I'm sorry, young Kingfishers! Return, and I'll show you how sorry I am!"

And then they were gone at last from the Otherworld and from the green land of Sylvan.

They arrived in an empty stone room.

Merlin appeared immediately. For once, he looked like a real wizard. He was dressed in a long, crisp linen cloak, and he had a knotted wooden pendant hanging from a long silver chain around his neck, and he wore simple leather sandals. No pointy hat, but that didn't matter, because his head tattoos were alive with anticipation and enchantment.

The old wizard barely noticed the battered and exhausted party as he demanded greedily, "Well, do you have it? Where is it?"

Kay yelled, "What? Look at Artie, Gramps!"

And the wizard did look, and Kay could tell that his eyes only saw the hand of the forest lord. Before Merlin could take it, she held it away from him. "Look at Artie, you jerk!"

Merlin shook his head and finally comprehended the wounded king.

A surge of relief washed over Kay. "By the trees, what happened?" He gasped.

"No time to explain. Get to work," Kay ordered.

The wizard nodded and did just that. He repeated the glowing-spinning-floating trick, and before they knew it they were in the hospital room with Bedevere, who was still unconscious. The glass partition was back in place, and this time it was Kay who stood on its far side with Thumb, watching Merlin ply his trade.

The wizard moved in a blur, flickering from one side of Artie to the other. He placed his hands all over him, making tiny adjustments like a weird chiropractor. His tattoos swirled along his skin. His hands glowed and darkened and glowed again.

Artie's body twitched and twisted as the wizard tended the cooked leg. He chanted and turned his hands around the blackened mass of flesh. It glowed and then changed color, becoming red and white and pink. Merlin lowered his hands and smoothed them over Artie's leg. He reached for Excalibur's sheath, which leaned against the bed frame, and laid it over the wound. And there, before their very eyes, Artie was good as new. Asleep, but healed.

Merlin finished by placing moss all over the leg, and he doused this with a green liquid from an oblong decanter.

He said more words, and then he clapped one time and came to Kay and Thumb.

"He'll be fine," Merlin said. "This time tomorrow he'll be running laps."

Kay let out the biggest breath of her life as Thumb jumped up and down on her shoulder.

Then Merlin said, "I'm sorry for obsessing over the key. Understand that I've been here for so long, and I am so eager to see the outside world. Please forgive me, Kay."

Kay smirked and said, "I'll try, Merlin."

"Thank you. Well, where is it?"

She held out the hand. "Right here."

Merlin took it. The wrist's stump dripped bloody mud and trailed grassy sinews and revealed a bone of ancient petrified wood. Merlin looked so happy. He regarded Thumb and Kay and Artie with obvious pride, then frowned. "But where is Excalibur?"

"Gone," Kay said apologetically.

"Gone?" Merlin breathed.

"She got it. We still have the pommel though. It's a long story."

Thumb said, "They've just been through a lot, my friend. Let Sir Kay settle."

Merlin stepped back and smoothed the front of his robe. "It is a pity that she got the sword. We will have to get it back as soon as possible. Were you able to find out the whereabouts of Qwon?"

Kay hung her head. Thumb, who realized that he didn't know the answer to this question, looked at Kay. "It wasn't Numinae who took her," she said. "It was Morgaine."

Merlin shook his head and placed a reassuring hand on Kay's shoulder. He said deeply, "Kay, I will find her and the sword. Since Artie is healing, and since all of you need your rest, let me leave this place and do what I can to find them. Come, we must finally break the bonds of this invisible tower!"

"To the back door, then? To Mrs. Thresher?" Thumb asked excitedly.

"Yes! To Mrs. Thresher!" Merlin answered.

Merlin whisked them through the amazing, percolating rooms, and in no time they landed in the simple chamber at the end of the wizard's underground lair.

Merlin knelt in front of Mrs. Thresher and flayed open Numinae's hand with a knife. He worked the skeleton of petrified wood from the mossy skin and placed it in front of him ceremoniously. In fact, he would have liked to do the whole breaking out of the invisible tower with a lot more ceremony—he had been stuck here for nearly fifteen hundred years, after all. This was a big deal. But he knew that the longer they waited to search out Qwon and Excalibur, the harder it would be to locate them.

He murmured a few private words and then looked at

Kay and said seriously, "It's too bad Artie can't be here now. Remember this well, Kay. Tell him. It is part of his legacy."

"You got it," Kay said eagerly.

The small door opened on its own. And then, for the first time in his life, Merlin leaned forward and passed the top half of his body through the opening. He reached for something and pulled it out.

It was a long block of white limestone affixed with a bright titanium handle. On its top along the nearest edge were five finger-sized holes.

"What're you doing, Merlin?" Kay asked.

"This is the tower's keystone, Kay Kingfisher. Normally keystones are found at the top of archways, but in this case it's down here. Once this is destroyed, the tower will be no more, and I shall be free."

He inserted Numinae's skeletal fingers into the holes, and once they were in place, the block began to tremble, and Mrs. Thresher began to swing, banging back and forth between the keystone and the wall.

This was it. His eyes widened as the forest lord's hand shook in the stone sockets. And then it began to crack. Merlin smiled—such an eager, broad, expectant smile— and turned to Kay and Thumb.

Already he looked different. Thumb barely recognized him. He held out his hands, and his robe draped down from him like wings.

"I am finally free!" he wailed. "Freeeeee!"

Wild-eyed and terrifying, he yelled, "Four things, most important all! Do not leave these caverns until the noise has stopped! Do not search for Qwon or Excalibur or venture to the Otherworld until you hear from me! Turn the moss on Artie's leg in exactly three hours! And above all, mind the store, my friends! Thank you all, and mind the store!"

Then, a searing flash blinded Kay and Thumb for more than a few minutes. During their blindness they heard first the flaps of giant wings retreating through and out of Mrs. Thresher. And then the room shook, and they had to deal with the worst, most spine-rattling series of crashes and crumbles and quakes they'd ever had to endure.

32 IN WHICH THE KINGFISHERS TRY TO RETURN TO NORMAL LIFE

𝕰very police car and fire engine this side of the Ohio River—and quite a few more from the other side too—rushed to the old Vine Street Cable Railway Building. They responded to the frantic calls placed by hundreds of people reporting huge blocks of white rock tumbling from—from—well, no one knew exactly where they were tumbling from.

Those who saw swore on a stack of holy books that giant chunks of limestone simply started to appear in the air above, only to career earthward. When that course of stone fell, another revealed itself, and it fell, and so on. In the end exactly one thousand blocks came crashing to the ground, destroying cars and buses and damaging buildings and scaring the you-know-what out of just about everyone.

Miraculously, only minor injuries were reported. Scrapes and near misses were everywhere. For the rest of their lives, hundreds of people would tell the story of how they were nearly killed by the falling invisible stone blocks.

The authorities initially suspected terrorism, but no one came forward to claim responsibility. Even if someone had done so, the general consensus quickly settled on the notion that, while disturbing, dropping several thousand tons of gargantuan bricks on a city like Cincinnati wasn't so much terrifying as it was just plain weird.

Not to mention really, really difficult.

Theories explaining their appearance multiplied like rabbits. None were very convincing. It didn't take long for most people to pass the whole thing off. Of course, the people closest to the incident would never forget it, but, like the world at large, they preferred to engage in a collective exercise of self-delusion. For perhaps the one trillionth time in its history, the human race exhibited its uncanny and baffling ability to believe just about anything. Some big old rocks had fallen from the sky, that's all. Stranger things had happened, right?

Back in the basement of the Vine Street Cable Railway Building, things weren't getting stranger but were instead getting more normal. As Merlin promised, Artie got better quickly. Kay flipped the moss on his leg and he woke up and they talked about all that had happened. But mostly they talked about Qwon. Artie couldn't stop talking about Qwon. He felt so bad that they hadn't found her.

In the following days, as crews worked nonstop to clean the rubble from around Merlin's store, Bedevere healed and finally spent as much time awake as he did asleep. He had beaten back the threat of infection. Artie and Kay had only a few days before school started (School! After everything!), and Kay spent most of her time with Bedevere talking about things like baseball (which for some reason Bedevere knew a lot about—not the teams, but the game itself), milk shakes, and *SpongeBob SquarePants*. Who knew? Bedevere had never seen cartoons before and he was just crazy about that little yellow sponge.

Kynder, Lance, and Mrs. Onakea immediately rushed to Cincinnati once they heard that Artie, Kay, and Thumb were back. Kynder brought Kay a *whole case* of Mountain Dew! When he handed it over, Kay said, "Man, Kynder, you must feel real bad about all of this. Thanks! But don't sweat it, okay?" All Kynder did then was hug his wonderful daughter as hard as he could.

Understandably, Mrs. Onakea was a wreck. Kynder had to use his smarts and his newfound potion-making skills to keep her heavily sedated. Artie suffered for the loss of Qwon, but Mrs. Onakea was simply devastated by it. Not to mention she was having a pretty hard time accepting all the crazy stuff these people were telling her.

Early on the morning that they had to return to Shadyside to start up the school year, Artie found himself alone with Mrs. Onakea. She was in a comfy chair and covered with a light blanket. Because of her sedation, Mrs. Onakea wasn't much on conversation, and so Artie had been sitting with her for some time in a deep, shared silence. Right before he had to leave, Artie took her hand. She smiled weakly. Artie said, "I'll find her, Mrs. Onakea. I swear to you that I will find her and bring her back."

Mrs. Onakea squeezed Artie's hand. With a heavy dose of conviction she said, "I know you will, Artie. I know you will."

Artie tried to say something else, but Mrs. Onakea put her fingers on his lips and said, "And please, never call me Mrs. Onakea again. My name is Pammy."

Artie promised he would and left.

The next day Kynder drove his remarkable kids to school. Bedevere, who'd decided to try school, knowing he could always go back to the Otherworld if it didn't work out, came with them. Kay, who sat with Bedevere in the backseat, thought he looked pretty spiffy in his jeans and plaid shirt with the empty folded sleeve and the two top buttons undone.

Artie was up front with Kynder, and all he could think about was Qwon. Being at school was going to be really hard, and Artie just wasn't ready.

As if he could read their minds, Kynder said, "Listen up, guys. I'm not going to pretend I have the right to lecture you after all you've been through, but I do want to get this off my chest. I know you're different now, and preoccupied, and probably off in space a little bit. That's totally fine. But . . ." He trailed off. The Kingfisher-kids-plus-Bedevere didn't know what to say. Kynder continued, "Just try to pay *some* attention, okay?"

Kay said, "You got it, Pops," and Bedevere made a jovial grunt. They got out and waited for Artie on the curb.

Kynder looked at his boy, who'd so recently come from such a strange place, and done such strange things. He said, "Try not to think about her, okay, Arthur? You'll get her. Merlin will come back soon, and you'll get her together."

Artie lifted his head and smiled. He said weakly, "I know. I just really want to be there."

"Of course you do. But you were nearly killed before. We should listen to Merlin and wait. I'm sure he's working hard for us right now. I'm sure he'll contact you soon."

"I hope so, Dad."

Kynder reached across the car and ruffled Artie's hair. He looked out the front window and saw someone that Artie didn't. Kynder said, "All right, then. Go get 'em, tiger."

Artie fixed his hair and got out. He joined Kay and Bedevere, and they started down the sidewalk.

Artie looked at the ground, twirling Excalibur's pommel in his hand, and Kay and Bedevere nudged each other with some private joke when suddenly, from some distance beyond the carpool drop-off, came a familiar and annoying catcall.

"Yo! Kingfisher! I missed yoooooooou. . . ."

They looked and saw none other than Frankie Finkelstein about twenty feet away.

It was weird, but in a way Artie had never been happier to see someone. For a moment, he forgot about Qwon. For a moment, he was Artie Kingfisher, bully target.

For a moment.

Finkelstein had grown taller and a little fatter. Probably stronger too.

But Artie couldn't have cared less.

He pocketed the pommel and raised his chin at Finkelstein. The bully barked, "What? You want some of this? Al*ready*?" He nudged some freckled sidekick Artie had never seen before and let out a mocking laugh.

Bedevere began to ask, "Who is this gnat, sire, and what can I—" but Artie held up his hand.

Kay turned to her brother, who she'd had to rescue so many times before, and asked, "You want help with those Dr Pepper heads, Art?"

Without looking at the best big sister in the world, Artie answered, "Naw. I got this."

Artie clenched his fists. Kay chuckled and guided a craning Bedevere toward the school's entrance, reminding him to lay off the *sires* and *majestys* and *lieges* while they were on this side.

Artie stared at his so-called nemesis for a second more. Then he pulled a friendly smile across his face and walked casually but intently toward Finkelstein.

What got the bully most, and what he would never forget for the rest of his life, was that through the whole fight Artie Kingfisher never said a single word.

𝔄𝔰𝔥𝔢𝔫 𝔞𝔫𝔡 𝔟𝔯𝔢𝔞𝔱𝔥𝔦𝔫𝔤 𝔰𝔥𝔞𝔩𝔩𝔬𝔴𝔩𝔶, 𝔱𝔥𝔢 old mage slumped against a massive tree trunk. A breeze tickled the leaves and combed the grasses and weeds, but didn't wake the man. Merlin had never slept so soundly.

He was enjoying his freedom, and enjoying being lazy.

He may have slept longer, if it wasn't for the watery nymph cooing at him over the Lake's breeze-tossed wavelets.

He woke but didn't open an eye. He demanded quietly, "What is it, Nyneve, can't you see I'm trying to sleep?"

"Ambrosius, it *is* you." Ambrosius was one of Merlin's names from the old days.

"Who else, my dear? None other is so marked." He rubbed his head to indicate his tattoos.

"You've far more markings now," the Lady intoned.

"What can I say? I've been busy. Bored, too. A thousand-plus years is a long time, even for those as patient as us." Finally he opened his eyes and raised his head.

The young-looking spirit was half out of the Lake at the water's edge, propped on her elbows. Her skin was light blue, and her whole being was shrouded in water. Where her body met the Lake, her flesh fell away. Merlin knew that she was the Lake and the Lake was she, of course, but this had never been more impressive than it was in that moment.

Her face was cruelly young. Many, many years ago this spirit had fooled Merlin, and taken him on a vacation under the glassy surface, and almost kept him there, but he got away. He couldn't believe she was still so potent.

He shook off the Lady's charms and spoke. "What's the news, Nyneve?"

"The new boy-king came some time ago. A fortnight, perhaps more."

"I know."

"You sent him?"

"I did." Merlin straightened and put on his shoes.

"You have seen the sword?" she asked casually.

"I have. Thank you for keeping it."

"Of course. It was easy to care for. Its sangrealitic essence made it so."

"Of course," the old man echoed, getting to his feet.

"You and the sword are a perfect pair, Nyneve. Both ancient, both exceedingly exquisite." He frowned.

Her manner clouded as she said, "True." She wasn't much for modesty. "And where, may I ask, might the sword and its bearer be on this day?"

"Arthur—Artie—is on his side awaiting my orders. As for the sword—I was hoping you might help me with that. You see, we've lost it."

The spirit frowned, and it cut Merlin to the bone. "Shame, Ambrosius," she scolded. "You know the blade only comes for purposes at hand. I know surely where it is, but I wouldn't deign to tell you more than you already guess, for I fear that your purposes and Excalibur's are set against each other." She said this with such dark authority that Merlin felt like nothing more than a man. He slid down the tree's trunk and plopped onto his bottom.

"Tell me, mistress, what you can."

Nyneve retreated into the water to her shoulders. Her glistening hair fanned out in the Lake behind her, laying flat just below the surface. She smiled an awful smile and said, "The sword wants three things, Ambrosius. To be claimed by the rightful king." Merlin nodded. "To reopen the worlds." Merlin tilted his head. "And . . ."

She paused. Merlin could barely take it. He asked desperately, "What, my lady?"

The nymph said, "You are old, are you not, Ambrosius?"

"You know that I am."

"Yes. You have lived many lives, and endured many deaths."

Merlin was impatient. His weariness quickly faded and was replaced by a power that gathered in his toes and fingertips. He felt as though soon he might like to destroy something. He said, "You know this is true. The same is true of you, my dear."

"Perhaps, but I am not at all human, whereas you are at least partly such. Do you know why you have lived for so long, old wizard?"

The answer to that was easy. "Power, Nyneve, and the wits it has provided."

She shook her head, throwing clean, cold droplets of water. "No. You are powerful, of course, but that is not why. You have skirted death for one reason only—because that which has the power to kill you has never marked you for death. In fact, it has long been your friend. But no more, dear Ambrosius. No more."

Merlin stood and stamped his foot. "What are you talking about, nymph? Out with it!"

Nyneve was cool and calm. "Why, the sword, of course. It is the only thing that can strike you down. That's the reason you were imprisoned and not destroyed. Morgaine didn't have the sword back in those days and she couldn't get it. Besides, it wasn't ready. But now—"

Merlin was flabbergasted. "What are you saying?" He took two long strides toward the Lake's edge.

"The third thing the sword wants, my dearest, is *to kill you*."

Her deep, unsympathetic eyes bore into Merlin's as she retreated into the water. Merlin could tell that as far as Nyneve was concerned, he was already dead, and she was not sad about it at all.

Merlin wasn't happy about this. He raised his hands and brought them down forcefully, palms first. A jolt of orange and blue electricity gathered from the ground into his hands, and he flung it at the water nymph with lightning speed. It struck the surface of the Lake, and the water there boiled and steamed. But he was too slow, and it was pointless anyway. The Lady was the Lake and the Lake was the Lady, after all. He could not destroy her.

His chest shot through with pain, his teeth chattered, his lips quivered.

But it wasn't fear that racked him. It was rage. Merlin was suddenly brimming with rage. The rage felt familiar, and it felt fantastic.

He had to get going. He had to see Artie right away.

ACKNOWLEDGMENTS

Thank you, James Frey, for so many, many things, including letting me pilfer the way you write your acknowledgments. Thank you, Sarah Sevier and Tara Weikum and Jon Howard and everyone at HarperCollins. Thank you, Kathryn Hinds. Thank you, Brian Thompson. Thank you, Ray Shappell. Thank you, Abigail Bowen. Thank you, Jessica Almon. Thank you, Eric Simonoff and William Morris Endeavor. Thank you, Jenny Meyer. Thank you, Courtney Kivowitz. Thank you, David Krintzman. Thank you, Richard Pine and Inkwell Management. Thank you, thank you, thank you.

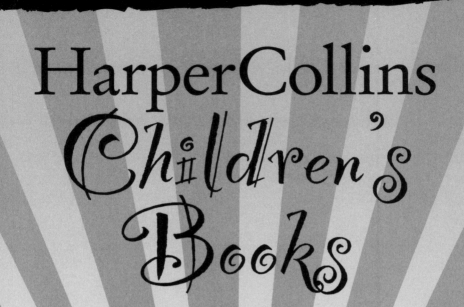